Prologue

LUNA

The noise of the crowd is a deafening roar, so loud it's like being inside the barrel of a wave, but it still can't silence the screams in my head.

Twenty minutes ago I was feeling calm and confident, and now I'm falling apart. It shows me just how shaky my new sense of self was. I was a badly constructed Jenga tower, and someone has pulled a block from the very bottom and I'm collapsing in slow motion.

Adrenaline pounds furiously through my veins, making it hard to breathe or think straight. I take a swig from my water bottle, hoping it might drown the million ants that have started to burrow and scratch beneath my skin. I thought I had it under control, was managing to swim with my head above water, but just like that, I've been dragged under.

The idea of walking onstage in front of seventy thousand people is suddenly an impossibility. How can I—knowing someone out there wants to kill me?

How did they slip unnoticed into my dressing room? How did they get past my bodyguard? Everyone with backstage access is meant to have been security-checked. No strangers should be able to get back here, so whoever it is must work for me. But who do I know that could secretly hate me that much?

The roar in the distance grows louder, making me think of a hungry crowd baying for a gladiator's blood. I have to go out there. I don't have a choice. The clock is ticking.

I think of Will to help calm me and wonder where he is right now. If he's happy. Closing my eyes, I allow myself to picture him—focus on recalling every detail, pulling them out of my memory like treasures from a box. I see the soft curve of his lips and the rough scratch of his beard, how it felt when he kissed me. I remember the exact sensation of his hands gliding down my body, coming to rest on my hips, the way he'd tug me toward him. I can visualize the warmth in his smoke-gray eyes as he looked at me, seeing all the way through the outer layer to the real me inside.

For a while we were free, on the run together, never glancing over our shoulders or looking back, but only focusing on the present and each other. The rest of the world could have gone to hell. It was just us. I smile as I recall those days of dizzy escape, but then the smile fades. I always knew deep down that they'd have to end. You can't be a fugitive from your life forever. One day you'll get caught and sent back to do your time. I just wish it hadn't happened so soon.

I wish we'd had longer.

ELEVEN MONTHS AGO

WILL

There are few things worse than being forced to spend a whole evening with a bunch of strangers, but I promised that I'd show my face, so here I am, gritting my teeth and trying to get through it.

"Will!" I hear my name being called as I'm walking up the steps to the front door of the biggest house I've ever seen. I turn around and find my best friend, Tristan, arm in arm with my sister Zoey.

It still messes with my head seeing them together, but I have to admit they really do seem happy. And I know Tristan—he's a good guy. I always worried Zoey might end up with someone like my dad, because they say that's what happens to kids who grow up with asshole fathers; they gravitate toward what they know, not what they deserve. It gives me hope, because they also say that the sons of asshole fathers often end up modeling their father's behavior, and I'd be lying if I didn't admit that I secretly sometimes worry that I might turn out to be a violent asshole just like him. It keeps me up at night.

I keep those concerns to myself, obviously. They're not ones you want to share, even if I were the sharing type.

Zoey hugs me like a long-lost relative, even though she only saw me a few hours earlier. I can tell she's relieved I made it to the party, and that makes me realize she thought I wouldn't show. It bothers me. I guess that no matter how many times I apologize for joining the Marines and explain why I thought it was a good idea at the time, she'll never fully be able to trust me not to abandon her again.

"How's it going?" Tristan asks, and I pick up on the concern in his voice. His worry isn't obvious, but I'm good at reading people. You get good when you have a father like mine, whose moods flipped on a dime. You also get good at it when you have to stand guard outside a Marine base.

"Okay," I tell him. "Finding my feet."

I've only been out of the Marines a couple of weeks. They warn you it'll be strange returning to civilian life, and they are definitely right about that. I'm still getting used to not having to get out of bed at the crack of dawn, or wearing a uniform, or carrying a weapon with me wherever I go.

But I don't miss a thing about being in the Marines. I couldn't wait to get out. I figured I would feel like a free man, like the guy in the *Shawshank Redemption* movie who hightails it to Mexico after being released from prison to live on the beach and build his own boat. I have similar ambitions, but unlike the guy in the movie, I don't have a stash of cash hidden away to help me achieve my dreams.

Until I have a job and some money and start paying off my debt, I'm stuck here. Not that Oceanside is bad—as its name suggests, it's by the ocean. But it's just not what I've been dreaming of for the last seven years.

"You'll get there," Tristan tells me with more confidence than I feel. "Did you talk to Kit?"

I shake my head. I haven't seen Kit yet. He's busy with the restaurant and the new baby. I don't want to get in the way.

"You should ask him for a job," Tristan says. "He's always looking for people to work at the restaurant."

"I can't cook," I say, pulling a face. "And I'm not sure I'd make much of a waiter." I'm not the best at dealing with people, especially difficult ones. I don't have the patience for rude idiots. But more than that, I don't want to have to ask Kit for a job. It's embarrassing.

"I'll find something. Don't worry," I tell Tristan, forcing a smile. It's not his problem.

We enter the house, which is packed with so many gold helium balloons that it's like we're swimming in a giant glass of champagne. Waiters drift past with trays of drinks and fancy-looking burgers the size of quarters, and a DJ is playing somewhere in the distance. There must be over a hundred people, but I spot Tristan's twin sister, Dahlia, immediately as she rushes toward us through the crowd.

I used to have a crush on Dahlia, back when we were all fourteen and at school together, and I wonder if she ever suspected. I was pretty good at hiding my feelings, and I never worked up the courage to tell her how I felt because I figured she'd never feel the same way. Why the hell would she? I was the kid who was always getting into trouble, the one with the shameful family secret, who'd often show up to school with black eyes and bruises and act all sullen when questioned. I figured my survival rested on being both watchful and quiet, habits that have stuck with me.

I was surprised Dahlia invited me to the party, to be honest, as I haven't seen her since I was sixteen and quit school to enlist. I'm guessing Tristan pushed for the invite, trying to get me out of the house. But Dahlia throws her arms around me and hugs me tight, and I realize that maybe she did actually invite me herself, without being prodded to.

She pulls back to look at me, holding me by the shoulders. "My God!" she shouts over the music, squeezing my biceps. "Look at you! Someone's been to the gym." She eyes me up and down approvingly. "Like the beard. It suits you."

"Hey, Dahlia," I say, rubbing a self-conscious hand across my scratchy beard. I haven't bothered to shave in two weeks because I don't have to anymore and it feels good to not have to follow orders. "You look just the same."

She winces. "I hope not. I was the ugliest, dorkiest teenager. But now I've blossomed. Don't you think?" She twirls in front of me with a big grin.

I smile. "Yes. You've lost the dorkiness. At least, mostly."

"You have to meet the birthday girl," she says, and pulls me by the sleeve away from Tristan and Zoey and over toward a striking-looking, elfin girl with blond hair, who stands in the center of a half dozen people, like a brilliant planet being orbited by lesser planetary bodies.

"This is Emma," Dahlia announces. "And this is my friend

Will," she says, introducing me. I know this girl is Dahlia's girl-friend and that she's an actress. This is her house, so I'm guessing she's a successful one.

"Hey," I say, feeling incredibly awkward as all eyes land on me. "Happy birthday."

"I used to have the biggest crush on him." Dahlia laughs.

I glance sideways at her, bowled over by the news, and by the fact she's announcing it to the world, including to her girlfriend.

"She's only saying that to be nice. I was the weird kid on the block," I mumble, already wondering how long I have to stay. It's not that the party doesn't seem fun and buzzy and all those other adjectives people use to describe parties, but it really isn't my kind of thing. I prefer small groups—one-on-one conversations, and even those I find difficult most of the time. I'm also not good at chitchat, and that's obvious after several strained minutes of standing like a lemon making small talk with Dahlia and her friends. I don't feel out of my depth here, so much as in the wrong swimming pool.

Emma suddenly inches over to me. "You don't like crowds, I can tell."

I look at her, surprised. "I guess I'm just not used to them."

"You're an observer, like me."

I nod. "Yeah."

She sighs. "I've had to learn to play the role of an extrovert, but secretly I'm not one at all."

"I hear you," I say, smiling as my eyes roam the room. It's another habit from the Marines. I'm used to always being on the lookout for threats coming my way, so even in a party in a fancy house owned by a film star, I'm behaving like a sentry on the base.

"Dahlia told me you were looking for a job," Emma remarks.

I take a deep breath in. For crying out loud, does everyone know my business? "Yeah," I grunt, before telling myself not to get so upset. It's not like it's a secret. I'm just sensitive to the idea of anyone worrying about me or taking pity on me. I can take care of myself.

"I think I can help," Emma says. "I know someone who's looking to hire someone in your"—her eyebrows lift—"area of expertise."

What could that possibly mean? I squint at her. Then I realize that whatever friend she's talking about is probably part of this celebrity world—a world I want nothing to do with. But before I can dismiss her, someone calls her name from across the room. Emma quickly squeezes my shoulder. "We'll talk later, okay? It really is a great opportunity."

"That would be great," I murmur politely. "Thanks."

Emma hurries off, darting through the crowd like a silver comet. And I stand in the corner, watching people talking and dancing and flirting. I feel like I'm on the outside of a galaxy, looking in, like some piece of floating space debris.

I watch Tristan and Zoey slow-dance but have to turn away when they start kissing. My gaze falls through open French doors that lead into the back garden. Outside I catch a glimmer of an azure swimming pool, and then a flash of neon purple streaks past. It's a girl with dark hair pulled into a sleek topknot. She's wearing a clinging purple dress that reveals slender arms and a tiny waist. I can feel myself automatically leaning closer to get a better look at her. There's something about her that catches the eye, beyond the dress and the body. She's talking to someone who I can't see, but it looks like they're having an argument.

I can only see her in profile, and I find myself wanting to see her face-on. She starts to walk off, out of sight, but a guy suddenly appears. He chases after her and yanks her by the arm, pulling her back around to face him. He's yelling at her, saying something I can't catch, and she's trying to pull away, but he won't let her go.

I'm moving before I can think about it, pushing past a couple of people making out by the window and walking out the French doors onto the terrace.

The guy, who is skinny and blond, with hair sprayed into some weird shape that looks like he walked backward through a wind tunnel, is still holding on to the girl. "Leave me alone, Jamie!" she yells.

Instinct kicks in. "You heard her," I say, stepping toward them and staring at the guy. My heart rate drops even as adrenaline seeps into my veins. "Let her go."

I'm aware of them both turning to look at me, the boy's face twisted up with anger. I'm aware, too, of his hand still gripping her arm, and I'm aware of the music and the sounds of the party, but only as a distant thrum beneath my own heartbeat. I move, lightning fast, and break the hold with a snap of my hand against his elbow.

The guy lets out a yell and falls back, clutching his arm and looking up at me, with a touch of fear flashing across his face as well as indignation. "What the hell? You just attacked me!" he shouts, looking around as though for witnesses to our exchange.

"I told you to get your hands off her," I answer quietly. I turn to the girl, ignoring him. "Are you okay?" I ask, searching her face.

I can't read her expression. She seems relieved but also

angry, though I can't tell at whom. I have my back to the guy, but I sense him as he comes up behind me, and I turn in time to catch his fist as it plows toward me. Keeping his fist gripped in my hand, I twist his arm up and behind his back. He lets out a high-pitched howl in response, but I don't let go.

"Ow! Get off!" He flails, trying to get free, but I hold him tighter, unsure if he's going to try to hit me again.

"Stop it!" the girl says to me. "Let him go."

Reluctantly I do, shoving him a little so he gets the message not to try anything.

I turn back to the girl. She has mascara streaked down her cheeks, but even so, she's breathtaking, with huge brown eyes, bronzed skin that's smooth as butter, and lips so full that I can't stop staring at them. I almost lose my train of thought. "You want me to walk you inside?" I finally manage to stutter, giving myself a mental slap.

She shakes her head and then looks away, as if she doesn't want me to see she's been crying. "No," she says, sounding annoyed.

I feel my simmering anger at the guy start to bubble up, irritated that she's making me feel like I did something wrong. Did I? "I'm only trying to help," I tell her. What was I meant to do, let him hurt her?

"I don't need your help," she spits. "I'm fine."

"Really?" I ask, sarcasm dripping off my voice as I glance at her arm.

She stops rubbing it. "We were just having an argument. It's none of your business."

"Yeah," the guy pipes up. "It's none of your business. So why not get lost?"

I raise an eyebrow at him. Get lost? That's the best he can come up with? Are we in grade school?

"Or I'll have you arrested for assault," he adds, fronting up to me, obviously keen not to lose face in front of his girlfriend.

"Are you going to tell the cops you also assaulted your girlfriend?" I ask him, managing to get a handle on my anger and keep my voice low.

"He didn't assault me," the girl interrupts. "Look, just go away, would you?"

I open my mouth, wanting to argue with her, but she's waving her hand at me like a princess dismissing a peasant, and even though it pains me, I force myself to say nothing and back off, shaking my head.

"Right," I say. "Well, good luck." I shoot a glance back at her boyfriend, who sneers at me. "Asshole," I mumble under my breath, but loud enough for him to hear me.

I head back inside. Tristan and Zoey are still slow-dancing and kissing, so I slip around the edge of the room, following a waiter as he heads into the kitchen. Once away from the party, I dart out a side door and make my way to my car.

When I was overseas, Zoey always used to write me emails. She'd sign them off saying, "Don't be a hero." From now on, I'm going to follow that advice.

WILL

The gates are wrought iron and ten feet high. Shards of broken glass stud the top of the walls on either side.

"It's like being back in Afghanistan," I mutter to myself as the sullen old guy in the security booth waves me through and up the long, winding driveway.

Up ahead I catch a glimpse of a house framed by palm trees and fringed with a bright bloom of pink bougainvillea. It's Spanish style, two floors, with lots of windows and balconies. Though the security might be on a par with an Afghan military base, the house is one hundred percent Beverly Hills.

I pull up beside a fountain that is almost as big as a swimming pool and sits in the middle of a circular driveway in front of the house. My beat-up old Bronco is wildly out of place in such manicured, high-end surroundings. I don't want to dirty up the view.

I follow the driveway around the side of the house, hoping to find somewhere to park around back, but as I do, a bright yellow Porsche screeches up, spraying gravel in its wake. I slam on my brakes, but this person doesn't seem to notice that they almost drove into me.

The Porsche pulls up in front of the house. The windows are tinted black, so I can't see who's driving and music pounds from inside; a stream of rap that drowns out the jazz track playing on my radio and makes my Bronco vibrate as though King Kong is rocking it. I shake my head and follow the drive around the house, tempted for half a second to reverse and get the hell out of here. I wonder if whoever is driving the car is the person I'm supposed to be interviewing with, and I worry that I'm doing the wrong thing. I don't want to work for a selfish asshole.

But instead, I pull into a shady parking spot beside a truck filled with gardening equipment and get out, pausing to scan the grounds, noting the team of gardeners grooming the bushes and clipping grass in the distance and a man dredging leaves from a glistening blue pool. My eyes skip over the menagerie of colorful floaties on the surface of the water and land on the perimeter wall, hidden in places by thick stands of eucalyptus and palms. I clock the half dozen cameras camouflaged in the trees and the one above the back door, as well as the touch-pad entry system and the reinforced glass windows. This house has more security than the military base I just spent the last year on, and over there we were facing bomb threats. But maybe that's normal in this world?

The back door opens as I start walking toward it. A woman in what I'm guessing to be her late twenties, wearing skinny jeans and high heels, stands on the threshold. She frowns at the sight of me, looking me up and down, and I pull off my sunglasses and arrange my face into what I hope resembles a smile. She doesn't smile back. Instead, her mouth tightens with disapproval. I guess maybe I should have shaved.

She's wearing stiletto heels and has more jewelry on display than the front window of Tiffany and Co. Diamonds drip from her fingers and ears, and a gold chain that could double as a bike lock hangs around her neck.

"You're the guy Emma sent?" she asks.

I nod and hold out my hand, forcing the smile to stay fixed on my face, even though she isn't reciprocating it. "Yes. I'm Will Ward."

She appears to be frowning, but her brow stays smooth as stretched latex. It's the pursed lips that give away her consternation. "You're very young," she remarks, and I pick up the trace of a Hispanic accent.

"Twenty-three," I tell her, wondering how old she is. At first glance I took her to be in her late twenties, but now I'm wondering if she's older, maybe even in her late thirties or early forties, with just really good skin.

"You were in the army?" she asks.

"Marines," I answer. "Just finished my fourth tour."

Her eyebrows rise the smallest amount. "Where were you deployed?" she asks.

I squint against the harsh sunlight. "Afghanistan mainly. Helmand Province. Iraq, too, for a while."

I wonder if this is the actual interview and it's being conducted here in the doorway. Maybe they don't let *the help* inside the house.

There's a long pause where she seems to be weighing me up before she steps aside and gestures for me to enter the house.

I have to admit I think twice about it. So far, nothing is making me feel like working here will be worth the hassle, but curiosity gets the better of me. I'm here now and I drove all this way, so what's ten more minutes?

When we walk into the cool interior of the house, my first thought is that it feels like entering a tomb. Despite the sunlight streaming through the windows, there's something airless about the place. All the windows are sealed tightly shut, killing the summer breeze, and instead of the balmy seventy degrees of outside, it's as cold as a morgue in here. The tile floors and white walls aren't helping to dispel that notion either, nor is the huge vase of white calla lilies on the table in the atrium-like hallway.

I hate those flowers and what they signify. The sight of them in their tall black vase takes me instantly back to the four funerals I've attended, all for brothers in the Marines who never made it home. I shiver involuntarily, fighting the urge to escape this place and get back outside into the sunshine.

The woman, who has introduced herself as Mrs. Rivera, leads me into a living room filled with giant white sofas and a grand piano. She gestures for me to sit on one of the sofas, and she takes a seat opposite me.

"So," the woman says to me, straightening the diamond-crusted watch on her wrist. "I take it you know what the job entails."

I shake my head. "No."

Emma didn't tell me much beyond the fact that someone she knew was looking for someone to work security. She said it would be an easy, fun job and that it would pay well. Right now I'm holding out hope that the third of those might still be correct.

The woman's lips tighten into the smallest pout of displeasure. "My daughter is receiving threats," she says.

Her *daughter*?

"The threats aren't public knowledge," the woman adds

hastily. "And this conversation that we're having is obviously confidential."

"Of course," I answer.

"I'll have our lawyer send you an NDA," she goes on.

"A nondisclosure agreement?" I interrupt.

"Yes." She nods. "It's standard. You don't have a problem with that, do you?"

"I don't need to sign an agreement. I just gave you my word."

She shrugs. "And with respect, I don't know you, and everyone in Luna's orbit has to sign one. That's the deal."

"With respect," I say to Luna's mother, "I was in the military for seven years—I know how to keep a secret."

Mrs. Rivera eyes me with a jaded expression. "And do you know how many times people have told me to trust them and have then sold my daughter out to the tabloids or gossip sites?"

I stay quiet.

"As I was saying," she goes on, "my daughter has been receiving threats."

"What kind of threats?" I ask.

Luna's mom stands up and walks over to the window. She takes in the view for a few seconds, then turns to me, and for the first time her face expresses an emotion that's clear to read: one of pure fear. "Death threats."

LUNA

'm starving and I have nothing to wear, and all I want to do is crawl into bed and watch *Queer Eye* while eating a gallon of ice cream, but I can't. I glance at my phone, which is lying on the bed. I promised myself I wouldn't go near it for at least twenty minutes and it's only been about five, though I'm not exactly sure because to check how long it's actually been, I'd have to look at the phone.

I step toward the bed but then stop myself. If I pick up the phone, I'll get sucked in. But what if Jamie has texted? He's probably awake by now. What time is it in Japan anyway? No. We broke up. We're over, this time for good. Last week at that party we got in a fight. It wasn't even over anything big. I wanted to go home and he wanted to stay. I didn't really know anyone, and I don't feel comfortable around strangers. I'm always too nervous to relax, too aware that I'm being watched like some rare species in a zoo. Jamie's the opposite. He thrives on attention. It's his oxygen. He loves knowing people are staring at him, and he becomes a different person in public, loud and kind of obnoxious, and that night I'd had enough.

I force myself to back away from the phone and focus instead on the problem of what to wear tonight. I don't want to go and I've already tried getting out of it several times, but standing up to Marty is like trying to stand up to Thanos.

Standing in the doorway to my walk-in closet, I glance at the rails of clothes and boxes of shoes stacked all the way to the ceiling like an architect's model of New York City skyscrapers, but instead of feeling excited about getting dressed up, I feel only a creeping sense of dread. My breathing is shallow, and it feels as if there are rocks pressing down on my shoulders and an army of ants on the march beneath my skin. I glance at my reflection in the mirror.

If only I could wear these sweatpants and a hoodie tonight. I laugh under my breath, imagining what people would say if I did. When I take a step toward the mirror, it's easy to see myself the way other people do, because it's like looking at a stranger. The girl in the mirror smiles at me, a big, broad dazzling smile. And it is so genuine that for a second I feel envy at how happy she is and wish I could feel that way myself.

Wanting to ease the antsy feeling, which is only getting worse, I head downstairs, making a beeline for the kitchen. I hurry to the freezer and yank open the door. Someone has been shopping. There are six tubs of Ben & Jerry's ice cream to choose from, one Cherry Garcia and the rest Chunky Monkey. Cruel. Carla knows my weaknesses and is exploiting them.

I hear the back door opening and spin around. Carla bustles in with her hands full of fresh pink and red roses she must have just cut from the bushes in the garden. Or maybe the gardener, Francisco, gave them to her. I've seen his eyes follow her when she wanders outside.

"Are you hungry?" she asks me, setting the flowers in the

sink before crossing to the fridge. "Let me make you something. You can't have ice cream for breakfast."

I slam the freezer door. "I wasn't going to," I say indignantly. "I'm not hungry."

Carla ignores me and starts pulling food from the fridge: eggs, tomatoes, chilies, cheese.

"I'm serious," I tell her. "I'm not hungry." But my mouth salivates all the same.

"Well, I'm going to make something anyway for Matias," she says. "I'll make you some too. You don't have to eat it."

I glower at her, but she is busy moving around the kitchen, gathering bowls and whisks and frying pans, and oh no, I realize too late what it is she's doing. . . . She's making huevos rancheros. She hums as she cracks the eggs into the bowl, and I watch as she starts to froth them with the whisk, adding liberal shakes of salt and pepper.

I did do a two-hour workout this morning, so surely I can cut myself a break just this once? Grudgingly I take a seat at the kitchen counter and watch Carla as she starts chopping a green chili, smiling a little smugly and very annoyingly to herself.

"Who's the cute guy talking to your mom?" Carla asks as she drops the chili into the egg mixture.

My head pricks up at that. "I don't know," I say, hopping off the stool and heading for the door. My suspicions are raised.

"Will you call your brother?" Carla asks, seeing me heading for the door. "Tell him breakfast is almost ready."

I mumble a yes, but I make straight for the living room, tiptoeing closer to the door. I can hear my mom talking in a low voice, but I can't make out what she's saying. I peek through the crack in the door and see a man with broad shoulders sitting on the sofa. It takes me a few seconds to place him, but then . . .

"No, no, no," I whisper to myself—it's the guy who inserted himself into my argument with Jamie at the party. What's he even doing here? How did he get in? Panic weaves through me.

". . . already been through three bodyguards," I catch my mom saying to him.

"Three?" he responds, sounding vaguely amused, vaguely horrified.

My stomach lurches. My blood starts to boil. I storm into the room. "What the hell is going on?" I demand, glaring at my mother. "What are you doing here?" I say, turning to the guy, who double-takes when he sees me, his mouth falling open.

My mom looks up at me, alarmed. "Luna," she stammers. "I thought you were out."

"Clearly," I answer, anger rising like a geyser in my chest.

"This is Will," she says now, gesturing toward him. He forces a smile, only it comes out as a grimace. He recognizes me too.

"Hey," he says with a trace of what looks like a smirk. "I think we met before."

My mom looks at him and then me with what can only be assumed is a frown, though it's impossible to tell because all the Botox she's had has frozen her face, so she always looks blank. "I thought you didn't know her," she says to him.

He shakes his head, and his nostrils flare in dislike. "I don't," he says. "We ran into each other at a party. I had no idea who she was."

Oh, nice. I laugh, though it comes out as a snort. He didn't know who I was? I'm sure he interrupted Jamie and me on purpose, wanting to know the juicy gossip and what we were arguing about, so he could spread it all around.

"What's he doing here?" I demand, without looking in his direction.

My mom glares at me, her eyes bulging because she thinks I'm being rude. "I'm hiring him to provide security," she says.

"I don't need security," I spit back, feeling my cheeks burn and adrenaline bursting through my veins, making me feel like I might explode. "I've already told you I don't want anyone. And definitely not him."

My mom nods. "I know. But I disagree, as does Marty."

"I don't care what you or Marty think. It's *my* life."

My mom takes a deep breath, then lets it out slowly, as though counting to ten. I bet she learned that in her one-to-one yoga class. "I know it's your life," she says calmly. "But Marty and I are making an executive decision."

I bite my lip, tears stinging my eyes. "No," I say. I feel like a toddler, and that I actually might stomp my foot. It's the injustice of it, the complete lack of control over my own life. It's a helpless feeling that makes my skin crawl. I don't want someone spying on me and reporting back to my mom on everything I do, or worse, selling me out. It's suffocating and humiliating, but no matter how many times I try to explain all this to her, I can't seem to make my own mother understand it.

"You don't have a choice in this," my mom answers.

"Screw you!" I manage to yell as a sob bursts out of me.

I turn around before she can see me crying, only to find Will standing in my way. I charge toward him, desperate to get out of the room, and he steps smartly aside, but I've already started to swerve around him and so we bump into each other. I shove him with my hands and he stumbles back, hitting the edge of the coffee table.

"Luna!" my mom shouts after me, but I ignore her and run up the stairs, tears streaming down my face.

WILL

I watch Luna run from the room. She's like a human hurricane, whirling in, wreaking havoc, then storming off to no doubt wreak havoc someplace else. What are the freaking odds? My heart leaped and sank at the same time when I saw it was the girl from the party. I'm tempted to get up and leave right now, but before I can, her mother starts talking at me again.

"I'm sorry," she says, turning back to me. "I was meaning to talk to her before you came, but she went out early this morning before I could."

I shrug. "That's okay." I hesitate for an awkward moment, then hold out my hand. "It was nice to meet you."

"You're not leaving, are you?" she asks, surprised.

I glance toward the door that Luna just ran through, crying. "Well," I say, "I figured that she doesn't want a bodyguard, so—"

"What Luna wants doesn't matter," her mother interrupts.

I laugh to myself. "It kind of does. I can't do this job if the person I'm paid to protect doesn't want me around."

Her mom sighs and gestures to the sofa. I don't want to sit down, though, because I just want to get out of here. I'm not a fan of drama. I've had enough of it to last a lifetime. "I think I should go," I tell her.

"Please," she urges. "Let me at least tell you what's going on." Before I can stop her, she gets up and walks over to the door and closes it, cutting off my escape.

I glance at the window with its triple-thick glass, then sigh and sit back down.

Once she sees that I'm no longer about to bolt, she sits down too, perching on the edge of her seat, ready to leap to her feet if I try to flee again.

"Letters started arriving about two years ago," she says. "They were nasty—abusive, but they weren't threatening her life. We thought it was just an angry fan."

"A fan?" I ask. "Why would a fan send nasty letters?"

"I mean, a fan of Jamie's."

"Who's Jamie?" I ask, confused.

Mrs. Rivera gives me a look like she wonders if I'm joking. "Are you serious?"

I nod.

"Have you been living in a hole for the last six years?"

"Kind of," I answer, deadpan. "I've been on deployment, remember?"

She flushes. "Of course. I'm sorry."

"It's okay."

"I'm talking about Jamie Whitstone. He's a singer. He just had a Billboard number one. His album has been in the top ten for sixty-three weeks. He recently launched a clothing line. He's her boyfriend."

"Oh," I say, trying to hide my reaction. "We met at the party. Nice guy."

Her mother's face doesn't change. Not even a flicker. She has an even better poker face than I do. I wonder if she likes the guy or not, or if she knows how badly he treats her daughter.

"They're on and off a lot. *A lot*." She rolls her eyes.

"Are you sure he isn't behind the threats?" I ask, thinking back to Jamie's behavior at the party and the way he was dragging Luna back by the arm.

Mrs. Rivera shakes her head at me. "It's not him. They get hand delivered, often when Jamie's overseas. The police have already investigated."

"I was about to ask if the police were involved."

She nods. "We spoke to a detective a while ago, but he wasn't able to trace the letters, and until the person who sends them actually does something more than send letters, until he threatens her in person, there's nothing more they can do, apparently."

"So, if it's only an angry fan, or someone who's jealous, why not just ignore them?" I ask. It sounds like middle school–level drama to me when I compare it to what I've seen in Afghanistan—a place where threats are usually followed by an IED explosion. Even the police didn't take it seriously, which tells me something.

"You don't understand," Luna's mom goes on. "At first we thought they were letters from a jealous fan of Jamie's, or someone who just hates Luna. You'd be amazed at the nasty things people post online."

I don't have social media, but I can guess. I know enough about people to know that most of them aren't very nice, and they're even less nice when they can hide behind anonymity.

"I tell Luna not to read the comments online, but short of taking away her phone, I can't stop her. But then the death threats started," she goes on. "And they were detailed. Extremely graphic. Explaining what this person wanted to do to her." She swallows hard, as though even recalling it is difficult, and then she looks up at me, and I see her eyes are welling up with tears. "I mean, I know you must have seen some awful things in your time, but this was pretty much the worst thing I've ever read. And this is my daughter we're talking about. I'll do anything to protect her."

I nod because I get it. I'd do anything to protect my family too. Though, admittedly, when they needed me most, I was overseas—I wasn't there for them. If it weren't for Tristan, they may not even be here at all, but I force myself to avoid thinking about the past. If I don't, I'd spend my life beating myself up over something I can't change.

"These letters, they were sent to the house?" I ask, forcing myself to focus.

She nods, and I can see she's struggling to keep composure, obsessively twisting the diamond rings on her fingers. "Yes. Whoever sent them found out our address. But they also send letters to the hotels we stay at when we're on tour or traveling. Luna even found one in her dressing room. We have security on-site, so whoever sent it managed to get backstage and into her private space. It really scared me. And a month ago someone broke into her tour bus. . . . They slashed the seats with a knife, threw red paint all over everything. It looked like a slaughter-house. It was horrific."

I take that in, feeling a buzz of irritation. "Where was her bodyguard when all this happened?"

"He was distracted, watching Luna rehearse."

Sounds like a real pro. I shake my head in disgust.

"We got rid of him, obviously," she adds.

"You mentioned there were three bodyguards. What happened to the other two?"

"One sold gossip about Luna to the *National Enquirer*, so I fired him."

I wonder what kind of gossip, but I don't ask.

"And the third one quit."

"How long did he last?" I ask, alarm bells ringing loudly.

She hesitates. "Eight days," she finally admits. "He found the job too challenging."

I can't think why.

"Whoever is doing it has to be someone who knows Luna," I say. "Someone who knows her schedule, and someone who doesn't look out of place wandering around backstage."

Mrs. Rivera nods in agreement.

"So, it should be easy to figure out who it is," I say.

She lifts her chin at me. "You would think so, but there are dozens of people it could be: assistants, makeup artists, stylists, PR people, managers, agents, advertisers, brand strategists, musicians."

She keeps reeling off job titles, though I have no idea what even half of them mean.

"It could be anyone," she admits, throwing her hands in the air.

"Why is Luna so against having a bodyguard, given the situation? Is it just because she doesn't trust them to do the job properly?"

Mrs. Rivera sighs loudly again, and I see it's a sore spot for her. "Well, it's not as if the last three have given her much confidence. And she thinks they get in the way of her living her life, that they're there to spy on her. We've also kept a few of the more recent letters from her, not wanting to scare her."

I take that in. Maybe she should be told; it might help them convince her she needs security.

Her mom looks at me. "So, will you take the job?"

LUNA

don't need a freaking babysitter. I'm nineteen! How many times do I need to tell my mom that I'm an adult and I can make my own choices? I'm sick of her and Marty and their *executive decisions*. To them, I'm not a person with feelings; I'm a money-making robot. If they could turn me off and not have to deal with me until it came time to wheel me out and push me onstage, they'd be a lot happier. They always think they know what's best, and I'm sick of it.

I know I've had threats, but those were a while ago, and it's not as if anyone can get near me when I'm home, thanks to all the security cameras and alarms. I hardly go anywhere either, so what do I need a bodyguard for? It's not like they've stopped any of the threats or figured out who is behind them, not to mention the fact they're never reliable or trustworthy. The first guy perved on the dancers and let someone walk onto my tour bus and deface it. And the second one sold me out to the tabloids. The last guy I acted like a total diva toward, in the hopes of making him quit, and it worked.

My mom's using the threats as an excuse to employ someone

to spy on me. The fact that I don't want yet another man giving me orders, spying on me, and interfering in my life is of no concern to her or to Marty or to anyone.

I throw myself down on the bed and bury my face in a pillow before I let out a howl of frustration. I bet that guy Will is going to go and tell all his friends about me. He'll probably post something on Twitter about what a bitch I am, and how I'm not half as pretty in the flesh.

That's what they always do. *And they're right*, the voice in my head pipes up with a friendly reminder.

My phone buzzes. I sit up and grab for it. It's a reminder from Marty about my schedule for this afternoon. The ants are crawling over and under my skin, and I pace my room, hands on hips, trying to catch my breath, but it feels as if I'm wearing an iron corset and sipping air through a straw.

There's a knock on my door. "Go away!" I shout, feeling lightheaded. I don't want to see my mom right now.

But then there's another knock. This time more of a thud. I run over to the door and pull it open. It's Matias, in his *Star Wars* pajamas. His lip is trembling and he looks like he's about to burst into tears. "Why go away?" he asks plaintively.

"I didn't know it was you," I tell him. "I'm sorry."

He gives me a timid smile, and I pull him into the room, closing the door behind him. He runs and dives onto my bed, already laughing, and I jog over to the remote and throw it to him.

"Gumball!" he shouts with excitement as he flips to his favorite cartoon. I sit next to him on the bed as he cranks the volume up, and I smile despite the fact the sound is deafening because the joy on his face is so infectious.

I stretch out beside him and watch the cartoon as Matias

bounces on the bed, guffawing with laughter. Lying here beside him helps distract me from the ants and the tightness in my chest.

People find Matias to be hard work, or at least some people do. He's been through almost as many occupational therapists and special needs teachers as I have security guards. But Matias, despite his size—he's taller than me and he's only twelve—and his uncoordinated movements, isn't difficult to manage, not if you get to know him, which most people don't. He's the sweetest boy on the planet, and easily my favorite human, which isn't hard because most people I meet are Grade A assholes with their own agendas who can't be trusted not to screw me over.

Matias just doesn't know how to communicate quite like other children his age. Most people can't be bothered to engage with him, so they make up ideas about him that aren't true. I guess Matias and I have that in common.

Carla knocks and enters a few minutes later, carrying a tray laden with plates of food and glasses of fresh-squeezed orange juice.

"I thought you and Matias could have breakfast in bed," she says, crossing to the bed, where she greets Matias with a big smile. "Good morning!" she says.

"Good morning." Matias grins back. He loves Carla more than he loves cartoons, which is saying something. Besides me, Carla's the only person who actually bothers to make an effort with him. I can't help that voice inside me wondering if it's because she's paid to.

"Did you sleep well?" Carla asks Matias.

Matias nods and reaches for a spoon and his special bowl— a blue plastic *Ninjago* one he eats all his meals out of—where

Carla has piled his food, already thoughtfully cut up into bite-size pieces. "Eggs!" he shouts in delight.

Carla turns to me and nods at the other plate on the tray. "Eat it while it's hot," she says.

I frown. Carla—a trained special needs teacher—has worked for us for the last eight years, mainly to look after Matias, but she seems to think that gives her permission to order me around too.

"You can't live on Diet Coke and air," she adds, hands on hips.

"I don't," I protest, albeit weakly because I have tried this diet in the past.

"You don't eat enough."

She sounds like my mother, except my mother is usually telling me to watch what I eat.

"Are you pining for Jamie?" she asks, a strong note of disapproval in her voice.

I huff. "No." Pining suggests I'm a dog sitting on a doormat, waiting for its master to come home, tongue lolling out. And I'm not doing that. Not really.

"Good, because you deserve better than him. He doesn't treat you the way you deserve to be treated."

I shrug. I don't know about deserving better. Who else would put up with me? But this time I am determined to stay broken up with him. It's not as if we make each other happy. I think we just get back together out of habit. We've been together so long and we've shared so much, it's hard to break that habit.

Back when we first got together, before either of us were so well known, things were different. He was sweet and genuine, and we were best friends, supporting each other. It's tough for people who aren't in this world to understand the pressures, and he did because he was dealing with the same level of public scrutiny.

But in the last two years, his ego has grown out of control. He seems to thrive on adoration, and he's adopted this swagger that he never used to have. Maybe part of the reason I go back to him is because I keep hoping that the old Jamie will resurface sometime.

"There's extra hot sauce on your eggs," Carla says, switching topics back to food.

To appease her, I sit down on the bed. I am hungry, and so I give in to her evil temptress hot-sauce ways. Carla looks on approvingly as I take my first bite.

"Did you find out who the cute guy is?" she asks as I swallow.

I frown. "No one," I say.

Carla makes a *hmmm* sound and starts busying herself picking up items of clothing from the floor, as well as bits of stray knitting. I know she's just hanging around to make sure I finish my food.

"And he wasn't handsome," I mutter.

"You need an eye exam, then." She chuckles as she throws my dirty clothes into the laundry basket.

I start to protest, but the eggs go down the wrong way and I start coughing. Matias slaps me on the back so hard I almost bounce off the bed. "Saved your life!" he announces proudly when I'm done coughing.

I glare at Carla, who is still smirking with amusement. "Hot," she comments.

"He is not hot," I splutter.

"I meant the eggs," she says, laughing as she walks out the door.

WILL

Mrs. Rivera is still waiting on me to answer her about whether I'm taking the job, but I don't know what to say. I'm torn. Half of me wants to say no and walk away. I want peace and quiet, and neither Luna nor her world fits that description. But on the other hand, now that I know the threat she's facing, I don't feel like I can walk away. What if I did, and something happened to her?

But this is not the same situation as the one my family was in, and I have no obligation to Luna. In fact, considering how rude she's been to me, it's clear she doesn't want me around, so why would I say yes?

"I think you'd be perfect."

I frown at her. How does she even know that? She doesn't know anything about me. As far as she's concerned, I could be as bad, or worse, than any of the other guys she's previously employed. "Why?" I ask her.

"For one, you're not impressed," she answers.

"Excuse me?"

She gestures at the house. "By her. By the house. You don't seem to care. A lot of people are drawn to this world because they think it's exciting, because they want to be around it, and all the glamour. They're more interested in the fame and the celebrity than in the actual job. That's not you."

I nod. She's got that right.

"And I don't think you're the kind of person who will be intimidated by my daughter either."

"Intimidated?" I say, trying to keep the smirk out of my voice. Luna's about as intimidating as a mosquito.

She nods. "Yes. Luna is good at getting her own way. She's very stubborn."

I can see that.

"Luna's sometimes her own worst enemy," she continues. Her gaze drops to the ground and for a brief second she's lost in thought, but then she looks up at me. "But most of all, she needs someone she can trust not to betray her. Someone who will do the job, watch over her and keep her safe, but keep a professional distance. I think that's you."

I meet her gaze. I can't help but feel like Mrs. Rivera is trying to manipulate me into taking the job. She's trying to flatter me into saying yes, and there's nothing I hate more than feeling like I'm being manipulated. "How do you know that's me?" I ask.

"I ran a background check."

"What?" I ask, feeling my irritation levels spiking.

She gives me a cool, unbothered look in response. "I run checks on all potential employees."

My hand grips the car door until my knuckles bleach. I try to steady my breathing, but I'm pissed. How dare she do something like that without my permission?

"I know that you're highly decorated. You received a Silver Star."

Blood starts to pound in my temples.

"And your superiors spoke very highly of your integrity, loyalty, and leadership skills. I also know that you overcame some early challenges."

My breathing becomes shallow, as it always does when I enter a state of high alert.

"Your father is in prison."

I maintain a steady gaze, but all my senses are primed for fight or flight, and I have to tell myself to breathe and relax.

"I'm sorry," she says. "I know that must have been hard for you."

I make no response, but my teeth are gritted.

"I know, too, that you were providing for your mother and siblings, sending them your wages, and that you're in significant amounts of debt."

I swallow hard, my face heating up. Whoever ran a background check somehow got hold of my financial history, which makes me angrily indignant as well as embarrassed because that's no one's damn business but mine.

I joined the Marines for the signing bonus. I gave it to my mom, hoping she could use it to get away from my dad, but my dad found the money and took it. He spent it on a weekend in Vegas.

When my mom, my sisters, and my brother did finally get away from him, they were housed at first in an emergency shelter, but it wasn't safe and I was worried, so I took a loan out to help them get their own place. I told my mom that it was money I had saved, but it wasn't. It was one of those high-interest loans. I've been struggling to pay it off ever since, never managing to even make a dent, thanks to the skyrocketing interest payments.

"I'll pay you double," Luna's mom says.

I freeze. *Double?* I have no idea how much the rate was to begin with, but double? I think about the weight of all the worry I'm carrying around and how nice it would be to not have that on my shoulders anymore.

Still, I'm furious at the invasion of my privacy. How dare she dive into my financial records?

"How about if you agreed to just a six-week contract? Initially?"

My shoulders involuntarily relax. That's definitely more appealing. I could earn enough to make a dent in those interest payments, and I wouldn't be signing away my life.

"And a bonus of five thousand if you stay the whole six weeks," she adds, seeing my hesitation.

I hesitate some more, doing the math. Five thousand dollars as a bonus? That would go a huge way to clearing my debt. I could do six weeks. I've done a lot worse for a hell of a lot less, after all.

"And you can stay in the apartment over the garage. Rent-free," she says, sensing that she's close to convincing me. In fact, she already has.

I nod. "Six weeks. But that's it." I should feel relieved that I've finally got a job, but a sense of foreboding hangs over me that I just made a huge mistake and am walking into a situation I'm going to regret.

Mrs. Rivera takes a relieved breath. "Thank you."

"When would I need to start?" I ask her.

"Today. Tonight," she says.

"What?" I say, surprised. "I don't have any of my things with me. I—"

"I can send a driver to pick your things up," she interrupts.

"Seriously?" I ask, bemused. "Oceanside's an hour and a half away."

She waves me off as though it's no bother. "There's an event tonight. Whoever is sending these letters warned us that they'd be there. I want you to be there too, with Luna, to make sure she's safe."

"Why is she going if threats have been made?" I ask.

"She has to," her mother answers in a firm voice.

"Why?" I ask, confused.

"It's a big deal," she explains. "An award ceremony. Luna's giving out the award for best music video."

"Can't she pull out?" I ask.

"No," Mrs. Rivera says with a shake of her head. "She's contracted to do it."

I shake my head too, still confused. It sounds ridiculous. "I don't get how these things work," I say as politely as I can, "but it seems to me that nothing's that important, and surely if the organizers knew about the threats, they'd be okay with releasing Luna from any obligation?"

Luna's mother laughs at me as though I've said something naive. "You're right." She pushes herself up to stand. "You really don't get how these things work. But you'll learn."

I bristle at her tone.

"I'll have Carla show you the apartment," she says, already turning away and heading back toward the house.

"Oh, Will?"

I look back around. Mrs. Rivera has stopped by the back door and is glancing over her shoulder at me.

"Yeah?"

"You'll need a tux for tonight."

LUNA

The girl in the mirror has bright red lips and a brilliant smile. Her eyelids are crusted with sequins, and her skin glitters like ice. Her hair is twisted up into an ornate updo that exposes her neck and shoulders. The dress is cobalt blue in some light, purple in others, and clings so tightly that I wish I hadn't eaten those eggs earlier, or anything in fact for the last week, and can only send prayers for the invention of Spanx. There's a slit up the side of the dress, thankfully, so I don't have to teeter terribly on these ridiculous shoes with their heels like skewers and overly complicated straps.

"It's very gladiator mermaid." Natalie beams, dusting my shoulders with some more glitter.

Just the look I've always wanted to try, I think to myself.

"You look amazing," she says. "Do you like it?"

"I love it!" I say, startling myself with the force of my enthusiasm because inside I feel as flat and deflated as a ripped helium balloon.

Marty barges into my bedroom without the courtesy of even knocking first. He looks me up and down, appraising me like I'm a mannequin. "That looks good," he finally says.

Not *You look good*. *That looks good*. Whatever air was left in the balloon whistles out, leaving me feeling like a piece of trash lying on a dirty sidewalk.

"You ready?" he barks.

I nod, no longer smiling. "I guess."

"Cheer up," he answers in his gruff English accent. He holds open the bedroom door and I walk through it.

Marty claims to be cockney, born and bred in East London, but I've heard him on the phone once or twice to his mom when he didn't know I was in the room, and he sounded very different, like an actor reading Shakespeare. I wonder if he's playing a part as much as I am, in his case the role of the pop star's manager.

He's older, but he dresses like he's in his twenties in too-tight T-shirts and ripped jeans. He likes to pair them with pointy leather shoes, and he sports a diamond earring in one ear. All in all, having him compliment my look doesn't fill me with confidence.

"Let's go, then. Don't want to be late," he says, ushering me toward the stairs. I freeze at the top, spotting Will standing in the hall below by the front door, wearing black tie. I grip the banister to stop myself from tripping. What's he still doing here? And why's he wearing a tux?

My mom exits the living room just then and looks up at me. I glare at her. My fury meets her stone-cold defiance and bounces right off it as though she's made of Teflon-coated rubber. She doesn't care what I want; that much was already clear. She must have hired him after all, and he's coming with me tonight. Great.

"All right, Luna?" Marty asks, his hand on my elbow, trying to hustle me along. I shake his hand off and start walking. My legs quiver, though, as I descend the stairs, and I have to hold tight to the banister because I'm scared I might fall.

When I reach the bottom in one piece, Will opens the front door for me. I feel like yelling at him that I can open a damn door, I don't need his help for that. I stride past him, glowering pointedly in his direction, but his expression remains totally blank. It's as though he's looking through a pane of glass. He doesn't even see me.

I storm through the door, heading for the limo parked in front of the house, and somehow, before I get two paces, he's one step ahead of me, his head moving on a pivot left to right as if he expects an assassin to leap out of the fountain.

He opens the car door for me, and I climb in, determined to ignore him. As we set off down the drive, I ignore my mom, too, who is waving from the front door, and I try to tune out the nonstop chatter of Natalie sitting beside me as well. It's easy enough, since now that we've started to leave, I suddenly feel sick, my skin crawling with ants and my stomach churning. I'd been holding off thinking about walking out onstage tonight, but now there's no more ignoring it.

I take a deep breath, but in this dress it's impossible to breathe properly, and my head starts to spin. I want to put my head between my knees, but I can't really bend, either, due to how tight it is. I have to comfort myself with leaning forward, tapping Will on the shoulder, and asking him to turn up the AC.

He complies without a word.

"New bodyguard?" Natalie asks in a loud whisper, poking me in the ribs until I'm forced to tune back in. She nods toward Will. "What's his name?"

I shrug. "I don't know."

"I hope he sticks around longer than the last one," she whispers.

"I hope he doesn't," I mutter. I'm already planning on acting the diva so he quits, like the last guy did.

Will turns his head then, just a fraction, giving me a glimpse of his profile. Did he hear? He turns again to face forward. He isn't hot. What are Natalie and Carla thinking?

WILL

I can hear Luna and her friend with the red hair whispering in the back of the limo, but I tune it out. My phone buzzes and I glance at the screen. It's Dahlia, asking about the tux. After Mrs. Rivera told me I needed one for tonight, I called the only person who I thought might have an idea where I could get one on such late notice. She hooked me up with a stylist friend of hers, who lent me one for the evening. I feel like a penguin in it and it's too tight in the shoulders, but that's okay. I don't think anyone is going to be looking at me. It's safe to say all eyes will be on Luna tonight.

I text Dahlia, then stick my phone back in my pocket and concentrate. As we pull out through the gates, I check for any cars lurking on the street that might be following, and what do you know, a white truck parked a block down switches on its headlights and pulls out behind us. It follows us all the way down the canyon and onto Hollywood Boulevard.

I wonder if it's a fan or if it's the person who's making the threats against Luna. I turn to the driver, a guy in his fifties, and tell him to take the next right. He's in the left-hand lane, and he looks at me with a frown.

"What?" he asks.

"Take a right. Just do it," I tell him.

His gaze falls to my holster, which I know is visible, thanks to the tightness of the jacket, and then he obeys, swinging across lanes and making Luna and her friend let out shrieks of alarm. When I turn around, Luna is staring right at me, eyes narrowed.

"What's going on?" she demands.

"Detour," I tell her, looking in the side mirrors to see if the white truck that was following us is still on our tail. It is. It jumps the red light to follow us.

"That's Donny," Luna says, sighing.

"Excuse me?" I say, eyes still on the mirror.

"He's a photographer."

I glance her way. She jerks her head out the window toward the truck behind us. "It's Donny, behind us in the white truck," she says.

She knew we were being followed?

"So if you're done with the *Fast and Furious* driving tactics," she snarks, "can we get to where we're meant to be going? I'm already late."

Face burning, I turn to the driver and offer him an apologetic shrug. He purses his lips and sighs, taking the next right to bring us full circle back to where we were. There are giggles from the back seat.

"Donny's always following Luna," the girl with the red hair says. "We joke that she pays all his bills."

I shake my head, confused.

The girl smiles at me. "He's a paparazzo," she explains. "A photo of Luna can earn him five hundred dollars. He sells them to magazines, newspapers, gossip sites."

I shake my head at the weirdness of a stranger following you around taking pictures of you with a zoom lens and the even greater weirdness that people pay that much money for a photo of Luna, or of anyone.

"I can speak to him if you like," I say, looking over at Luna. "Make him stop."

"No," she answers, without even looking in my direction. "It's fine."

I guess she likes the attention. I glance at the red-haired girl, who smiles at me some more and gives me the eye. She's not shy about it either. She's pretty, with sharp cheekbones and wide-set brown eyes. I smile back at her, then turn to glance once again in the side mirrors. There's Donny right behind us in his white truck, still on our tail.

My phone buzzes again. This time it's my sixteen-year-old sister, Kate, who's found out about my new job and is now harassing me for insider intel. She's already sent a dozen texts demanding gossip. I ignore this one just like I ignored all the others. I'll call her tomorrow when I have some downtime. If I have any downtime. I've been told I'm on call 24/7. Wherever Luna goes, I go. I'm not to let her out of my sight whenever we're in public.

When we arrive at the award ceremony, I'm momentarily thrown. There's an actual red carpet and hundreds of people crowding the sidewalk, held back behind metal railings. As we pull up in front of the theater, I'm half-blinded by flashes going off and wish I'd had more time to prepare a plan. I only had thirty minutes to go over the location's blueprints and to map the exits in my head, and I had no idea there would be this level of pandemonium outside. There must be over five hundred people in the crowd.

Before I can get out of the car and assess for threats, I hear the back door of the limo opening. I leap out and find Luna already stepping out. A man in a suit, wearing an earpiece, is about to open the door for her. I push in front of him.

"I've got this," I tell him.

He steps aside and I block Luna's exit from the car with my body. I scan the crowd quickly, my eyes skipping over faces. I don't know who I'm looking for, or what, but I'm trained in VIP protection and it's the first thing we do before we allow the person we're protecting into a public space. We assess the situation for danger. Right now I'm scouring the faces in the crowd, memorizing them, looking for things out of the ordinary. Given the threats made against her, ideally I'd have wanted her to enter via a private back door or side entrance, away from the crowds, but when I mentioned it to Marty earlier, he dismissed the idea with a snort, saying something about not wasting a good PR opportunity.

A middle-aged man in the crowd stands out like a sore thumb and immediately grabs my attention. He's the only man among a sea of screaming teenage girls. But then I see he's holding hands with two young girls and that he looks pretty bored, and I figure he's probably their dad, accompanying his daughters here against his will.

I'm knocked back a step as the car door smashes into me. Luna, tired of waiting for me to open it, has shoved all her weight against it. She gives me a death stare as she steps out, but then she turns toward the crowd and the glare is gone. In its place is a megawatt smile. Luna waves, and the screaming from the sea of teenage girls gets louder.

As she walks forward onto the red carpet, ushered by a

woman in a cocktail dress who is holding an iPad, I start to follow, at a distance to give her space but staying close enough to reach her if I need to.

Luna poses in front of a cluster of photographers, hand on hip, her chin raised and tilted slightly. She's smiling and laughing and acting like she wouldn't want to be anywhere else in the world but right there in front of them, having her photo taken. The transformation from the sulky girl in the back of the limo is so extreme that I am mesmerized by it, by *her*. She comes alive under the lights, her skin glittering like she's made of diamonds, but it's more than the makeup doing it. She seems to glow from the inside, and it's hard to pull my eyes away in order to do my job. For the first time in my life I understand the meaning of the phrase "star power." Whatever it is, Luna has it in spades.

Annoyed at letting myself get distracted, I go back to checking off faces in the crowd, mentally examining everyone I see and filing their images away in my memory bank. When Luna stops posing and moves on up the red carpet, I follow, keeping her in my peripheral vision, ensuring she's only ever a few steps away from me, just in case.

As we near the door to the theater, instead of heading inside as the woman with the iPad is trying to get her to do, Luna walks over to the crowd gathered behind the railings. It's another crowd of teenage girls, all of whom are holding up their phones, snapping photos and videos.

Luna poses for selfies, shakes hands, offers hugs, and signs T-shirts and even someone's arm with a Sharpie pen. I step closer, ready to intercede, because some of the girls look close to overexcited and are starting to push and shove to get nearer, but Luna shoots me a warning glare, ordering me to keep my distance. I stop where I am, still within arm's reach, watching the edges of the crowd where I notice it's starting to surge as people shove each other in order to get closer to Luna. I look around for whoever is doing crowd control, but the venue's security people are mostly at the other end of the carpet.

"We should go," I whisper to Luna.

"Leave me alone," she hisses, moving to sign more autographs. And as I begin to reluctantly step back, out of the corner of my eye I see a young girl, no older than eleven, get thrown against the metal railing as the crowd surges. I rush forward, watching in horror as the girl is knocked to her knees and disappears beneath a trample of feet and legs. I leap the railing, shouting at the girls to get back, shoving my arms down into the mosh pit and hauling the girl up by her collar. I heft her up over my shoulder and lift her over the crowd, which pushes and buffets like a storm around me.

The venue's security guards have finally noticed the commotion and they race over. One takes the girl from my arms, and others yell at the crowd to back off. I jump the railing again back onto the red carpet side and crouch down by the girl who was almost crushed.

"You okay?" I ask her, checking her for any sign of injury.

The girl sniffs back tears and nods.

Luna is suddenly beside her on her knees. "Are you hurt?" she asks the girl.

The girl's mouth drops open as she beholds Luna kneeling beside her. She's rendered speechless, and when I look at Luna, glittering in front of her, I can see why. She looks like some kind of angel.

"Here, let's take a photo," Luna says to the girl, giving her a

Mila Gray

warm smile, and because the girl is too starstruck to move, Luna takes the girl's phone and hands it to me.

I follow orders, snapping a photo of Luna with her arm around the girl, and when I hand the phone back, I catch Luna's eye. For a moment I think she is about to say something to me, maybe thank me for saving the girl's life, or even for just taking the photo, but she doesn't. She gets to her feet and smiles and waves at her adoring fans, before striding off down the red carpet.

I follow at a safe distance.

LUNA

He's breathing down my neck. Wherever I turn, there he is. Even with my back to him, I can feel him hovering behind me, like a stalker. I look over at him, standing a few steps away from the makeup table, his hands folded in front of him, head on a swivel like the freaking Terminator wearing a tux. He's tall, but unlike the normal crew-cut, clean-shaven guards I've had before, he has a beard. It makes me wonder whether he's growing it to look cool. But it's scruffy, so I wonder if it's just that he can't be bothered to shave. Jamie's tried for years to grow a beard and never succeeded in growing anything more than a few pale wisps.

"Did you see him leap over that railing?" Natalie asks, nodding at Will as she applies fresh lipstick to my lips.

I shake my head.

"It was like he was in *Mission: Impossible*," she says, swooning.

Will looks over just then at Natalie as though he's heard her, and I feel a sharp twist of annoyance that he'll look at her but not at me. Whenever he looks in my direction, his eyes just skip over me, as though I'm a blank wall. I am pretty sure he hates me. But that's okay, because I don't much like him, either, and I want him to hate me. That way he'll quit.

The woman with the iPad who has been hovering by the makeup table appears at my side. "Five minutes," she tells me.

I nod, feeling the worms writhing in my gut and the nausea starting to build. My entire life is regimented by people with iPhones and walkie-talkies. I wonder where Marty is, but he doesn't need to be here with me because the responsibility for getting me here was his and he did his job. The responsibility for getting me onstage is now this woman's. I look at my phone. I want to text Jamie. It's habit, rather than necessity. When I'm anxious, I usually turn to him to distract me. He understands what it's like to feel nervous before going onstage, though he doesn't get panic attacks like I do.

I am determined not to cave, though, so I glance at Will, who is looking in the opposite direction, and then I tell the iPad woman I need the bathroom.

She looks a little worried, given there's only five minutes to go before I have to present onstage, but I don't give her the chance to argue, as I'm already walking as fast as I can toward the exit.

Once through the door, I up my pace, darting down a hallway filled with waitstaff who are too busy carrying trays of glasses and canapés to pay me much notice. I don't know where the bathrooms are and I don't want to waste time by asking. Up ahead I've seen a green Exit sign and so I shove my way toward it, then through it and into a loading bay. A couple of waitstaff are hanging around a dumpster, vaping. I walk past them, inhaling the heady smell of weed, and around a corner into a parking lot, where I duck into a shadowed recess and lean my head back against a wall.

How many minutes do I have left? Three and a half? Two and

a half if I want to make it back in time. I can feel my heart beating like a kettledrum being hit by someone with bad rhythm.

I start to tug at the ring on my finger. It's a huge black onyx, and when it comes off, I flip it open, revealing a hidden compartment inside, like a jewel box hiding secret gems, in this case two blue Xanax pills.

I break one in half because I only need a little to manage my nerves. I'm so anxious about walking onstage that I need to take the edge off. If I go on like this, I won't even be able to open the envelope without my hands shaking or my knees buckling. I put the pill in my mouth and tip my head back to swallow. When I open my eyes, I find Will standing right in front of me.

"You okay?" he asks.

Did he see? Now he's probably going to sell the story to the *National Enquirer*. LUNA RIVERA DOES DRUGS! Even though Xanax is perfectly legal, it's all about twisting the truth.

"I'm fine," I say, starting to move around him, heat blazing across my face.

"Hey," he says, blocking my way. He's scowling. "You shouldn't run off like that."

"I'll do whatever I want," I say slowly, making sure he hears every syllable before pushing past him.

"It's dangerous," he answers.

I roll my eyes and storm off, heading back toward the fire exit door. I push against it, but it won't open. Shit. I'm going to be late. I thump on the door with my fist, hoping someone on the other side will hear and open it.

"Here." It's Will, edging past me to wave a security pass at a card reader by the door handle. How did he get that? The door clicks and I shove it open before he can.

I make my way down the hallway toward the backstage area, but it's crowded now with dozens of event staff and I can barely squeeze a path through. I'm going to miss my cue to go onstage. I can already hear Marty's voice in my head, yelling at me for screwing up, and my heart is going crazy, trying to tunnel a way out of my chest. I wish I'd taken that pill sooner so I'd feel calm right now, but instead it feels as if my ribs are splintering. I can't breathe. My vision swims.

A waiter carrying a tray of hot shrimp and sauce bumps into me, and it almost all goes sliding down the front of my dress, but luckily, Will's suddenly by my side, pulling me out of the way, and then he's taking my hand and pushing through the crowd, forcing a path through somehow, and then we're in an empty corridor and I find that I can breathe again. I have no idea where we are, but Will seems to know where we're going, so I let him lead me. He makes a series of turns, and God knows how, but he gets us to the backstage area.

"There you are!" the woman with the iPad says. Her eyes are wide and panicked, and she rushes over and takes me by the elbow. I feel like I'm a relay baton being passed from one runner to the next as she pulls me toward the wings of the stage.

My hand slips from Will's. I look back over my shoulder for him, relieved to see he's only a few feet behind me.

The pill is starting to work, its little atoms speeding through my bloodstream, spreading peace. My heartbeat has slowed, my lungs can inhale their fill, my vision no longer swims. The cheers of a thousand people are a muted white noise in the background, and it's only when I'm nudged by the woman with the iPad that I realize they're saying my name. I throw back my shoulders and walk, or rather, float, out of the wings and onto the stage.

WILL

Luckily for me, I have practice standing on parade, so I grin and bear it, or just bear it. The grinning is not happening. I've found an out-of-the-way spot, half-hidden behind a large fern, where I have a view of the whole room and all the exits within reach. If only I could escape through one right now, instead of having to stand here listening to the deafening din of rich people talking about themselves.

After the award ceremony we moved to an after-party at a swanky hotel. Luna is easy to keep an eye on as she's the focal point of the entire room. She's like the moon with her silver-sparkle gleam, except, unlike the moon, everything and everyone revolves around her rather than the other way around.

I'm trying not to seethe about her sneaking off earlier. The truth is, though, that I'm not so much mad at her as I am at me for almost losing her. My first day on the job and I'm getting distracted by this wild world I've been dropped into.

I look at Luna now, smiling as her manager, Marty, introduces her to some other man in his late thirties with a slicked-back hairdo and a flashy diamond watch. Luna smiles at him and politely shakes his hand, but I can see the muscles in her back stiffen, and her body language can't hide how she's trying to keep her distance from him.

"Drink?"

I turn and find the girl with the red hair offering me a champagne glass. I saw her doing Luna's makeup earlier backstage and deduced that maybe the two of them aren't friends but that, like me, the girl's just *the help*.

"No thanks," I say, my eyes darting back to Luna. I can't afford to lose her twice in one night.

"Are you having fun?" the red-haired girl asks, finishing her own champagne and setting the empty glass down on a passing waiter's tray.

I shrug. I don't want to be rude, but I'm not here for conversation. I'm working. She doesn't seem to notice, though, as she moves to stand beside me.

"Not your kind of thing, hanging with A-listers?" she asks with a sardonic smile as she nods at the crowded room and starts sipping from the glass she offered me a moment ago.

I look around the room with a frown. I probably wouldn't recognize anyone in here, even if they were standing in front of me wearing a name badge. Everyone is definitely above-average attractive, though, that's for sure, and they also exude confidence and privilege in a way that makes me wonder what pills they're all popping. I wonder what Luna was taking earlier too. Is that normal in this world?

"I'm Natalie," the girl says, holding out her hand.

"Will," I say, shaking it, looking at her only briefly before I turn my head back to scan the room.

"What's your story, Will?" Natalie asks, leaning her back against the wall beside me.

"How do you mean?" I ask, watching Marty maneuver Luna to another corner of the room to meet yet more people.

"Who are you? Where are you from? How'd you get this job?" Natalie asks, peppering me with questions. "I'm guessing you're ex-military," she says before I can answer. "You guys all are."

"Yeah," I say.

"I'm guessing you miss wearing camouflage."

"Excuse me?" I say, turning briefly to look at her.

She grins at me. "You're trying to blend in by hiding behind a potted palm." She leans in so her shoulder brushes mine. "Hate to tell you, it isn't working."

I fidget at my suit cuffs self-consciously. Is it the tux? Do I look as ridiculous in it as I feel?

Natalie gestures at the room. "They're all desperate to be seen and you just want to hide, which automatically makes you stand out. It's ironic, I suppose." She laughs softly under her breath. "Those who want it the least get it the most."

I follow her gaze toward Luna. She sure seemed happy being the center of attention earlier. On the red carpet she was lapping it up. But here, I notice, with the crowd now two deep around her, it seems like she's trying to shrink away from the limelight. Marty's hand on the middle of her back seems to be forcing her to stand in place. It's odd.

"Don't."

I look at Natalie. "Don't what?"

She gives me a hard stare, her eyebrows raised. "Fall for her."

I frown, confused. She nods toward Luna. I double-take and then laugh out loud. "Believe me, there's no chance of that," I reassure her.

"Why?" she asks, tilting her head in my direction as though her curiosity has been aroused.

I shrug. "She's not my type."

"What is your type?" she asks, turning to face me full-on. Her breath, sweet with champagne, fills my nostrils and I can't help but glance down at her lips. She notices and smiles.

"Not sure I have one," I answer lightly.

"But you know she isn't it?" she asks, cocking her head.

"Yes." I nod. I only like people who are straight up and who aren't wearing a mask. I also like people with manners who say *please* and *thank you* and don't treat me like I'm shit on the bottom of their shoe. I keep this to myself, though. For all I know, Natalie and Luna might be friends, despite the working relationship, and anything I say could get repeated.

"Well, that's good," Natalie answers, reaching up a hand and brushing away some lint from the shoulder of my tux. Her hand lingers and the look she's giving me isn't a hard one to decipher. "I'll give you my number," she murmurs. "Maybe we can hang out sometime."

"Maybe, yeah," I say, glancing around the room and trying to avoid her eye. She's attractive, yes, and maybe if I wasn't working, I'd respond to the flirting, but I'm on the job, which makes it impossible. But maybe I should take her number. I don't know anyone in LA, and it might be helpful to have someone I can call on. And who knows? Maybe a date could be fun, if I ever get time off. It's been a long time since I went out with a girl. I hand her my phone, and she inputs her number before handing it back.

"I should stay close," I say, moving past her and toward Luna, who is now at the far end of the room.

"Oh, Will?" Natalie calls after me.

I turn.

"I found this on the dressing table when we arrived," she says, pulling an envelope out of her handbag. It has Luna's name written across it in a childish scrawl, the letters shaky and block printed with a black Sharpie.

"What is it?" I ask, reaching for it.

Natalie shakes her head. "I don't know, but Luna's mom told me if a letter showed up for Luna, I was to give it to you, not to her. I'm sorry. I totally forgot."

"Thanks," I say, tearing the envelope open and pulling out the piece of paper inside.

"What is it?" Natalie asks, trying to peer over my shoulder.

I'M WATCHING YOU, BITCH. THIS IS YOUR LAST WARNING. NO MORE APPEARANCES OR YOU DIE.

"Nothing," I mutter, shoving the letter back in the envelope. "Where did you say you found it?"

Natalie shrugs. "On the dressing table."

"You didn't see who put it there?"

"No," she says, reaching for the envelope. "What does it say? Who's it from?"

"It doesn't matter," I say, snatching the envelope away before she can grab it. "Are you sure you didn't see anyone around?"

Natalie frowns, thinking. "There was a guy wearing a hat. But I think he works for the venue."

"What did he look like?"

"I don't remember. He was walking away, so I didn't really see him. I just noticed him because usually roadies aren't in the green room area."

"What color was the hat?" I ask her.

"Black, I think."

Mila Gray

"We're leaving," a gruff voice says behind me.

I look around. It's Marty and he's scowling at me while Luna stands beside him, glowering unhappily in my direction.

"She wants to go home," Marty says, jerking his head in Luna's direction.

I stuff the envelope in my inside pocket, hoping she didn't see it, before leading Marty and Luna toward the exit.

"This isn't a club, mate," Marty says to me as we push through the crowd. "You're not here to pull."

"What?" I ask, my eyes on Luna, who has been waylaid by the guy from before with the slicked-back hair and diamond watch.

"You're not paid to chat up women," Marty tells me as we wait for them to finish their conversation. "If you want to get laid, do it on your own time."

"I wasn't," I splutter, indignant.

"Of course you weren't," Marty says, slapping me on the arm. "Just do your damn job."

Gritting my teeth, I pull out the envelope from my pocket. "This showed up earlier."

As soon as Marty sees it, he snatches the envelope straight out of my hand. "Where'd you find it?" he demands.

"Her dressing table," I tell him.

As he reads the letter, I pull out my phone and text the limo driver, telling him to pull up to the front of the hotel.

"Where's your car?" I ask Marty.

"I valeted it."

"Give me the ticket."

"Why?" he asks.

"You go in the limo," I tell him. "A decoy. To be safe. I'll take Luna home in your car."

"It's a brand-new Tesla," Marty says.

"Okay," I answer with a bemused shrug. "Can I have the valet ticket?"

Grumpily he hands it to me, before shoving the envelope into his back pocket. "Keep your mouth shut about this, all right?" he says warningly.

I glance at Luna, who is still locked in conversation with the slicked-back-hair guy. Up close I can see his scalp and realize he's trying to cover his encroaching baldness. He's got his phone out and appears to be asking her for a selfie. Luna poses with him, and he puts his arm around her as he leans in close and snaps away.

I shove Marty aside and make a beeline toward them. When I reach them, I step on the guy's foot hard and fast, grinding my heel into his toes. He yelps and drops his phone, letting go of Luna to dive for it. I push between them and am rewarded with the look of relief I see on Luna's face.

"What the hell was that about?" Marty growls as I steer Luna toward the door, my arm a buffer between her and the crowd.

I glance at Luna. She knows I saw that sleazeball's hand inching lower and lower down her back and that's why I stepped in, but from her pleading expression, she doesn't want me to tell Marty.

"Nothing," I grunt, shoving open the door to an industrial kitchen with my shoulder and glancing backward to make sure the guy isn't following us. He isn't—he's hopping on one foot and swearing about his smashed phone screen.

"Do you know who that was?" Marty demands angrily. "He's only the biggest music producer in the world."

"So what?" I ask.

"You just broke his damn foot!"

"I didn't break it," I say quietly. If I had wanted to break it, I think to myself, I would have broken it, and next time I see him put his hands on a girl without her permission, I'll do more than break his damn foot.

I throw open an emergency exit door and lead Marty and a stone-faced Luna out into a back alley behind the hotel, where the limo driver has already pulled up. I open the back door, and Luna is about to climb in when I stop her.

"Marty's taking the limo," I tell her, waving the valet ticket. "We're taking his car."

"If you crash it, I'll kill you," Marty says, wagging his finger in my face as I shut the limo door on him.

I nod, whatever, and watch the limo drive away.

"Why are we not going with them?"

I turn and find Luna looking at me, with a slightly fearful expression on her face, as though she's afraid to find herself alone in the alley with me. I'm not sure what to say. I don't want to tell her about the letter. "Standard protocol," I blurt. "Come on, let's find the valet stand."

She pulls a face at me and then, huffing, struts off down the alley on those dangerous-looking skyscraper heels.

LUNA

I can still feel Craig's hand on me like a thumping bruise from a recently occurred injury. There's a thump in my head, too, not from champagne, as Marty wouldn't let me have any, but from something else. Rage. I can't believe I let Craig touch me like that and I didn't say anything, didn't tell him to get his hands off me, or push him off. I froze.

I'm glad Will did what he did, but Marty's right. We can't afford to upset Craig Matthers. I'm meant to be recording a song with him in the new year. He's one of the biggest producers in the world. I tell myself that's why I didn't say anything to him myself. It wasn't because I froze.

Will opens the door to Marty's Tesla. His tux is way too tight on the shoulders, like he's deliberately trying to show off his physique. It's something Jamie does too, wearing too-tight T-shirts.

As I slip into the passenger seat and pull down my skirt to cover my legs, I realize that I'm being a pot calling the kettle black. I know that my body and the way I look is all part of the image I have to project and that, as Marty says, showing skin sells records. I tried to argue that things were changing, name-dropped a few female singers who don't conform to beauty or fashion standards, and Marty scoffed and told me that they got away with it because they had unique sounds and unique personalities, which is basically him telling me that I have neither.

I take off my shoes, unbuckling them as Will gets in the driver's seat of Marty's Tesla beside me. Two minutes later I'm barefoot with my feet tucked under me, and we're still sitting at the valet stand.

"Are we going to sit here all night?" I ask, worrying that the whole decoy car thing will be moot if I'm spotted.

"I've never driven a Tesla," Will says with an embarrassed laugh.

"You push that button," I tell him, pointing and rolling my eyes.

He presses the start button and the screen lights up. He stares at it. "It looks like a spaceship." He starts to press the buttons on the screen, like a kid with a new toy at Christmas. "I thought these things were meant to drive themselves," he mutters.

I am about to laugh, but then I remember him talking to Natalie back inside the hotel and the way he was flirting with her, and my laughter dries up. I don't know why it's annoying, but it is. Am I jealous? No. I'm not jealous. It's more envy. Natalie is beautiful. I can see why he'd be interested in her. And maybe, too, I'm upset as no one ever really talks to me like I'm a regular person. I can never have a normal conversation with anyone, not even a barista when I order a coffee.

Will finally figures out how to drive the car, and we pull away from the valet stand. I sink back into my seat and retrieve my phone from my bag.

I swipe on Instagram, although the voice in my head is warning me not to because nothing good ever comes from a late-night scroll through Instagram. Almost immediately I am slammed by a deluge of messages and tags, all of them leading to a photograph someone has posted online of Jamie with some girl. She's pretty, way prettier than me: Japanese, and stylish in a way that looks artless but is undoubtedly artful. Jamie has his arm around her, and they're sitting in what looks like a bar or a restaurant booth. My heart almost explodes in my chest, and I get a panicky sensation that there isn't enough air in the car and that I'm going to suffocate within seconds.

Who is she? No one online seems to know, either. My hands shake as I scroll through the comments. Everyone is wondering if the mystery girl is Jamie's new girlfriend, and a few people are asking what that means about Jamie and me, and if it's confirmation that we've broken up for the millionth time.

It has to be a mistake, I tell myself. She's probably just a fan. I go back to studying the photograph, zooming in on every detail. They're sitting so close she's practically in Jamie's lap. His arm is across the back of the booth, but his hand is resting on her shoulder. Is that friendly or is there something more to it? They're not even posing for a photograph. It looks like it was taken surreptitiously, with a long lens when they weren't looking. I tell myself to shrug it off. It doesn't matter. We're not together. He can do what he wants.

"Can you stop at In-N-Out?" I blurt.

Will glances over at me. "The burger place?"

"Yes," I say. "There's one on Sunset."

I feel an overwhelming urge to eat a burger. I'm starving and my head is spinning and I don't want to go home just yet, where

Marty will be waiting and no doubt will want to talk through my schedule for tomorrow.

I have to give Will directions to In-N-Out, because he doesn't know his way around LA, and teaching him how to use the built-in GPS will probably take an hour. When we pull up outside five minutes later, I take one look at the twenty-five-car line for the drive-through and tell him to park instead.

"Can you get me a cheeseburger?" I ask.

"Sure," he says, sounding amused. "You want ketchup or fries? Anything to drink with that?"

Is he being sarcastic? I can't tell. His face is inscrutable, but his top lip seems to be twitching into a smirk. "No, just a cheese-burger," I say.

"Sure?" he asks.

I roll my eyes. "Yes."

"Don't go anywhere," he tells me as he gets out of the car.

Ha ha, I want to shoot back at him. As if I could. Even if I had a pair of shoes I could actually walk in, I can't go any-where. Firstly, I've got nowhere to go. I don't have any friends who I can call. Secondly, I'm locked on a schedule, and as Marty reminds me every opportunity he gets, I can't let people down. Not my fans, not the people who work to make me a success, by which he mainly means himself, and not my family, either, who need me.

But oh my God, how much would I love to jump behind the wheel of this car right now and take off? I'd love nothing more than to disappear, for a month or a year, or maybe forever. I'd love to stop being Luna Rivera and be someone else, try out a different life, a normal one. But how would that ever be pos-sible? There's nowhere on the planet that I could disappear to where I wouldn't be found or recognized or where someone wouldn't stop me for a selfie. And on top of all that, how could I ever leave Matias?

I watch Will head inside the fast-food restaurant, noticing the looks he gets from a group of drunk women in their twenties whom he holds open the door for. They flirt with him like middle-graders, cackling something and then giving him suggestive glances over their shoulders as they walk away.

I dig out my phone again and let my finger hover over the dial button. I shouldn't call Jamie. I should have some self-respect. But the buzzy feeling in my chest is getting worse. I'm so antsy I feel I could scratch my skin off. I need to know what's going on and if this girl in the photographs is just a random or someone he's hooked up with, or someone he's dating. Even though I know this makes me look desperate, I can't help myself.

I write and rewrite at least a dozen texts without managing to land on the right wording—the whole time the voice in my head berates me for being pathetic, yelling at me that I'm a loser—before Will shows back up with my burger. He gets into the car, and the smell of grease hits me immediately, and my stomach growls in response. I haven't eaten a thing since the eggs Carla made this morning, and now that I no longer have to worry about squeezing into this ridiculous dress, I'm free to splurge on calories. I reach over to grab the brown paper bag from his hand, but he holds it tantalizingly out of reach.

"What?" I say, snatching the bag from him, irritated.

"You're welcome," he answers sarcastically.

"What is this?" I ask as I unwrap my burger. "It's not a cheeseburger."

"It's animal style," he says.

"Animal what?"

"Animal style," he repeats. "You've never tried one before?"

I shake my head. "I asked for a cheeseburger." Why can't he just do what I ask?

"Oh, that's a cheeseburger. The best cheeseburger you'll ever eat, I mean, from a fast-food restaurant. If you want to talk about real burgers, you'd need to try the ones my friend Kit makes."

I'm tempted to throw the burger at him or at the very least make him go in and get me the cheeseburger that I asked for, but I'm starving and it does smell really damn good. I take a bite and my eyes almost roll back in my head.

"Here," he says, passing me a napkin and pointing at my chin, where I can feel the grease running in a river toward my neck.

I take the napkin and wipe, embarrassed and then annoyed because he's not even trying to hide his smile.

"Good, right?" he asks.

I shrug, refusing to give him the pleasure of hearing me agree with him. "What's in it?" I ask.

"They put mustard in the patties. And extra pickles. It's on their secret menu."

"They have a secret menu?" Firstly, why? And secondly, how does he know this?

"Hang out with me, I'll let you in on all the cool secrets," he says, without any trace of irony.

Is he being self-mocking or does he actually think he knows all the cool secrets? His expression is so hard to read. I can't tell if he's joking.

"Yeah, I'm sure," I reply, smirking.

"I'm sorry about what happened back there," Will says after a few seconds of silence.

I cock my head to one side. Is he talking about Jamie? But no. He can't know about that. He must be talking about Craig.

"You broke his phone," I say.

"No, I'm not sorry about that," Will says, shaking his head. "I'm sorry he groped you," he mumbles. "And I'm sorry I didn't notice it sooner and stop him."

I swallow. I don't know what to say. I'm embarrassed that he saw and also angry that he's reminding me that I did nothing either. I don't need him to rescue me. "It's fine. People do it all the time."

"What?" he asks.

I shrug and laugh under my breath, trying to brush it off. "That's normal in this industry," I say quietly. "You learn to deal."

"You shouldn't have to deal with that," Will says. He seems genuinely concerned, as well as angry, and it makes me warm to him. Very slightly. I don't need him telling me something that I already know. Still, I shrug, because dealing with assholes is part of the job, as Marty's always reminding me.

Just then there's a screech from outside the car. I look up, startled. The drunk, loud women who were flirting with Will over by the door are now gathered in a gaggle in front of the car. All of them have their phones out and aimed right at me. Shit. I shove the burger into the paper bag. "Let's go," I say, ducking my head and covering my face with my hands.

The women are all screaming with delight, like bird spotters having caught a glimpse of a dodo in the wild. I can hear them yelling my name, telling me to look up and smile. A couple of them are belting out one of my songs and starting to twerk to the lyrics.

"Just go!" I yell at Will.

Will starts the car, and as we pull out of the parking lot, I sink farther down in my seat.

Damn it, why the hell did I decide to stop at a fast-food restaurant? This is what happens whenever I try to be normal. Once we're half a mile down the street, I sit up and scrabble to open the window, desperate for air. I stick my head out the window and breathe, my heart rate starting to eventually slow after a minute. That's when I notice the chill of the wind hitting my wet face and discover that I'm crying. I wipe the back of my arm across my face, and it comes away smeared in makeup and glitter. My dress is splotched with ketchup too. I'm a mess.

"Here."

Napkins land in my lap. I swipe surreptitiously at my face with them, then at the stain on my dress, but soon give up. It looks like I've been shot in the chest. This dress is for the trash can, and even though I don't particularly like it and won't ever wear it again, I don't want to throw it away.

"Are you okay?" Will asks quietly.

Am I okay? I stare at him blankly. It's so rare that anyone actually asks me that, and I don't know how to answer.

He glances over at me while he drives, and his expression is one of such sweet and genuine concern that for the briefest of seconds I buy it and think that he actually cares. I start to shake my head, more tears threatening to spill, but then I force myself to get a damn grip.

"I'm fine," I say, turning my head to look out the window.

WILL

Luna jumps out of the car, slamming the door behind her, and runs up to the front door. I watch her go and then let out the breath I've been holding. Five weeks, six days to go, I tell myself. I can manage. My tours of duty were ten times that.

I wonder if I should have kept quiet when she was crying and not asked her if she was okay, not spoken to her at all, in fact, because the look she shot me was almost lethal. I guess she prefers the help to be seen and not heard, but I thought she was having a heart attack, the way she was gasping for breath. Now that I think about it some more, though, I wonder if she wasn't having a panic attack. My mom had a few when I was a kid, before my dad was arrested and sent to jail for domestic assault. Maybe that's what Luna takes the pills for. Maybe it's medication to help soothe anxiety.

I glance down at the discarded burger on the floor of the car and the crumpled-up napkins. I suppose I need to clean that up before I give the car back to Marty. Sighing, I drive around to the rear of the house and pull up by the back door.

I empty the trash out of the car, finding Luna's shoes beneath the burger bag. They're childlike in their size and have several complicated buckles and straps. They honestly look like implements of torture that have been given a glittery makeover by Barbie-obsessed toddlers.

"It's like Cinderella."

I look up to find Marty walking toward me. He nods at the shoes I'm holding.

"You brought her back okay, then?" he asks.

"Yeah, she's gone inside," I answer, nodding toward the house.

"I meant the car," he answers, walking around to inspect it.

I hand him the keys. "It's fine, apart from the scratch on the bumper."

His eyes boggle and I let his face turn the shade of an eggplant before I say, "Joking. The car's fine."

He snatches the keys from my hand. "You're not Prince Charming, you know," he says, nodding at the pair of shoes I'm still holding. "She's Cinderella, but you're more like a peasant who works in the castle."

I grit my teeth and stare at him.

"By that I mean you're supposed to melt into the background and do your job without getting in the way of the main actors. Understood?"

I get what he's saying, and it irritates the hell out of me. He's insinuating I'm interested in the limelight or in being some kind of savior, when neither idea could be further from the truth. Although, maybe I'm feeling so triggered by his insult because there is some truth to it. Not the limelight, but needing to be a savior.

"You don't touch the merchandise, not even the free testers," Marty says, spelling it out even more by jabbing his index finger into my chest. "By that I mean Natalie, too. Keep your fingers out of the pies."

Pies? Is he really describing women as pies? "I've already told you I'm not interested," I say, forcing my tone to remain even despite my rising anger.

He narrows his eyes at me, disbelieving. "That's what they all say."

I'm about to walk off, not wanting to endure another second of his lecturing, when Marty notices the crumpled burger bag in my hand. "I see you stopped for a midnight feast," he grunts, moving past me and opening the car door. "Great, now my car stinks."

"Luna wanted something to eat," I say by way of explanation.

"You shouldn't have let her," Marty says, wiping at an invisible mark on the interior of the door.

I shake my head, confused. "What?"

"She can't eat that junk. She'll put on weight."

"She's tiny," I say in disbelief.

"And she needs to stay that way." Marty grinds his teeth.

It takes a lot of willpower to bite my tongue. I watch Marty move to get into his car.

"Hey," I call. "What about the letter?"

"What about it?" he asks grumpily.

"What are you going to do about it?"

"That's my problem, not yours," he tells me.

"But that's why I've been hired, isn't it?" I ask.

He shakes his head. "You've been hired to drive her about, keep wild fans away from her, and watch her so she doesn't do anything stupid."

"That sounds like a babysitter."

"Listen, mate," he says. "You want this job or not?"

He's calling me *mate*? After wagging his finger in my face and poking me in the chest and telling me to keep my fingers out of all the pies?

"It's a good job," he continues. "And what's a kid like you gonna do otherwise? Sign up for another four years in the army?"

My back stiffens. "The Marines."

"Whatever." He gestures backward, toward the house. "This is a damn lot better paid, and you've got a lot less chance of being blown up."

I work to keep my cool, riled because he doesn't know jack about me or why I joined the Marines. He's assuming I'm an idiot who can't get another job . . . which makes me want to tell him exactly where he can stick this one, but I stop myself. I need the money, I tell myself, trying to ignore the voice in my head whispering that he's right. What *would* I do other-wise? I'm definitely not signing up for another four years in the Marines. It's bad enough I have to do eight more years in the reserves.

Marty's tone shifts all of a sudden and becomes friendlier. "You seem like you've got a fairly good head on your shoulders," he tells me. "So, I'm trusting you to do your job."

I nod, thinking of the money. "But what about the threats?" I press. "The letters. How serious are they?"

Marty rolls his eyes. "They're not."

"How do you know?"

"It's just some obsessed fan who has a thing against her," he says, sighing loudly. He throws his hands in the air. "Maybe they hate that she's rich and successful and they're not. I honestly don't know. But what I do know is that the police have already told us that it's nothing to worry about, and I'm listening to the professionals."

I'm not a fan of the police. My father was a cop. His badge gave him protection. His buddies in the department turned the other cheek when my mom tried to press charges, and it took him almost killing her before they decided to take it semi-seriously. Even then he received a shorter prison sentence than he should have and was let out early, which led to him terrorizing my whole family for a second time. "It's never serious, until it is," I tell Marty.

Marty sighs again, even louder, as though I'm being over-dramatic.

"We need to find out who it is, make a list of suspects, and eliminate them," I tell him, ignoring his sighs. "Natalie said she saw someone, some guy in a black cap."

"Look," Marty says, interrupting me. "I'm not paying you to play Hercule Poirot," he says. "The threats aren't important. It's someone trying to mess with Luna's head, that's all. Just do your job and don't let anyone get near her, and if you do come across any of these letters, hide them from her. We don't need her any more stressed than she already is. She's very highly strung."

I think back to the pills I caught her taking. "What are the pills for?" I ask Marty.

"Her anxiety," he mumbles, seeming surprised that I know about them. "She gets them prescribed. Again, that's between you and me."

I nod, but at the same time I'm wondering why, then, if they know she suffers from anxiety, are they putting her in situations that make her anxious?

He walks toward his car. "A warning, by the way," he says before he gets in. "Tomorrow she's going to be in a bad mood."

"How do you know?" I ask, while wondering what mood she was in today.

"Because her boyfriend just cheated on her."

"Jamie?" I say.

Marty nods. "That's the one. He's a right pillock. Don't tell her I said that."

I nod. I wasn't intending to. "I thought they broke up?"

"They break up and get back together all the time. It's their schtick. They first started dating around the time they were both breaking out. Was a match made in heaven—PR heaven, that is. Two cute, talented young kids. People were obsessed. Still are. And I'm warning you, tomorrow she'll be a right grumpy pants," Marty tells me.

And that's different from normal, how? I think, but don't say out loud.

"Don't take it personally," Marty reassures me. "It's not about you. And next week, when Jamie gets back from Japan, it'll be back to normal and she'll be all smiles and sunshine again."

With that, Marty finally gets into his Tesla and drives off. After he's gone, I head up the stairs to my new apartment, mulling over everything he just told me. I think about Luna as I walk around my new digs, taking in the neatly made bed with my bag beside it, then the bathroom, filled with all the amenities I'll ever need and some I never will. But I'm still thinking about Luna when I slide into bed. I picture her walking up the red carpet, posing for photographs and chatting with fans.

She was so at home there and she seemed so happy and confident, but then I saw another side to her entirely, outside the venue and again in the car, someone vulnerable. Is she putting on a mask when she's onstage and in front of her fans? If so, that mask is better even than my own.

LUNA

look like I'm wearing a death mask. My eyes are red-rimmed and bloodshot, my skin dull across my cheeks and greasy on my forehead. My hair hangs limp even after I drag myself into the shower and wash it. It's almost midday, but I only managed to fall asleep around dawn after taking a sleeping pill stolen from my mom's cabinet.

I spent most of the night online, scouring for more photos of Jamie and reading the comments on Instagram. It's a form of torture, like picking a scab, but I can't stop myself.

Secretly, deep down, I believe that I deserve it, that every one of the terrible things people say about me is true, that it's merely confirmation of what I already know: I'm a terrible singer, ugly, worthless, and that no one could ever love me. Jamie moving on with another girl only proves that. I know not all the comments are negative, but even if one out of a hundred is, I can only seem to focus on that negative one. The voice in my head takes it and amplifies it a million times.

Now I feel groggy and nauseous. The only thing to pass my lips in the last twenty-four hours was two bites of that burger.

But it's probably thanks to that I now have a greasy forehead. I need Natalie to come and fix things. I search for my phone and text her, noting that there are no texts or missed calls from Jamie.

I ended up leaving him two messages last night and now I regret it. It's best to play it cool. I need to get out and show the world I don't care. Retail therapy is the cure for all ills—isn't that what they say? And at least shopping will give me something to do other than sit in my room alternating between staring at the walls and staring at my phone.

Natalie shows up thirty minutes after I text her and finds me knitting, which I do whenever I feel myself becoming anxious. It's meant to make me feel calm—at least that's what Carla said it would do when she first taught me—but I find myself more often than not getting stressed because I'm so bad at it that I have to constantly untangle knots and unpick stitches. Definitely not a zen-inducing activity.

"What are you knitting?" Natalie asks.

"It was a blanket. Now it's a scarf. I think."

She cocks her head to one side. "It's awesome."

I sigh at the blatant lie and toss the knitting down.

"Has Jamie called?" Natalie asks, sitting down at my dressing table and unzipping her carry-on suitcase filled with makeup.

I shake my head. She knows all the drama between Jamie and me because she's witnessed it and is often the one I call on to help me cover up the damage caused by a night with no sleep or a day spent crying. I hate the fact that I have to bother with my appearance just to go shopping, but the truth is, the paparazzi will be out like hawks trying to get a shot of me, and Marty will yell at me if I go out looking less than perfect.

"Well, let's make him regret what he's missing out on," she says, smiling at me. Natalie chatters away as she gets to work, applying foundation. "Is Will around?" she asks.

"How do I know?" I grunt.

She shrugs off my terse tone. "He's nice. We were chatting last night. I'm going to see if he wants to go out one night when he's got an evening off."

I force a smile. "Cool," I say. "I'm not sure when he'll have a night off, but go for it."

"What's the plan for the rest of the day?" Natalie asks as she applies the last slick of lip gloss and then starts packing up the tools of her trade.

I glance in the mirror and smile at my reflection. She's done a great job at hiding the dark circles under my eyes, and she's even somehow managed to make my skin glow.

"Retail therapy," I say.

"Oooh," she coos, her eyes growing round. "Need a partner in crime?"

I think about saying yes, because it might be fun to go shopping with her, but then I think about the fact that I will need to take Will with me. "Next time," I say to her.

Her face falls a little, and I wonder if I'm making a mistake. It's been so long since I had a girlfriend or anyone to confide in, and why do I care if she and Will hook up? In the end, though, I decide I want to be on my own. I don't take my phone with me because I don't want the temptation of calling Jamie, and because I don't want to turn into a version of Jamie, constantly checking my social media to make sure I'm still trending.

When I walk into the kitchen, I stop short at the sight of Matias, Carla, and Will sitting at the counter eating what looks like Spanish tortilla and chatting away like one big, happy family. Carla beams at me. "Good morning. Do you want something to eat?"

I shake my head even though I'm starving and turn to grab a Diet Coke out of the fridge. The sight of Will sitting there has riled me for some reason I can't explain. My skin feels hot, and I relish the chilly refrigerated air against my face as I take my time rooting around for a cold can. I'm embarrassed about last night, I think, that Will saw me crying and witnessed one of my anxiety attacks. What if he's said something to someone about it?

"Look what Will showed me!" Matias says, rushing over to me and waving something in his hand. "I can make this quarter disappear."

I force a smile. "Oh, really?"

Matias nods and then proceeds to show me his magic trick, except he hasn't quite mastered the sleight of hand required. I act like he has, though, and marvel at the trick. "That's amazing!" I smile. "Wow."

"I want to be a magician when I grow up," he boasts proudly.

"I'll show you another trick if you like," Will says to him, and when Matias bounces over to him, grinning, I feel a pang of resentment.

"I'm going shopping," I say, tossing my head and moving toward the door.

Will slides off his counter stool. For the first time I realize how tall he is. He's probably six foot one or two, and I notice, too, that he moves with a kind of stiffness as well as an alertness, like he's about to snap to attention at any moment.

"I guess I'll show you that trick later," he tells Matias, who immediately starts to melt down, his grin vanishing and a grimace replacing it.

I glare at Will. Matias doesn't have much of a sense of time. You can't tell him you'll do something and then change the plan like that. I start to say something, wanting to calm Matias down before he loses his temper and starts to shout, but before I can, Will is in front of him.

"You need to work on that other trick," he says, looking Matias straight in the eye. "Get it as good as can be. Then when I get back, I'll test you on it, and if you pass, I'll show you the next one."

Matias pauses, his face bubbling on the verge of a volcanic eruption, but then he cocks his head to one side like a puppy being offered a treat, and nods. And like that, the whole crisis is averted and the volcano stops spewing. I stare at Will in shock. How the hell did he manage that? Carla and I share a bemused glance before Will looks over at me. It takes me a second to come back to the moment and realize he's waiting on me. I fluster and walk out the door.

"I'll drive," I say as we head outside with Will behind me. "Seeing how you don't know your way anywhere."

"There's this thing called Google Maps," he says under his breath.

I turn to look at him. He's not trying very hard to hide an amused smirk.

"I'm still driving," I say, getting into the car. I'm determined to keep up the diva act, in order to make him quit.

He hesitates before getting in the passenger side. He looks uncomfortable squashed into the bucket-size passenger seat and unhappy, too, when I turn the radio on and crank it full volume. I put my foot to the floor, kicking up gravel, and notice his knuckles turning white as they grip the door handle, but he still doesn't say anything.

Even though Will is trying to keep his feelings under wraps, I can tell how much he hates me. I saw the look on his face when I interrupted his conversation with Natalie last night and the look on his face when he saw me swallow that pill and when I asked him to get me a cheeseburger. He was judging me. Just like everybody else.

WILL

Marty doesn't seem to have been right about Luna being in a bad mood. If anything, she seems in a good mood: upbeat, smiling, and chatting with the people serving her—and serving her is what everyone she encounters seems eager to do.

I feel ridiculous lurking in a corner of the store, holding bags, like an animate coatrack, and my irritation grows when I think about how much she just threw down on a handbag. How can anyone spend that much money on a handbag? It cost more than I owe in debt, and more than I'll earn in six months.

"What do you think?"

I glance over at Luna, who's just exited a changing room. I look around, but she seems to be talking to me. "Excuse me?" I respond.

"What do you think?" she asks.

I look her up and down, not that there's much to look at because the snake-effect leather dress she's wearing is minuscule. I'm stumped for what to say and struggling hard to keep my face from giving away my real feelings. "Sure."

It seems like a reasonably neutral response.

"Sure?" she demands, hands on hips. "Do you like it or not?"

I shrug. "My opinion isn't important." Why is she even asking me?

She turns to look in the mirror. She's got a great body, a dancer's body, lithe and toned, and in that dress, there's no way of hiding it either. But the dress itself? It's like a boa constrictor ate Vegas Barbie.

"What do you think?" she presses again.

I run a hand between my neck and my collar. This is way beyond my comfort zone. I've never been asked by a woman, let alone one who employs me, what I think of what they're wearing. I'm guessing the smart thing to do would be to lie, but I'm not good at that. "Well, I wouldn't wear it," I tell her, hoping for a laugh.

She rolls her eyes at me. "You don't like it?" she asks, huffing loudly.

I shake my head. "Not really, no."

She blinks at me in surprise, and I wonder how many people ever tell her the truth. It almost makes me smile.

"What would you choose?" she asks with a sneer, gesturing at the racks of clothes. "Go on, pick something for me. Play stylist."

She's trying to find a way to humiliate me and it's childish and silly, but I decide to take it seriously. And besides, it's better than standing in the corner like a coat stand. I start strolling around the store, looking over the racks of clothes.

She's probably thinking that as a guy I'll opt for her to try on something skimpy and tight, so I deliberately go the opposite direction. I choose a dress that's soft as silk but made of cashmere or some other kind of wool. It's moss green and it looks comfortable, too—loose, with a turtleneck and long sleeves.

I pick it off the rail, almost dropping it when I notice the price tag contains three zeroes before the decimal point, before handing it to her.

She looks at it, holding it up to inspect it. "Wow. I love it."

She does? I have to admit I'm surprised.

"I can wear it for Halloween," she says. "I can go as a nun. A blind nun. Who grew up in a Mormon sect."

"Guess I'll shelve that ambition I had to be your stylist," I tell her dryly.

She pulls a face and hands me the dress before heading back inside the changing room. Feeling more dejected than I should, I hang the dress up. I didn't think it was that bad. If she'd tried it, she might have discovered it suited her. But what do I know?

"Will?"

I turn, surprised to hear my name and even more surprised when I see Luna sticking her head out of the door of the changing room, calling to me. I didn't even know she knew my name.

"Come here."

I walk over to her, wondering if she ever says *please* or *thank you*.

"I need your help," she whispers.

I raise my eyebrows. What now? Carrying more bags? Picking clothes up off the floor? "What is it?" I ask, struggling to hide my impatience.

She glances over my shoulder, furtive, and then looks back at me. "I'm stuck."

I look around, unsure what she means.

"The dress," she hisses. "The zipper's stuck."

"Oh," I say. "Want me to get someone?" I start to walk away, meaning to find one of the shop assistants, but Luna grabs my arm and hauls me back.

"No!" she says. "They'll laugh at me."

"Why would they laugh?" I ask, confused.

"Look," she snaps impatiently, "can you just try to unzip me?" Her cheeks are bright red and I can tell she's genuinely embarrassed. I hide my smile at her predicament. Feels like karma.

She pulls me into the changing room with her, much to my surprise, and then shuts the door behind me. "Come on, help," she says, turning around. "I can't get it undone."

I take hold of the zipper, aware that her bare back is brushing my fingertips and trying not to focus on how smooth and golden her skin is. I pull the zipper, but it doesn't budge.

"It's stuck," I tell Luna.

"I know that," she hisses, annoyed. "That's why I asked for help."

I try again, tugging harder. "It's really stuck," I announce.

"Oh my God." She sighs loudly. "What am I going to do?"

"We could cut you out," I suggest.

She starts frantically wriggling, trying to pull the dress off over her head, but it gets caught around her shoulders and now she's even more stuck and it really is like a boa constrictor ate Barbie. I grin, unable to stop myself.

She pulls the dress down and glares at me, her cheeks flushing bright red. "Don't laugh at me!"

"I'm not laughing," I say, fighting to keep a straight face.

"Please," she says.

I see she's on the verge of tears and immediately stop smiling.

"I think we need scissors," I say to her.

"No!" she sobs. "This dress costs like ten thousand dollars or something stupid."

"Okay," I say, my mind blown by the price tag, but also recognizing that she's starting to panic and hyperventilate and that I need to keep her calm. "Let's try this again. Turn around."

She obeys and I take hold of the zipper. "Breathe in," I tell her.

She does and I wriggle the zipper and manage finally to free it. I slide it down, revealing the length of her spine. She isn't wearing a bra, and my gaze falls to her waist and then lower, to the top of her black lace underwear. For a second, I completely lose my train of thought and just stare, my throat going dry.

I look up and catch her looking at me in the mirror. Oh shit. Busted.

"There you go," I whisper, embarrassed.

"Thanks," she says quietly, still staring at me.

I nod. Then realize my hand is still on the zipper, my knuckles against the small of her back. I pull my hand away quickly and awkwardly leave the changing room, only to find a shop assistant on the other side of the door.

"I was just helping," I mumble by way of explanation. She smirks at me, clearly not buying it.

Shit. I hurry back to the bags and wait for Luna to emerge. I can't get rid of the image of her bare back from my mind, and I find my imagination going one step farther, picturing the dress sliding over her hips. I imagine it dropping to the floor. I shake my head.

Ten minutes later we leave the store, with yet more bags, though I'm not sure the boa constrictor dress made the cut. As we head for the car, someone shouts Luna's name.

I look up and see a short man in a dark hat and a Nike T-shirt striding toward us. He's holding something in his hand, and instantly I'm on alert. Luna, too, seems startled. She trips and I steady her, stopping her from falling by putting my arm around her waist and pulling her into my side so I can use my body to block her. She turns into me, her head buried against my shoulder, and I shield her with my other arm, even as I realize the man is only holding a camera and there's no real threat. He gets his photos, following us all the way to the car, at which point Luna pulls sharply away from me and jumps into the passenger side. I put the shopping bags in the trunk and walk around to the driver's side, wondering why she's letting me drive, but the question is answered as soon as I get in and find her clutching the seat and on the verge of hyperventilating.

"You okay?" I ask her.

She shakes her head, panicking, scratching at the door lock.

"Just breathe," I say.

"Oh really?" she pants, tossing me the keys. "What do you think I'm trying to do?"

I pull out of the parking space and into traffic. Behind I see the photographer climb into his white truck. It's the same guy who followed us last night. Donny. I wonder again why she didn't want me to talk to him about leaving her alone. To try to distract her, I turn on the radio, hoping music will help.

"Turn that off," she shouts as a song blasts through the speakers.

I reach to turn the dial, but she beats me to it.

"Sorry," I say, trying to figure out what I did wrong this time and telling myself *five weeks, five and a half days left.*

I wind the window down for her, knowing she likes air when she gets like this. She leans her face into the breeze and closes her eyes.

LUNA

feel the warm air blast my face. I'm embarrassed that Will saw me freaking out again. He must think I'm pathetic. I don't know why I reacted that way. It was only Donny, after all. It must be lack of sleep and forgetting to take my anxiety meds this morning.

After five minutes or so my breathing is under control, but I keep my eyes shut. I don't want to face Will. My mind wanders back to the changing room and the way he laughed at me. Something else to be embarrassed about. My skin tingles at the memory of his hand tracing down my back as he undid the zipper, and I try to push the memory away, angry at my body for reacting so stupidly. I don't even like him. Hopefully, he's going to quit anyway, so I won't have to see him ever again.

Will stops the car and I open my eyes, surprised to see we aren't at home. We're in a parking lot overlooking a beach, somewhere in Malibu.

"What are we doing here?" I ask, annoyed.

Will looks over at me and gives a little shrug. "I didn't want to wake you. And I figured some ocean air would be good. Always works for me."

I purse my lips. I'm irritated by him not having asked, but then my gaze is caught by the golden sand and beyond that, the sun starting to dip low toward the Pacific. "I haven't been to the beach in years," I mutter, more to myself than him.

He frowns at me. "You live ten minutes from it."

"I know, but—" I break off. "Never mind." It's not like he'll understand.

"I've got a cap you can borrow," he says, pulling it out of his inside pocket. He must have intuited what stops me from coming to the beach. It's the fear of being recognized.

He offers it to me and I notice that it's a Lakers hat.

"You're a Lakers fan?" I ask, surprised.

He nods. "All my life."

What do you know? We actually have something in common. I don't tell him, though. I take the hat and pull it on, stuffing my hair into it. We get out of the car.

It's fairly late in the day and the surf is choppy, meaning the only people at the beach are surfers and a couple of older people walking dogs. I take a deep breath of sea air and let it out, feeling myself relax, ever so slightly, for the first time in weeks. At the edge of the sand, we stop and take off our shoes. We start walking the length of the beach, and as my toes sink into the sun-kissed warmth, I smile. It feels so good.

"This reminds me of where I grew up," I say before I can stop myself.

"Yeah?" Will says. "Where was that?"

"Florida. A place called Buenaventura Lakes."

"What was it like?" he asks.

I shrug. "Hot. Humid as hell in the summer." I sigh wistfully. "But it was fun. I remember watching the fireflies over the lake and going to the beach to watch the rocket launches from Cape Canaveral." A pang of longing hits me in the chest when I think back to those days. There was no golden cage then. I can smell the ocean spray, feel the damp hot air on my skin, and hear the buzz of mosquitoes at night through my open window as they bat against the screens.

"Sounds like you miss it," he says.

I nod. "Yeah."

"Do you like LA?"

I'm taken aback by the question because it's the first time anyone has asked me that. For most people, LA and Hollywood are the dream, the destination they long to reach, a symbol of achievement, so why on earth would you ever want to leave?

"Of course," I say, pulling a face. "Obviously. I'm so lucky to be here. It's my dream."

Will's eyebrows shoot up, and he looks at me with amused skepticism. I realize that I've switched into the mode I go into when I have to do an interview. I'm throwing out soundbites of what I think people want to hear, giving the rote answer. I can't seem ungrateful. I must always seem amazed by my success, or people will think I'm arrogant or rude and will turn on me.

"I hate LA," he admits with a casual shrug.

"Why?" I ask.

"I don't like cities. Too many people. Too much noise. I like being in nature. By water."

I nod. I get that. I veer toward the water so I can let the surf wash over my feet.

"Actually," I admit, "I don't like LA much either."

He glances at me curiously. I look away, annoyed I just

blurted that out. And to him, of all people. His honesty is contagious, I guess. "Why?" he asks.

"It's like living in a cage," I explain. "You see what it's like. I can't go anywhere or do anything without being spotted." Will looks at me blankly and I stop. How could he ever understand? He's a normal person, with a normal life. "Where's home for you?" I ask, changing the subject.

He hesitates, then says, "I grew up near Phoenix. But I wouldn't call it home."

"Where is home, then?" I ask.

He shrugs. "I don't really have one. I just got out of the Marines."

I already knew that from Carla, but I find myself curious to know more. "Where were you based overseas?"

"Iraq. Afghanistan. Different places," he says. "I worked in close protection at the US embassy in Kabul. I was assigned to protect a general as well, on a tour of the Middle East."

Hearing him talk about his work makes me look at him in a slightly new light. "That sounds dangerous," I say.

He gives another small shrug, which seems to be his trademark gesture. Nothing seems to really bother him or ruffle his feathers. He seems to be able to shrug everything off. I wish I could be more like that.

"Where is your family?" I ask.

"My mom lives in Oceanside, with my little sister and brother."

I notice he doesn't mention a dad and wonder if he's still around or if he disappeared like my dad.

"You know, I can talk to Donny," he suddenly says, surprising me at the turn in the conversation. "Tell him to back off and leave you alone."

"No," I say, shaking my head. "It's okay."

"Are you sure?" he presses.

I shake my head again, impatient. "He needs the money. He has a family. Three kids. His wife died. If a photo of me helps him pay the bills, then . . . whatever."

Will stops walking and I glance over my shoulder at him. He's looking at me like he doesn't understand something. "How do you know that?" he asks.

I shrug, borrowing the gesture from Will. "Donny was taking photos of Jamie and me one time. Usually Jamie loves being papped, but we were in the middle of an argument, so he confronted him and . . . he ended up breaking his camera."

Will raises his eyebrows in consternation.

"I paid for a new one," I add hastily. "And that's when he told me about his family situation. Ever since then, I've felt bad for him."

"You bought him a camera?" Will asks, bemused.

I nod. "Yeah."

"So he could keep following you around and taking photos of you?"

When he puts it like that, I guess it sounds strange. "I mean, it's his livelihood," I explain. "It would be like someone taking my voice."

Will nods, but he's looking at me strangely, like he thinks I'm irrational. I look away, feeling uncomfortable beneath his gaze, wishing I hadn't told him anything. It's none of his business. And besides, I was meant to be playing diva Luna and forcing him to hand in his notice. . . . Why am I suddenly in overshare mode?

Just then a seagull dive-bombs out of nowhere, seemingly thinking I'm dinner. I scream as its talons come way too close for comfort, and the next thing I know, Will is pulling me into his chest, covering my head with his arm and shooing the bird off.

Once it's gone, with a loud and angry squawk, I look up at the sky tentatively. "What the hell was that?" I ask.

"A kamikaze seagull." Will laughs.

"Even the birds are attacking me," I say with a sigh, before noticing I'm still sheltering against him. I leap backward. Time to put the distance back between us.

WILL

The wind teases strands of her hair out from under her cap as we walk back along the beach. She seems a lot calmer than when we were in the car. I'm still processing what she told me about Donny and paying for the camera Jamie broke. I guess I'm surprised. I keep seeing these contradictory sides to her; one minute she's blowing cold and acting like a princess, and the next she's warm and ... normal, for want of a better word. Maybe she's more than the spoiled celebrity princess I'd taken her for.

I remind myself I'm her bodyguard and I should be putting up boundaries. But at the same time, having her trust me is important. Maybe if I can build a bridge and let her see I'm on her side, she would be less prone to running off.

I am itching to ask her more about her childhood in Florida, and I'm also curious to know about Jamie and their relationship, but that feels like the kind of question a friend would ask. I'm also anxious that if we do have a deeper conversation, she might start asking more questions of me, ones about my childhood, and I don't want to have to answer anything about my dad. It's why I cut her off just now and changed the subject.

"You ever try meditation?" I ask.

She looks at me with a bewildered smile. "What?"

"Meditation," I say. "It used to help me."

"With what?"

"With dealing with stuff," I mumble, looking out at the surfers in the distance to avoid her inquiring gaze.

"What kind of stuff?" she probes.

I walked into that one. I should have kept my mouth shut. Two seconds ago I was telling myself that I didn't want to have a deeper conversation with her, and now . . .

"You know," I say, struggling to find the right words, "emotional issues." I don't want to admit to her that I had anger issues as a kid. "Meditation can help with stress and anxiety," I tell her. "Even just simple breathing techniques and learning how to clear your mind."

"Counting to ten doesn't work. I tried that," she answers with an impatient sigh.

"That's not what I'm suggesting," I say. "I mean, more like special breathing techniques."

"Like inhale, exhale, you mean?"

She's being sarcastic.

"More like breathe in for seven, hold it for four, breathe out for eight. It calms the nervous system. It's good for getting to sleep, too, if your mind is going wild with all the chatter."

There's a flicker in her eyes—curiosity and also surprise. "You get insomnia too?" she asks.

I nod. "Sometimes. When I've got a lot on my mind."

She's paused to look at me with an intrigued expression, like she wants to know what keeps me awake at night, and I pray she doesn't ask me, because then I would have to lie.

"I get insomnia all the time. It's like I can't turn my brain off," she admits, almost shyly.

"Things always seem worse at night."

She nods. "Yeah, a hundred times worse. I get into these panic attacks—" She stops abruptly and shakes her head. "It doesn't matter." Her expression changes, hardens. "Let's go back to the car."

"I'm sorry," I blurt, surprised by the sudden shift in her mood. Having not wanted to overstep a boundary, I've clearly gone and done it, though I'm not sure why she's reacting like this. It's not like I haven't seen her deal with anxiety attacks. "I was only trying to help."

"Thanks," she spits angrily, "but I really don't need your help. I'm fine."

"Right," I say to her departing back, wondering why she's suddenly acting like this and being so resistant to my suggestions. "You really seem like you've got it handled." I regret the words the second they leave my mouth.

She wheels around to face me, her eyes wide, and I take a step back. "What the hell?!" she demands. "It's none of your business. You're my bodyguard, not my therapist. Maybe you should remember that!"

She storms off and I watch her go. She really is a human hurricane. I only wish that the tiny glimpse she just gave me of the real her, right before she pushed me away, hadn't been so damn appealing.

LUNA

'm terrible at knitting, but I force myself to keep going, despite dropping several stitches. I can't stop thinking about Will and our conversation earlier at the beach, playing it over on repeat. He was pushing me to open up to him about my anxiety and panic attacks, and I'm scared it's because he's trying to find out gossip on me that he can sell to the papers. I tell myself I'm being paranoid, but it's not like it hasn't happened before. The other possibility is he's been asked by Marty and my mom to report back on me.

I drop another stitch and am trying to figure out how to fix it when my phone explodes beside me on the bed. I drop the knitting and grab for it.

"What the hell?" I whisper in horror, staring at my phone screen and then clicking on the alert to open up the tweet. Oh dear God. I read through the comments beneath the photo, of which there are hundreds, my panic mounting with each one.

The photograph Donny took of me coming out of the store with Will is front-page news, not in any newspaper but across the entire internet, and the headline accompanying it screams LUNA'S NEW BOYFRIEND!

My whole body shakes as I zoom in on the photograph. Will

has his arm around me, his other hand raised as though to stop the photographer approaching. He's holding all my shopping bags, but much worse is the expression on my face as I look up at him. I'm almost certain the photo's been altered because I don't ever remember looking at him like that. Why would I ever look at him like that? I look like a pathetic damsel in distress staring up at her rescuing prince. It's so cringeworthy I can feel my insides curdle with embarrassment.

The comments are coming thick and fast, quicker than I can read them, and all of them are speculating on who my new man is. No one, it seems, has worked out yet that he's my bodyguard or that I pay him to carry the bags. They all think I'm dating him. Some people are guessing that he's an actor or a model, and one swears blind she saw him on a police procedural show. A few people are gossiping that I'm on the rebound and claiming this is a pathetic attempt to make Jamie jealous.

Their speculation isn't too far off. I wanted people to think I was happy and carefree and that I wasn't bothered by what people were saying about Jamie. I wanted him to see too that I didn't care about him having a possible new girlfriend.

Oh God, it was a pathetic idea, though. What if Will sees? What if he hears what people are saying? What if he is furious about being dragged into all this drama? He might even have a girlfriend, and if he does, what will she think of it? But it's Jamie I should be worrying about. Not Will.

I pace the room, wondering if I should text Jamie to let him know that Will is working for me and to reassure him not to read into anything, but then I stop and mentally kick myself. Jamie and I are done. Why do I even care what he thinks? But I do know—fear. Fear that he'll finally walk away for good. And, despite me saying I'm done with him, I'm not. I need Jamie.

He's the only person who gets what it's like to live this life. He's the only person who remotely understands me. And if I push him away, I'm scared I'll be alone for the rest of my life. Jamie is what I know—he's comfortable and familiar. Anything else is too daunting.

I'm standing by the window when I look up and see Will outside. He's kicking a soccer ball around with Matias. I watch them for a long time, realizing I've never seen Matias play soccer before. He's not the most coordinated as a result of his brain injury, but Will is patient and kicks the ball slowly. He cheers when Matias makes contact with it, and he runs after the ball when Matias kicks it in the direction of the pool. I laugh as he mock dives to save it from going in and misses it accidentally on purpose so that Matias laughs even harder when he has to fish it out from the deep end.

My phone vibrates in my hand and I jump. It's a text from Jamie. I open it, breath catching in my chest like barbed wire. **Hey babe**, he writes. **Whassup?**

Finally! The relief bounces off me, making me feel light-headed. I had been on edge this whole time, worrying that I'd pushed him away for good, but the door has cracked open. The panic that had been buzzing behind my sternum like a trapped hornet escapes into the daylight. I feel a million times lighter.

Then I pause, wondering at the timing of him sending the text. Did he see the photo of me with Will? Is that what spurred him to suddenly get in touch? That has to be the reason. He's jealous.

An idea sparks in my head, streaking through like a comet. The second after I have it, I push it away. It would be wrong. But then again . . .

WILL

Matias goes off for a lesson with his tutor, and I have time to kill. I'm guessing Luna is upstairs trying on her new outfits.

As soon as I'm back in my apartment, I realize I've still got a lot of pent-up energy. Kicking the ball around with Matias helped dispel a little of it, but I continue to feel antsy and I can't sit still. I've already unpacked my meager belongings into the closet and drawers and made the bed. I've been through the kitchen, familiarizing myself with all the contents and all the expensive appliances, including a state-of-the-art coffee maker that took half an hour to figure out but makes an excellent espresso.

I don't have to go out for groceries because the kitchen was stocked with all the essentials, and Carla made me breakfast and lunch. The kitchen has a small bar counter with stools, and on the other side is a living area with a sofa and a wall-mounted television. I play around with the remote for a few minutes, but I'm not much of a TV watcher, so I end up turning it off. I try meditating, but that doesn't work either. I can't concentrate—I keep playing over the conversation with Luna at the beach and wondering why her mood shifted so dramatically—but I can't figure her out at all, so instead I make more coffee and idly scroll through the internet on my phone.

I type in Luna's name, more out of curiosity than anything else, and click through to YouTube to watch one of her music videos. My eyeballs are assaulted by strobe lights and music that has a headache-inducing tempo. And then there's Luna, wearing a pink wig, a silver leotard, and thigh-high boots, dancing on top of a glass table. Her voice is good, but it's also so synthesized that it's hard to tell for sure. And the lyrics are kind of idiotic, something about wanting a guy who makes her suffer for his love.

I know the guys on the base used to love watching videos like this, worse ones too. They'd all gather around to cheer and leer, and the suggestions that would come out of their mouths would turn the air blue. The idea of them doing that while watching this video and imagining the things they'd say about Luna makes me uncomfortable, so I click the video off.

I find the song stays in my head, though. Grudgingly I have to admit it's catchy, despite the manic house beat. I scroll through numerous links to gossip sites, not wanting to click on them and give them more advertising revenue. But then I see a link to the *National Enquirer* story that her mom mentioned, the one that her ex-bodyguard sold. It's easy to find and I wince when I do. It's not just a story—it's a photograph of Luna, eyes half-closed, lying sprawled against a toilet, her hair a mess and her makeup smeared. LUNA RIVERA ODS! screams the headline.

I don't assume the story is true because I know tabloids are usually making up gossip in order to sell more copies, and the thing that shocks me most is that her bodyguard, instead of helping her as she lay there passed out, decided to take a photograph so he could sell it to the highest bidder. Jesus. No wonder Luna doesn't trust anyone and doesn't want a bodyguard.

My phone buzzes as I'm scrolling through the article, trying to parse some information that isn't plain conjecture. It's my sister Kate. She's been sending me texts for the last day and a half, so I figure it's time I answer.

"Hey," I say, picking up.

"Oh my God, oh my God, oh my God!" she shouts down the phone. "Are you really dating Luna Rivera?" she asks.

"What?" I ask. "No. I'm working for her."

"That's not what it says online."

"On where?" I ask.

"On *Hollywood Scandalista*."

I take a sip of coffee. "What are you talking about?"

"It's a blog. There are pictures of you and Luna and you're dating."

I almost choke on my coffee.

My phone buzzes against my ear. "I just sent you a link," Kate tells me.

I click on it. My brain at first struggles to put it together, and I barely recognize myself in the photo, but then it all falls into place. It's the photo Donny took earlier today when Luna and I walked out of that store. But how has it ended up online? Donny must have sold it. But why would anyone think we're dating?

"You went shopping with Luna?" Kate squeals excitedly.

I rub the bridge of my nose as I read the headline that accompanies the photograph.

"So, are you for real dating her?" my sister continues. "What's she like? Can I meet her?"

"I'm not dating her," I answer crossly, reading the headline again.

"Then why is your arm around her?" Kate asks.

I study the photograph. My arm is around her, it's true. And Luna is leaning into me, her face pressed against my chest.

"Did she break up with Jamie for you?" Kate asks.

"What?" I grunt. "No!"

My phone buzzes again. I glance at the screen, ignoring the stream of high-pitched chatter coming from Kate. It's a text from Tristan. **Duuuuuude,** he writes. That's all.

My phone buzzes once more. This time it's a message from my other sister, Zoey, Tristan's girlfriend. **Are you really dating Luna Rivera?** she demands to know.

"Are you even listening to me?" I hear Kate yell down the phone.

I put the receiver back to my ear. "I need to go," I say.

"No!" she shouts. "Wait!"

But I hang up. My head is spinning, and for a moment I sit there, staring at the wall, trying to figure out how to handle the situation. The problem is that this is not like the normal situations I have to deal with. This isn't an enemy waving a gun in my face or wearing a suicide vest. My instincts are honed to look for escape routes, ways out of trouble, but in this instance I've no idea where the escape route is.

My phone keeps buzzing. Messages are flooding in. Some are from Kate, annoyed at me for hanging up on her, but others are from random people I haven't seen in ages, even people I went to school with. Word is spreading among all my friends and acquaintances like some deadly virus. Goddamn the internet. This is why I don't generally use my phone or go online.

What if Luna's seen it? She must have seen it. She's always on her phone. What will she think? Will she be mad? Damn. Why do I care? It's not my fault. Maybe I shouldn't have put my arm around her. But I was just doing my job.

If I don't get out of here, I'm going to tear a hole in the carpet from all the pacing. I jog downstairs to where earlier I spotted a punching bag and a weight bench. It looks like it's never been used. I quickly wrap my hands before I start pounding the bag.

Boxing was always my favorite sport. My dad dragged me to the gym when I was about seven, declaring that no son of his was going to ever lose a fight. I hated it at first, but my coach, Joe, taught me that to really excel at the sport, you had to use your brain first, then your fists. I slowly came around to it, channeling all the rage at my dad into the bag.

By the time I was fifteen, I'd bulked up, still not quite as tall or as broad as my dad, but I felt like I could take him on if I had to. The first time I tried to, though, my dad broke my nose.

The repetitive nature of hitting the bag helps calm my mind and release the pent-up feelings I'm carrying around. I'm not always good at talking about my feelings, so that's how I get them out. The boxing bag is my therapist.

My T-shirt gets drenched with sweat, so I tear it off and throw it down on the ground before going back to the bag, laying punch after punch after elbow strike on it. I'm frustrated and honestly, I don't fully understand why. It's a stupid photo, I tell myself. Why should I let it bother me?

A shadow moves to my right. I glimpse it out of the corner of my eye and swing around, fists raised. Luna startles and steps back.

I drop my hands. "Sorry," I say, embarrassed. How long was she standing there watching me take my anger out on the punching bag?

She opens her mouth and then shuts it, then opens it again. "I, um . . . ," she stammers, struggling, it seems, to look me in the eye. Shit. She's seen the photograph. That's the first thing that crosses my mind. What's she going to say? Should I bring it up first? She smiles, kind of nervously, and brushes her hair out of her eyes, then stares at the ground. "I wanted to say sorry," she says. "For earlier, at the beach. I shouldn't have snapped at you like that. You were only trying to help."

"No," I interrupt, feeling relief blaze through me. "I'm sorry. I shouldn't have said anything. You're right. It's not my business." I smile, trying to show her that all is forgiven. She looks away, staring nonchalantly around at the garden.

"I was thinking of going out, to see a movie," she announces.

"Okay," I say. "What time?"

"Soon," she says, still not looking at me.

I glance up at the sky. It's getting toward dusk. I must have been out here for almost an hour. Now that I've noticed the time, I also notice my shoulders are aching and the sweat is cooling on my chest and back. Then I become aware that I'm standing here half-naked. No wonder Luna doesn't know where to look.

"Sure." I nod and start to unwrap my hands. "You're the boss."

She frowns and then gestures at my hands as I unwind the long elastic bandages. My knuckles are grazed and red and my fingers swollen. I should have stopped before now. I'm lucky I didn't break anything.

"You need gloves?" Luna asks.

"Yeah." I had a pair, but they got lost somewhere in one of my moves.

"There's a speed bag in the garage too, if you want to use that."

I look at her, then back at the punching bag. "This is yours?" I ask, unable to keep the surprise out of my voice.

She nods.

"I didn't know you boxed."

"Oh, I don't," she mumbles.

I wonder why she bought all the equipment, then. Maybe when you're rich, you buy stuff you don't need and then never use it.

"You should ice that," she tells me, pointing to my hand.

I rub at the knuckles and try to flex my wrist to get some feeling back into it. "Yeah," I say.

"Who were you picturing?" she asks, glancing at the punching bag.

"No one," I tell her. I check my phone for the time. "What time's the movie?"

"Oh yeah," she says. Her cheeks turn pink and she starts scuffing the ground with her bare foot. "Let's leave around seven," she answers, smiling at me. "See you later."

LUNA

Where are you going?" my mom asks, stomping into my room as I'm getting ready to go out with Will.

"To the movies."

"Who with?"

"Natalie," I lie, not wanting to tell her the truth because I know she'll just get suspicious.

She hasn't even asked me about the photo of Jamie and that girl, or about what's happening between us, or how I'm doing. I wonder if she saw the photo of Will and me, but even if she has, she'll just be happy I'm getting publicity. It's unlikely she'd read anything into it, knowing how much the papers lie and how much I hate bodyguards.

She leans her body against the doorframe. "When's Jamie back?"

I let out a long sigh.

I didn't tell her we'd broken up, so it's possible she doesn't know about our recent split. "Next week," I say, a prickle of anxiety spreading like a rash across my skin at the thought.

"I'm leaving for the airport in five minutes," my mom says. "I just wanted to say goodbye."

Oh God, I'd forgotten she was going away for two weeks to a fancy spa for yoga and meditation. "Have fun," I say, feeling both massive relief that she's leaving but also a twinge of sadness because I can't remember the last time we went anywhere together. If she had asked, I most likely would have gone with her. But she never asks anymore.

My mom gives me a hug and a kiss on the cheek. "I love you. Carla's here to look after you and Matias while I'm gone. And Will is going to keep an eye on you. How are you getting along with him, by the way?" Maybe she has seen the photo after all.

I make a noncommittal grunting sound. "Fine."

"Marty will check in on you too. Be good."

I nod and smile. "Bye."

As soon as she's gone, I finish my makeup and hurry to the apartment over the garage. Will yanks open the door before I can knock. "Hey," he says. "I was just coming to find you."

I smile, noticing his hair is still wet from the shower and that he seems flustered. At least he's wearing a shirt, I tell myself. Earlier it was practically impossible to look anywhere else but at his chest, and I haven't been able to get the image of him shirtless out of my head, despite trying desperately hard.

"I wanted to bring you these," I say, holding up the boxing gloves I dug out of a pile of sports equipment in my closet.

He looks shocked. "These are new," he says, taking them.

I nod. I bought them for Jamie, just like I bought the boxing equipment for him as a gift since *Creed* is one of his favorite movies. But he never used them. I don't tell Will that, though. "I hope they're not too small" is all I say, glancing at his hands, which are bigger than Jamie's.

He smiles, looking genuinely happy, and I feel a warm-honey sensation spread through my chest. One of my favorite things to do is get gifts for people, not because I want people to thank me but because I love the satisfaction when I get it right. I like to think I'm an expert at it. It's one of the main ways I reconcile myself to having a lot of money, when so many people are struggling.

"Thanks," Will says, his eyes still on the gloves as he turns them over in his hands. They're good ones, the best I could find, and I did my research.

"You're welcome," I say.

Will sets the gloves down on a shelf by the stairs that lead up to his apartment.

"How are you settling in?" I hear myself ask.

"Good," he answers. "Thanks. The apartment's great."

There's an awkward pause where we both stand there in his doorway.

"What time is the movie?"

I blink. "Um." My mind goes blank. Movie. Time. Oh God. I knew there was something I was meant to do.

"I can't remember," I blurt.

"What's the movie?"

Crap. I don't even know what's playing. I pull out my phone. "It's—it's something I've been wanting to see for ages," I stutter.

As he closes the door and follows me toward the driveway, I frantically search for what movies are playing nearby. There's a big Disney animated kids' movie and something that looks like a rom-com, which I discount immediately because I hate rom-coms more than anything. My favorite movies are historical period dramas. I binge-watched *Downton Abbey* and *The Crown*. Jamie hates anything that isn't an action thriller with lots of explosions, fast cars, and fight sequences with huge body counts. Which is why I have an almost encyclopedic knowledge of the Fast & Furious franchise.

I stop by Will's Bronco. "You want to take my car?" he asks, sounding surprised.

I nod. "Sure."

"Okay, no problem," he says, opening the passenger door for me.

As he jogs around to the driver's side, I continue scrolling through the list of movies, landing on one with a picture of a little girl in a Victorian-looking dress.

"So, did you figure it out?" Will asks as he gets in the driver's seat.

"Yeah," I say, reading the title of the movie. "*Annabelle*."

He plugs in the directions to the movie theater and then turns on the engine. R&B music blasts out of the speakers.

"Minnie!" I exclaim. "You like Minnie Riperton?!" I can't help but burst into laughter.

He moves to hit the off switch, but I catch him by the wrist to stop him before he can.

"No, I love Minnie!" I say. "I would listen to her all the time when I was a kid. My mom used to play her and Patti LaBelle and Roberta Flack. We'd listen to the radio on Sunday mornings on the way to church—soul and R&B all the way. And then after church I'd dance around the house and pretend to sing with a wooden spoon."

I look over at Will and notice he's staring at me with his mouth hanging open. I don't know why I just opened up to him like that. He has this way of treating me like I'm normal, I guess. And I forget who I'm meant to be when I'm around him.

"Me too," he finally says. "I mean, not exactly the same, but my grandma had this collection of vinyl. She was a huge Minnie fan. She'd play us all her records when we came to stay, and we'd dance around the living room."

"Where does she live?" I ask.

His expression darkens. "Oh, she . . ." His grip on the steering wheel tightens. "She died."

I let a few seconds pass between us before saying an awkward "I'm sorry."

Will gives a sad smile. "Thanks."

"Where did she live?" I ask after a few moments.

"Atlanta."

I wait, hoping he'll continue, and thankfully, he does. "She was kind of a lighthouse for me as a kid."

A lighthouse? My eyebrows lift. "What do you mean?"

"Things were pretty rough at home when I was little." He hesitates and I know there's more to that story, but as soon as he begins to speak again, he clams up. I don't press the issue and instead we fall into silence.

I look out the window.

Will clears his throat. "You've got a really good voice," he says, breaking the silence.

I turn back to him and only then realize I've been singing along to the music under my breath. My face heats up. "Thanks."

"I mean," he adds hastily, "I knew you were a singer, and that you were good, but I mean, you can *really* sing."

"Thanks," I repeat. "I think."

"It's just—" He stops himself abruptly, as though he's caught himself before mentioning something he'd regret.

"What?" I press, shifting in my seat to face him.

"Nothing."

He turns into the parking garage by the movie theater.

"Tell me," I ask again, determined to make him spill.

He pulls into a parking space and turns off the engine. "I listened to one of your songs earlier."

"Which one?" I'm struck with how giddy I feel about the fact that he's sought out my music.

"I don't know," he says, shaking his head. "I can't remember." I frown.

"But you didn't sound like *that*," he says. "When you were singing right now."

My frown deepens. "You didn't like it?" I ask, unable to disguise my disappointment.

He scratches his beard nervously. "Not really," he admits.

It's like a knife nicking a rib, but I try not to show it hurts.

"It's not that you can't sing," he carries on, explaining himself. "It's just not my kind of music. Not that I've listened to your other stuff. Maybe I'll like that."

"You haven't heard any of my music except that one song?" I look up at him in surprise. No one ever admits that. Usually they lie and tell me they *love my music*. At least, to my face. Online it's another story.

He shrugs, looking a little embarrassed. "I inherited my grandma's vinyl collection. I never listened to anything else, so I don't know much about music after 1979."

I make a grunting sound and look out the window, turning my head away.

"Luna?"

I turn back at him, forcing an airy *I'm not in the least bit bothered by your opinion* smile, but the truth is, I am bothered. I try to tell myself I should be happy that for once I'm getting some honest feedback, but it hurts nonetheless.

"I'm sorry," he says, looking visibly uncomfortable. "And look, what do I know? You've won like, a hundred awards or something."

"Thirty-nine," I correct him.

"Who's counting?" he shoots back, a half smile brushing the corner of his mouth. "I'm sorry," he says again, looking painfully awkward.

I decide to shake it off and offer him a smile. "It's fine. A million other people will beg to differ with you, but it's fine."

He shoots me one of his signature smirks. "Do you like what you sing?"

I double-take. I've never been asked that before. "Um, yes, I guess. I mean, it sells."

"But do *you* like it?"

"Of course I do." And before I know it, I'm out of the car, slamming the door harder than necessary. I wish he'd lay off this topic of conversation. This movie outing wasn't supposed to be an interview.

He gets out too, and when I glance over, I see he's smiling to himself, like he knows he's gotten to me and he's happy about it. It's weird and disconcerting, not to mention annoying, that he, a near stranger, might be able to read me so well already. I can tell he knows I'm lying. I hate my music, and I've never admitted that to anyone.

As we walk toward the movie theater, I can feel Will glancing at me out of the corner of his eye and I turn to him. "What?" I ask, touching my face, wondering if I've got something on my cheek or toothpaste on my chin.

"You want to borrow my hat?" he asks.

I shake my head. "No."

He frowns and I know he must be wondering why I'm suddenly caring less about being spotted than earlier at the beach, when I made a big deal about being incognito. I clam up, hoping he won't press me on it.

"You like horror?" Will asks as we walk toward the movie theater.

"Huh?" I say.

"*Annabelle*. It's a horror movie."

What? I follow in the direction he's pointing and see the poster on the far side of the foyer. It features a terrifying doll. From the thumbnail-size picture on my phone, all I could make out was what looked like a child in a Victorian nightgown. I got that wrong. It's not a small child. It's a horrifying, evil-looking doll. I hate dolls. The only things I'm terrified of are dolls. Okay, also the dark and being buried alive. And death. So basically all the elements that usually make up horror movies.

"Yeah," I grunt, forcing the panic down inside my chest. "I love horror movies."

Will glances at me a little skeptically, but I breeze past him to the popcorn counter. The foyer is busy, and I see one or two people glance my way and nudge each other. After a time you develop a sixth sense for knowing when people have recognized you. I arrange my face into a smile because once you're spotted, it's only a short time before people are surreptitiously snapping photos while trying to pretend they're just looking something up on their phone.

"Are you meeting people?" Will asks, scanning the lobby as I order a large popcorn.

"Do you like butter?" I try to avoid his question.

"Um, sure," he answers.

"Coke?"

He shakes his head. I order a Diet Coke for me, then head to pay.

I can feel him standing behind, several feet away, and when I turn around with my drink and my popcorn, I spot him scouring the lobby and for a second I catch myself staring. The Terminator RoboCop thing might have been a little harsh. I take it back. He is undeniably attractive. Quickly I shake my head before the thought has time to gain a foothold in my brain. It's disloyal to Jamie. *Disloyal?* I mentally kick myself. Why am I still being loyal to Jamie?

The man at the desk checks the tickets. "Two?" he asks.

I nod and look over at Will, who seems very confused. I guess he figured I was meeting someone here and that he would be sitting in the row behind, keeping an eye on us like a chaperone.

"You're in the back row on the right-hand side," the ticket guy says to me.

I cringe. If it didn't look like we were on a date before, it definitely does now.

WILL

've never actually been to the movies with a girl, unbelievable as that sounds. I was a loner at school. I had just one friend, Tristan. And then I joined the Marines when I was sixteen.

I take a few measured in-and-out breaths, shifting in my seat a few times to crane over my shoulder to see where the exits are and also to scan the other people around us. It's an automatic response to look for threats, but I don't detect any. Most people look to be here on a date, which seems weird. I don't get why you'd go on a date to a horror movie. It doesn't seem like a very romantic thing to do, but I'm not exactly an expert on romance.

The trailers start and I glance over at Luna, who turns and offers me the popcorn. I shake my head.

"You have to share this with me," she says. "I can't eat it all on my own."

I shake my head again. This is too weird.

"You okay?" Luna asks, noticing.

I nod, but I'm lying through my teeth. I'm hyperaware of the oddness of the situation. It feels like a date. And I'm her bodyguard. I should be sitting behind her, or at the end of the row.

But the movie theater is packed, so there's no chance of moving.

She offers me her drink next. I tell her "no thanks" and focus on the screen, determined that I'm not going to look at her again for the entire duration of the movie. As the trailers continue, though, I find it harder and harder to focus on the screen and not on her. Her leg is an inch away from mine, and I'm more aware of her body than I am even of my own. It sounds stupid, but the feeling I have is the exact same feeling I get when I'm on patrol at night in a danger zone. Every sense is primed, and my situational awareness is off the scale.

The first stage of that is perceiving every aspect of your environment. In this case, I've checked the theater for threats and mapped all the escape routes, and now I'm fully occupied with perceiving my more immediate environment, aka Luna herself. As I sit beside her, trying not to look at her, out of the corner of my eye I'm still mapping every inch of her.

I glance sideways at Luna again and am struck by her profile. She's beautiful. Breathtaking, actually. It's not like I hadn't realized this before, but I'm starting to notice all the small details. Like the fact that she has a deep dimple in her right cheek, that her lower lip is slightly fuller than the top one, that she has an upturn to her nose, and that her neck is long and slender.

She turns and catches me staring, and I look away, more flustered than I want to admit. What is going on? Why did she invite just me, and not a friend? Does she often come to the movies on her own? Is this a thing she does? Or is it something that she likes to do but can only do with a security guard to make sure she doesn't get hassled? I can't imagine her being able to come to the movies by herself. I doubt, even if she wasn't famous, that she'd be able to go anywhere without being noticed. She's that kind of person, with that kind of face. People naturally look twice.

She was spotted as soon as we walked into the lobby, people elbowing each other and pointing at her. I moved to block a couple who were trying to take a photo without her knowledge, giving them a head shake to send them on their way. But she wasn't even trying to disguise herself, which is also weird.

As the movie starts, Luna shifts in her seat and places her hand on the armrest between us, bumping my arm. Was that deliberate? Or accidental? And why am I feeling an answering jolt up the length of my arm, like an electric shock?

I recognize that all this analysis is what occurs in the second stage of situational awareness—where you try to make sense of your current situation and what is happening.

I am failing to make sense of it, though, just like I am failing to make any sense of the movie, which seems to be about devil worshippers and a demonically possessed doll that some guy buys for his wife. A guaranteed recipe for divorce, no doubt.

The third stage of situational awareness is when you start to predict what might happen next based on what you've assessed in the first two stages about your environment. And so I glance over at Luna again, breaking my own rule for the second time in as many minutes. I look for clues as to what's coming. She has stopped eating the popcorn, and her hands are gripping the armrests. She looks like she might be about to throw up. It seems like she really isn't enjoying the movie that much, and I wonder why she wanted to see a horror movie in the first place.

"Are you okay?" I ask, leaning over to whisper in her ear.

She startles almost out of her seat and turns to me, wide-eyed. "Yeah, fine," she whispers back unconvincingly.

I go back to pretending to watch the movie, but all I find myself doing is focusing on her bare arm on the armrest by mine, close but not quite touching.

Luna suddenly lets out a scream, along with most of the audience, and grabs for my hand. I freeze. Her hand is warm and soft and her grip is tight. I don't know what to do, whether to squeeze her hand back or disentangle myself from her grip or just stay frozen, not doing either. I don't want to give the wrong idea, but I also don't want to be rude. My eyes find hers, and she jerks her hand away as though I'm poison oak and leans away from me.

Toward the end of the movie, though, she leans back again, near me. Adrenaline starts pumping as though I'm running a sprint. What the hell is going on? Why are my instincts firing like I'm on night patrol in enemy territory?

I jump out of my seat the moment the credits roll, and wait for Luna to gather her things. I tell myself to get it together and start thinking more professionally. I'll go home and meditate, clear my mind. That should do it.

I hope.

LUNA

am never going to sleep with the lights off ever again, not that I ever do, but now I think I'm going to need therapy to get over that movie.

"I hate horror movies," I say as we leave the theater.

"I thought you loved them?" Will asks.

Uh-oh. "I . . . um . . . I always think I do, and then after, I'm like *why did I watch that*?"

He nods. "They're not my favorite either," he says.

I frown at the thought that I've dragged him to something he didn't like. "Sorry," I say. "I didn't ask you what you wanted to see."

He shakes his head. "It's fine. You're the boss."

His words bruise. I don't like him thinking of me as his boss. But I'm not sure I know how else I'd want him to think of me. Sighing inwardly, I give myself a silent pep talk; I invited him to the movies for a reason, and that reason wasn't because I wanted to see a movie or hang out with him. I don't need to care what he thinks of me. And yet, annoyingly, I do care.

We reach the elevator to the parking lot, and Will pushes

the button. I see him casting his eyes about, looking out for any threats. And as I watch him, my stomach does a little flutter. It's nice to feel looked out for. The other guys my mom hired were all kinds of macho men who liked to draw attention to themselves with their swagger, which in turn drew attention to me. But Will, he's more subtle, with *arrogant* being the last word I'd use to describe him. He blends in. I appreciate that.

When the elevator arrives, the couple who followed us out of the theater make a beeline toward it, nudging each other. I doubt very much they actually need an elevator, but when they step forward, Will ushers me inside and then bars their entry. "Going up?" he asks.

"Yeah," they say.

"Sorry," he says, "we're going down."

They back away, looking disappointed, and Will steps inside the elevator and presses the button for down. The doors slide closed and I look at him and grin, grateful.

"Thanks," I say.

"You're welcome." He shrugs, as expected. "I saw them taking photos of you in the lobby. I tried to step into the shot to block them." He turns to face the elevator doors.

I wonder if he saw the photo of us that Donny took, and a worm of anxiety burrows frantically in my gut. That couple who were taking photos will definitely tweet them. I know that if I take out my phone right now, I will probably already be trending. It's what I wanted. It's why I asked Will to come with me to the movies. I wanted to be spotted with him again. I wanted Jamie to see and to know I wasn't pining for him, and yes, maybe I also wanted to make him jealous. But now I'm starting to regret it. I shouldn't have used Will for that. It's dishonest.

The elevator lurches violently, and I stumble into Will, who catches me by the arm and steadies me. "What's happening?" I ask as the elevator does another smaller wobble and then jerks to a stop.

"I think we're stuck," he responds.

Oh God. The light above us flickers on and off, plunging us into darkness, which makes me yelp and grab for Will again.

"I think there's a power outage," he says. "Don't worry. The backup generator will come on in a second."

We wait in the dark for close to a minute, but nothing happens. It feels like we're hanging by a thread over an abyss and might plunge downward at any moment. I wonder how many meters we would fall if the wire snapped. I close my eyes and try not to imagine it, but the more I try, the more extreme the imaginings become.

"How much longer?" I ask in a whisper, attempting not to give away my anxiety.

"I don't know," Will says. It's dark, but I can feel him looking at me.

My breathing has started to hike, and my heart is hammering so hard and fast that I wrap my arms around myself to try to lock it inside my chest. I feel like I can't move even the slightest, because if I do, I might cause the cable to snap.

And I hate the fact that I can't see anything. God, I hate the dark. I want to reach for Will's hand but restrain myself. I can hear myself starting to hyperventilate. Is there enough air in here? Will it last?

"In for seven," I hear Will say, but his voice sounds distant. Breathing is now impossible. It's as if my lungs have shrunk. What if we run out of oxygen? I feel like I'm drowning, and I reach for the doors, trying to find a way to open them and let the light and air in. I need to get out of here before I die.

I hammer my fists uselessly against the elevator door until I feel Will catch my hand in his. He holds it tight and pulls me firmly toward him in the dark. Then he puts his hands on my shoulders and holds me in place. Initially I fight him, feeling as if he's dragging me down like a riptide, but he won't let go.

"In for seven," he repeats calmly into my ear.

I hear him inhale and start counting, and it becomes impossible not to join in. We hold for four and then exhale for eight.

He counts the whole time, and I follow his lead. We do it a dozen times, and by the time he finally stops, I am feeling much, much calmer. My head isn't spinning and my lungs aren't shrinking. I keep breathing slow and deep, forcing myself to stay calm, as a wave of shame starts to build in place of the panic. He drops his hands from my shoulders, and I feel the loss immediately.

"I hate the dark," I tell him by way of excuse, though it sounds completely lame.

Will's face is lit up with a white glow as he looks down at his phone. "No reception," he says.

I pull my phone out and see he's right.

"What if we're stuck in here forever?" I ask, wrapping my arms around myself again. What will happen if we need to pee?

"We won't be, don't worry." His face is still illuminated by the phone, and he genuinely looks unbothered by the situation. How does he stay so calm all the time? "Do you want to sit down?" he asks.

I glance at the floor. It's not the cleanest, but who cares? I sit, crossing my legs and leaning against the back wall. Will sits down too, a few feet from me, his knees up, his arms resting on them. He puts his phone on the floor, keeping the flashlight switched on, and I'm grateful.

"Nothing to be afraid of," he says.

"Except plunging to the bottom of the elevator shaft," I comment. "I saw it happen in a movie once."

He smiles. "It won't happen. These elevators have very strong cables and emergency brakes. We'll be fine. Trust me."

I nod, though he's asking a lot. I don't trust anyone.

"Would you rather be at the beach or by the mountains?" he asks suddenly.

I glance at him. I know what he's doing. He's trying to distract me. "I don't know. I like both," I say. "It depends if there's a lake in the mountains. I like being by water."

He smiles. "Me too."

I feel my heart rate speed up. Is it the way he smiles at me? Or the fact we have something else in common?

"Would you rather eat pizza or sushi?" I ask quickly.

"Sushi. I've never had it."

My mouth drops open. "What? Are you serious? How can you never have had sushi?"

He looks abashed, and I feel bad for making him feel bad. "We didn't have much money when I was growing up," he explains. "We didn't really go out for dinner, except maybe to Red Lobster or McDonald's."

"Me either," I say quickly, trying to erase any embarrassment he might be feeling. "We were broke when I was growing up. We lived in a mobile home."

He looks up at that, surprised, and I nod, happy to have confounded his expectation of me. I know he thinks I'm a spoiled, overentitled brat. It's what I would think if I were him.

"I didn't know," he admits.

I nod. He shouldn't feel bad. No one knows the real me. Except Matias and Carla, and to some extent, Jamie, though I haven't told him everything about my past.

"Would you rather be invisible or be able to fly?" Will asks.

"That's easy," I answer. "Invisible, of course. Then I could do whatever I wanted. Go places without being stared at all the time." It would be a way to escape this golden cage. "What about you?" I ask.

"Fly," he responds. "Then I could go anywhere in the world for free."

I bite my bottom lip. I have a private jet at my disposal. I'm so lucky. It's easy to forget how lucky. I feel shitty for being so focused on what I don't have.

"Would you rather date Wonder Woman or Catwoman?" I ask next, sticking with the superhero theme.

"I don't date, so . . . I guess neither."

"You don't date?" I ask, even more surprised than when he told me he'd never eaten sushi.

He shakes his head.

"Why not?" I ask, confused.

He rubs the back of his neck. "I've been on deployment overseas for years." He's squirming, and I can tell I've made him uncomfortable. I narrow my eyes. I think there's another reason he doesn't date that he's not telling me.

"So you've never had a girlfriend?" I press.

"Nope," he confesses.

My eyebrows shoot up. "For real?"

"Yeah," he says.

"You've never been in love?"

He shakes his head again. I don't know what to say to that. It's both shocking and a little heartbreaking. Maybe he's a player and he doesn't date because he just has one-night stands. He probably doesn't want to admit that to me.

"That's sad," I say.

"I guess I saw my parents fight too much," he says after a beat.

"My parents fought all the time too," I admit. "Before my dad left."

"I wish my dad had left," Will mutters.

I glance at him. His frown has deepened and he's glowering at his feet. "My dad only calls me to ask me for money," I confess to him, then immediately wish I could take it back. It's too much information. I don't know if I can trust him to keep it to himself, and it also looks like I'm trying to one-up him in the terrible-dad stakes.

Will looks up. "That sucks."

It's my turn to shrug. I'm used to it, I want to say. People use you all the time when you're in my position. It's why I don't have any friends.

"I don't care," I tell him. "I just feel bad for Matias. He doesn't understand why his dad doesn't call or visit or care about him."

"That's rough. He's a great kid."

"You're good with him. Not many people bother."

"I have a brother around the same age. They're not so different. He's obsessed with soccer and cartoons too. And he found it hard when my dad . . . was no longer around."

I cock my head, surprised that we have this in common but also curious as to where his dad is. "What happened to him?" I ask, wondering if he's dead.

Will pauses, then says, "He's in prison."

"Oh," I say, blindsided.

"It's okay. It's where he deserves to be." There's a deep frown line etched between his eyes, and I regret having asked. It's obviously a sensitive topic. I wonder what his dad did to get sent to prison, though.

"My dad left us after Matias was diagnosed," I blurt. "Matias had a brain tumor."

When I look up, I see that Will is watching me, really studying me, and I feel a warmth spread through my chest. "He was two when they found it." My throat tightens as I speak. "We didn't have good insurance. So it took a while because of all the referrals and they kept moving us from one hospital to another . . . but we finally got the diagnosis and he had to have an operation to remove it. It was either that or he'd die, so there wasn't a choice, but they warned us that if we went ahead and he had the operation, there was a chance he could end up brain-injured. The tumor was really deep, and with those kinds of surgeries there's never a guarantee."

"I'm sorry," Will says.

His voice is soft and tender and filled with empathy, and I blink back tears. I've never shared all the details of that time. I've never told anyone how exhaustingly lonely it was.

"After the operation, it was clear right away that Matias wasn't the same," I tell Will. I gaze down at my lap, the memories flooding back, feeling like punches to the gut. I remember sitting in the waiting room as he had his operation, my mom beside herself with worry, praying to God he'd be okay. I look up. Will is watching me intently, waiting for me to continue.

"Before the operation Matias had been walking and he was

just starting to talk. He was really coordinated. I used to read to him and he'd follow my finger across the page. He could stack bricks and he was smart. He used to say my name and then 'story.' He always wanted me to read to him. But afterward—" I break off, shaking my head, my voice catching in my throat as I remember the days following the operation, when he came off all the breathing equipment and was conscious. How he couldn't follow a finger being held in front of his face, let alone grasp it. How he didn't seem to recognize me and how he wailed this strange noise that we'd never heard before, whenever he wanted something. "He was different," I tell Will. "He couldn't walk or talk. He was eight before he said my name again."

Will takes a deep breath. "I don't know what to say. I'm so sorry," he repeats.

Lots of people have said that—it's a stock phrase—but with Will, I actually believe it. He's so honest about everything, and I think, given what he's been through, he probably does get it.

"It's okay," I say. "He's alive. Most kids with his type of cancer don't survive. And we're getting him a lot of help. After we moved here, it got easier. He learned to walk and talk again. He has incredible doctors. And he has tutors and therapists. He's doing really well. If he stays in the clear, he'll officially be in remission in two years' time."

As soon as I finish, I worry again that I've shared too much, and I feel a butterfly swell of panic in my chest, erasing the warmth I felt before. "Please don't tell anyone," I blurt. "No one knows."

He nods. "Of course," he says, then pauses before adding,

"You know, I wouldn't ever tell anyone anything you shared with me. You can trust me."

I take that in. *Can I?* I wonder. I know I'm starting to, even despite my misgivings, but I've been burned so many times before that it's not that easy.

"Tell me about your brother and sisters," I say, wanting to move the conversation away from me.

He looks up, surprised I remembered he mentioned them.

"There's Kate. She's sixteen. She's a fan of yours, actually," he adds.

I give him a snarky look. "At least someone in your family is."

He flushes at that, something I find instantly endearing. "I didn't say I wasn't a fan," he protests.

"You're just honest," I laugh.

"I don't know how else to be," he answers simply.

I'm starting to understand that about him. "How many other sisters do you have?"

"Just one. Zoey. She lives in Florida. Her boyfriend, Tristan, is in the Coast Guard. He's training to be a pilot. They were the people who invited me to that party at Emma's house, where I first met you. Tristan's twin sister, Dahlia, is dating Emma."

I shake my head at the coincidence that Will and I, who are so different and move in such different worlds, actually have friends in common. "I wondered about that," I say.

"Didn't expect me to move in such circles, huh?" He's looking at me with this half-mocking smile on his face.

"I don't really move in those circles," I explain. "Or any circles. Emma knows Jamie. That's why we were there. And to be honest, I hate parties."

He looks bewildered. "You do?"

I nod. "I'd rather stay home."

"Me too."

He smiles at me, no longer a half smirk but a full smile. And there's a curious look in his eye, like I'm confounding him again. And I like it.

WILL

Almost everything Luna's told me has come as a surprise. I had the completely wrong idea about her. She's not the person I thought she was at first. She isn't the girl on the red carpet, the spoiled celebrity I first met at the party. When she opened up about her family and Matias, I felt like I was seeing the version of herself she keeps hidden from everyone. The peek I got at the beach. She was vulnerable and unguarded and honest. She dropped the act. The strange thing is just how much we have in common. I thought we were totally different people, but we're not so different after all.

I glance at my phone to check the time. We've been stuck in the elevator for almost thirty minutes. But thankfully, Luna seems to have moved past her initial panic.

"Not much longer," I tell her, though a part of me wouldn't mind staying stuck in here with her for days. I'm enjoying getting to know her better. I understand why she doesn't trust people and that the way she acts is a defense mechanism to keep people at arm's length. And it's no shock that she feels the need to do that.

"What would be your dream job?" she asks, leaning her head back against the elevator wall. She looks at me with a pointed expression. "Because I know it's not doing this."

She guessed that right. "I want to do something outdoors," I admit.

"Outdoors?"

"Yeah. I want to work in outdoor education. When I was a kid, around twelve or thirteen, I went to one. It was this camp for kids who kept getting into trouble."

"You were getting into trouble?" she asks, her voice rich with skepticism. "I can't believe it. What kind of trouble?"

I wonder if I should admit it. I worry what she might think of me, but then I opt to be honest. "Stupid stuff. I was getting into fights at school, ditching out all the time. But this particular time, my dad stole the money I'd earned washing the neighbors' cars. I was saving up to buy a Nintendo. I wanted it so bad." I shake my head, laughing bitterly as I recall just how excited I was, how that Nintendo was the only thing I had to look forward to. "It took me ages to save the money. But my dad found my secret hiding place, and he took it. Spent it at the casino."

Luna's mouth drops open and her eyes widen. "Whoa. Our dads could compete for the shittiest-dad award."

I laugh under my breath. She has no idea. I think mine would win hands down, but I won't go into further details.

"I'm sorry," she says quietly.

"Anyway," I say, moving on. "I got so mad at him that I threw a rock at his car. Only I missed and hit someone else's car. And they called the cops."

"Holy crap," Luna gasps.

"I got arrested. But they didn't charge me. I was only a minor.

Instead, they offered me the chance to pay for the damage, and then go to this camp. I didn't want to," I confess. "I thought it would suck. And I didn't want to leave my mom and my sisters, but it turned out to be the best experience of my life." I grin. "We were swimming in the lake every day and kayaking and rock climbing."

"So you're a regular action-man?" she says in a teasing way.

I pull a face, feeling self-conscious at the teasing. "I don't know about that. The teachers there, though," he says, "the camp staff, they changed my life. Them and Joe."

"Joe?" I ask.

"My boxing coach. They taught me how to deal with all the things I was feeling. All the anger I had."

"Toward your dad?"

I pause. I didn't want to share all this with her, but here I am, doing just that. "Yeah. They made me feel listened to and supported," I say. I take a deep breath, surprised to feel my chest tightening and my voice cracking. "I don't know where I'd be now if not for them." I pause. Luna waits, looking at me. "I want to do that job. I want to help other kids like me."

"You want to be the lighthouse."

My neck snaps up to look at her as I realize that she's understood something I hadn't ever managed to articulate to myself. And that she's remembered the conversation about my grandma. "Yeah," I say almost breathlessly. "Exactly."

She smiles and I smile back. Something passes between us, a spark. I feel my chest constrict, my heart skip a beat. She looks away, and her cheeks flush. Am I imagining this? A shift has taken place between us, that's for sure. It's not just that she's starting to trust me and open up to me. It feels like there's chemistry, but I shouldn't be encouraging it. I can't.

I get to my feet, stretching out. I need to remember this is just a job. She's a client. And she has an on-off boyfriend, too, who she's no doubt about to be back on with again.

Luna stands up too and stretches her arms in the air. I can't help but glance at her stomach as her sweater rides up. All at once I find myself imagining pulling her into my arms. I have an urge to feel her body against mine and to know what it's like to kiss her. I turn away, trying to shake the image and the idea from my head.

Just then, the elevator jerks to life and we both stumble. I fall against the wall and Luna falls into me. I catch her around the waist. She gasps. I'm not able to see her face properly or read her expression because it's too dark. She doesn't pull away, though, and I don't let her go, my hands on her hips, and time seems to freeze. I'm holding my breath and I can feel her holding hers.

The elevator lights flash on, and we both blink in the glare, and the elevator starts to move again. She jerks backward, dancing away from me, brushing a hand over her hair. "Thank God," she says, laughing with relief. "We can get out of here."

I mumble in agreement, but my heart is pounding like I just ran a three-minute mile, and I definitely don't feel the same relief she does.

LUNA

L una!"

I startle and look around. Twenty glistening faces are staring back at me. And all of them look really annoyed. I've missed my cue.

"Sorry, sorry," I say, catching Marty out of the corner of my eye scowling in my direction.

"Run it again!" he barks, and the choreographer, Marcello, hurries across the stage toward me while gesturing at the sound guys to line up the music one more time.

The dancers, all in their workout clothes, shake their limbs out and get back into position behind me. Guiltily I try to avoid their eyes. They're annoyed at me because I'm off my game. I was late getting here because I overslept. I spent all night tossing and turning, thinking about Will and our conversation in the elevator, and thinking even more about that moment when I fell against him, playing it over and over in my mind, convinced I made a fool of myself. Did he think I was going to kiss him?

Finally I got up and started scribbling down some ideas for songs before falling asleep at dawn.

Now we've been rehearsing for three hours straight, and I keep forgetting the words to all the songs and the steps I'm meant to already have learned. I can't concentrate, not just because of tiredness but because my focus keeps shifting toward the back of the rehearsal space, where Will is. Even though he doesn't seem remotely interested in watching the rehearsal, I can't stop looking his way. First I wanted to see if he was watching me, but now I keep hoping he isn't, because I keep screwing up.

I don't know what's going on, and it's confusing. He's the first person in such a long time who's actually listened to me, who I believed was genuinely interested in getting to know me, and not because of who I am. And he's funny, and interesting, and thoughtful, and kind. And when he looks at me, I feel seen in a way I haven't ever before. But I don't know what it means. Do I like him? How can I, though? I hardly know him. And he's my bodyguard! Who I was trying to not only use but also make quit, and who I now really want to stay.

"Do you want me to run through that again?" Marcello asks when he reaches my side. He's small and petite, built from pure muscle and sinew. He trained in Cuba with the National Ballet before fleeing to the US, where he's made a name for himself working with all the top talent in the business. And now me. I know I must be an enormous disappointment, not that he ever shows it because he's too kind for that. He puts his hand on my shoulder and looks me in the eye. "Take a break," he says gently, and I almost collapse against him from exhaustion.

"Thank you," I whisper.

He gives me a wink. "I've got your back. Now go."

I nod, and as I start to rush off the stage, I hear Marcello call to the dancers to get in position. "Okay, everyone," he says. "Let's run those moves again. Get them perfect. Because this is going to be the best show the world has ever seen!"

I jump off the stage and make a beeline for the dressing room. Marcello's pep talk to the dancers rings in my ears. The best show the world has ever seen? Talk about pressure. I know I can dance okay, but I'm not the best dancer in the world. It doesn't come naturally. That's why they employ all those backup dancers who can actually *really* dance.

In the dressing room I shut the door and reach for my phone. There's another text message from Jamie. I didn't reply to the one he sent yesterday, and now he's texted again. He's going flat-out with the heart emojis and the lolling tongue emojis. He's even thrown in an eggplant, like that's going to be the swing factor for me. I was right about the photo that couple took of Will and me at the movie theater. It did go viral. And that's the only reason Jamie is suddenly all up in my DMs. Which is what I wanted. And yet . . . now I'm not so sure it's what I want. I shouldn't have used Will.

My mind flips back to last night, to Will and the conversation we had. I liked talking to him. Whenever I go out with Jamie, he sits there on his phone all night, texting his friends or taking photos of himself or the food. We never talk, or at least not about anything interesting like we used to.

The door flies open just then and Marty storms in. As usual, he hasn't bothered to knock. "What the hell are you doing?" he demands. "There are fifty dancers out there working hard, and you're in here messing about on your phone."

"I'm not on my phone," I argue, even though I am still holding it.

"You've not got long before the tour starts!" Marty bellows.

I sigh. "I know. It'll be fine."

"You're distracted. If it's about that photograph of Jamie with that girl, forget about it. She's nobody. A hanger-on. Nothing happened between them."

I look at Marty. Does he think I'm an idiot?

"You need to be focused," he reprimands me, waving a finger in my face.

"I am," I protest, reaching inside the mini-fridge under the dressing table for a bottle of water.

"Doesn't seem like it. Are you taking your pills?"

I nod, annoyed.

"Do you need to see the doctor again?" he presses. "Change up your prescription?"

I shake my head.

"Look, you need to get back out there," Marty tells me.

"I just need five minutes," I explain, albeit weakly, as it's like trying to fend off a bear when it comes to arguing with Marty.

"You don't have five minutes. Those people are on the clock," he says, meaning the dancers. "I'm not paying them to stand around."

I want to point out that he's not paying them at all. *I* am. All the money for everything comes from me, doesn't it? From the ticket sales that people pay to see *me*. Even Marty's salary comes from me.

"Marty, please," I say quietly. "I just want five minutes."

"We're a team, Luna," Marty says. "And you're not being a team player. There's a lot of people working hard, slaving around the clock, to make you look good, to make you a success. Your tour is coming up. So get your finger out of your ass, stop messing around on social media, and get back out there."

Anger fizzes through me. "I'm not messing around," I say, but my anger is about as powerful as damp sparks hitting a concrete wall. Marty scoffs at me. The room starts to spin, and all the anxiety I've been keeping at bay starts to gnaw away at my insides. I try to do the breathing thing that Will taught me, but Marty is standing right in front of me, hands on hips, breathing heavily through his nostrils like a dragon, and I can't.

"Let me go to the bathroom at least," I mumble, and I shove through the dressing room door into the little en suite. I turn the lock, my pulse hammering so loudly in my ears that it drowns out Marty shouting something about me hurrying the hell up and then the sound of the door slamming.

I sink to the floor in the bathroom and put my head between my knees.

Did he have to remind me about how much is resting on this and how much I owe to people? It doesn't help. It just makes me even more anxious.

I struggle to my feet and unlock the bathroom door, peering out to check Marty is gone, before hurrying over to my bag. I reach for the water and am about to swallow two of my anti-anxiety pills when there's a knock at the door. I'm so on edge that I drop the pills and am down on my knees gathering them up when the door cracks open an inch. It's not Marty—of course it isn't; he wouldn't have bothered to knock. It's Will.

"Hey," he says, bending down to help me. He picks up a pill and hands it to me. I try not to look at him as I take it, afraid of what he must be thinking.

"They're for anxiety," I blurt, scared that he'll think badly of me.

He gives a small nod, but I don't see any judgment in his face, only compassion. "Are you okay?" he asks.

I swallow hard, unable to look at him. My instinct is to say, "Sure, I'm fine," but I find I can't lie to him, so I end up not saying anything.

We stand up at the same time and it's awkward. He's right there in front of me, and all I can see is his chest and his arms, and I have to check my reaction, which is an almost overwhelming desire to fall against him. I don't know why I want to do that, but I do. I want to press my head against his chest and hear his heartbeat and feel his arms come around me and have him hold me and do that breathing exercise with me again. I'm tired, that's all. I'm being stupid. I turn my back to him and reach for the bottle of water, then swig down the pills in one swallow.

"I need to get back," I mutter, moving past Will for the door.

He steps in my way, though, blocking my exit. "Why don't you take a break?" he suggests softly. "You seem like you need it."

I hang my head in shame. Is it that obvious how lame I am? "I can't," I say. "They're all waiting on me."

"They're not," Will tells me. "That dancer guy has them all practicing some weird moves."

I look up at him, unable to stop myself from smiling. "You mean, the dance?"

"If you want to call it that."

"You don't like it?" I ask, biting my lip.

He shrugs. "You really have to stop asking me if I like things. I told you, I don't know anything about music made after—"

"1979, I know," I interrupt.

"And I haven't been to a concert, in . . . maybe ever."

"Are you serious?" I ask.

He nods. "But you looked good up there."

My eyes fly to his. "Really?" I ask, flushing.

He nods. "Yeah, really."

"I can't dance," I say.

"Yeah, you can," he argues, and there's a look in his eye that makes my heart beat just a little bit faster than it was. "If you think *you* can't dance, you should see me."

I grin.

"Don't let Marty push you around," Will says now. "He's just a bully. I had drill sergeants like him. Loved the sound of their own voices. Always shouting. It's not worth getting upset over it. Let it go over your head."

I frown. "I try. It's not always that easy."

"When my drill sergeant would yell at me, I'd stare at the space between his eyebrows and I'd imagine myself on a desert island. His voice became the sound of the waves crashing on the beach. Same when my dad used to scream and shout," he continues. "I'd close my eyes and pretend I was someplace else."

My heart pangs at the thought of Will as a child, being afraid and having to deal with that. It's heartbreaking.

"I wish I didn't have to pretend," I whisper, and he nods.

WILL

I took a cold shower last night and again this morning, but nothing is back to normal. As soon as I stepped foot into the kitchen this morning and saw her, I knew I was screwed.

I try to tell myself it's an illusion, that I'm an idiot who's been bedazzled like a teenager by all the Hollywood sparkle, but that's not it. It's not the celebrity version of Luna that I'm drawn to—it's the version she keeps hidden. The version I catch glimpses of when she's around other people, but that she seems to only show to me when we're in private. I told myself I needed to start marking some clear professional boundaries, shaking my head at how relaxed I got last night in the elevator.

But all I wanted to do was take care of her, let her know she was safe.

Even now, as Luna seems to be on the verge of tears, I wish I could do something more than offer stupid advice about imagining she's on a desert island while she gets yelled at because, really, she shouldn't be putting up with Marty's bullshit. He's trying to make her feel small and reliant on him because he's scared. He's a bully, plain and simple. He knows she's his meal ticket. I'm surprised she hasn't figured this out, but it doesn't feel like my place to say it. I'm only the help, after all.

She nods, as though gathering herself, and I almost put my hand on her shoulder to give it a squeeze. There's something birdlike about her, and not just her fine-boned frame, but her fragility and the way she seems so hyperalert to danger, suspecting everything and everyone of being a threat. I feel like if I touched her, she'd startle and fly away. It's weird. When I first met her, I thought she was like a hurricane, and now I'm likening her to a bird. I guess that's Luna. A full-on contradiction.

"I better go," she says.

I step aside. She doesn't move. Her gaze flits from my chest to my face before she looks me in the eye. I feel that pull in my gut, the same as I had last night—a tension between us like an elastic band stretched tight and about to snap. But maybe I'm kidding myself and I'm the only one that feels it. She still isn't leaving, though. Is that a sign? I can't stop staring at her lips. I force myself to remember my boundaries and look away, and then I move quickly to open the door.

When I look back, her shoulders have dropped. She exits the dressing room, and I follow her back into the rehearsal space. How did things get so complicated so fast?

I spot Marty right away over by the stage. He stares at me with suspicion, like he thinks I'm up to something, and it's not entirely easy to pretend I'm not.

As Luna gets onstage and moves into position with the other dancers, he makes a beeline straight for me.

"I saw you two went out on a date last night," he says.

How does he know about that? "It wasn't a date," I argue.

He gives me a *Don't mess with me* look. "You remember what

I told you," he says menacingly. "She's got a boyfriend."

"I was on the job, babysitting her like you pay me to," I say, while wondering if that's true about her having a boyfriend, because according to my sister and the gossip blogs, they're broken up.

"You didn't tell her about the letter, did you?" Marty asks.

"No. You told me not to."

"Just checking," he grunts.

"What did you do with it?" I ask, curious.

Marty shakes his head, telling me it's not my business.

"She mentioned something about her dad last night," I say as he starts to walk away. Marty turns back around. "She said that he asks her for money. You don't think it could be him, do you?" I know the situation with my own father is making me think less than objectively, but it's surely worth mentioning so Marty can look into it. But he dismisses my idea.

"I doubt it's him. He's in Florida with his new girlfriend. The letters are all hand delivered."

I hadn't thought about that. "Maybe he's paying someone to deliver them?"

"Not likely. Why would you threaten to kill your own daughter?"

I bite my lip. My own dad didn't just threaten it; he attempted it. I think about the people who were there at the award ceremony. Natalie was the one who gave me the letter. Could she be a suspect? "What about Natalie?" I ask Marty.

"The makeup girl?" Marty asks, wrinkling his nose. "Why would she be sending hate mail?"

"I don't know," I say.

"Luna's her meal ticket."

That doesn't discount her. Maybe she's jealous. But she also seemed like she genuinely had no idea what was in the envelope. "What about the guy who Natalie mentioned, the one in the black hat?"

"Lots of people had access to the backstage area last night," Marty says. "It's easy to slip something to one of the stagehands and have them deliver it."

"We should be asking people, investigating," I say.

"I'm doing it," Marty says huffily, already walking off.

I watch him, wondering what exactly that means. I bet he's not doing a thing.

LUNA

By the time we get home, I'm exhausted. Will hasn't said anything in the car, and so I haven't either. I can sense he's putting distance between us, probably because I made a fool of myself yet again in the dressing room.

I get out of the car and slam the door, running up the front steps. I can hear Will come up the steps behind me, and I want to ask him what he's doing following me inside, but then I see he's picking up a large white box wrapped with a pink ribbon and stamped with the name of a bakery.

He glances at the card attached. "It's for you."

I take the box and open the front door. I can already guess it's from Jamie. As soon as I step into the hall, I see a huge vase of red roses, sitting like a crimson thundercloud on the table where the calla lilies used to be. Carla steps out of the kitchen when she hears us. "They just arrived for you," she says, her lips pursed. *Jamie*. He always sends this same bouquet, every Valentine's Day.

I glance at the card in the little white envelope propped among the thorns, and then I walk over and pull it out. I know he's only sending me flowers because he's seen the photos of Will and me and he's worried.

Luna, miss you, love you, J x

"What's that?" Carla asks, pointing at the white box I place beside the roses.

"It was on the doorstep," Will answers, walking over. I see him glance at the roses, but his face stays blank.

"It probably came with the roses." I shove the card back in the envelope before Will can read it.

Carla shakes her head. "No, they delivered them to the back door. I signed for them. And the security guard didn't let anyone else up to the house."

I glance between her and Carla. Will suddenly swoops in and takes the box. He carries it toward the kitchen. I chase after him, Carla on my heels. "What is it?" I say.

"Let me just take a look," Will explains.

I shake my head. "It's a cake," I tell him. "Why'd you need to look? It's for me." I often receive cakes and other food hampers and gifts from agents and publicists and journalists.

Carla takes my arm and tries to pull me back. She and Will exchange an odd look, like they know something I don't, and Carla's grip on my arm tightens.

"How did it get here?" Carla asks, worried. "Who delivered it?"

Will unties the ribbon gingerly, as if he is worried it might contain a bomb. I start to feel afraid. Why are they acting like this?

Will carefully opens the box lid. He looks at whatever is inside—I can't see—and then closes the lid again. I pull away from Carla and march over, reaching to lift the lid of the box, but Will's hand closes over mine. "Don't," he says.

His expression brooks no argument and leaves me shaky. "Why?" I ask. "What is it?"

"It's not a cake," he says.

Carla tries to reach for my arm again, but I'm so rattled and confused that I don't let her. "What's going on?" I ask, my voice rising. "Tell me!"

Will looks like he doesn't know what to say, but then he looks at Carla. "Can you get the security camera footage from the camera by the front door from the security guard? I want to know who delivered this."

Carla nods and hurries off.

"Will," I say, "are you going to tell me what's going on? You're scaring me."

As soon as I say that, his expression softens. "I'm sorry," he says. "You don't need to be scared."

"Please tell me what's in the box."

He bites his lip, trying to decide.

Irritated and impatient, I grab for the box. We wrestle for it. The box bursts open, and I let out a scream and leap backward as a dead bird falls with a thud to the floor, scattering feathers.

"Oh my God," I say, almost gagging.

The feathers are ruffled. It looks like it's been half eaten by a cat. I think I'm going to be sick. "Why would anyone send that?" I gasp, clutching my throat to stop the nausea shooting up.

I wonder if it's a mistake. Some cruel, cruel mistake. A malicious prank. I reach to snatch it, and again Will's hand closes over mine, stopping me.

"Who sent it?" I ask, glaring at Will as he bends to retrieve the dead bird, using some paper towels to pick it up and put it back in the box. The smell of it punches me in the nose, and I almost gag again. "I have the right to know."

"It doesn't say," he says, placing the box by the back door and washing his hands.

"So what does it say?" I ask, my voice barely steady as a hysterical sob starts to build in my throat.

"It's a threat. It's not serious," Will says.

I gape at him. It's obvious what kind of threat it is. I don't need to read the note to know that. I'm panicked; my head flies up and I look around in terror. "Oh my God," I say. "What if whoever sent it is still here? How did they get past the gate?"

"I'll figure it out, don't worry. We'll get to the bottom of it."

"Don't worry?!" I yell at him. "How can you say that? Someone just sent me a decapitated pigeon." It sounds almost funny, and there's no hiding the hysteria in my voice.

Will offers his usual half-shrug gesture, but this time it doesn't charm me; it infuriates me.

"It's the same person, isn't it?" I stammer. "The person who threatened me before? The same person who trashed my tour bus?"

I shudder at the memory I've worked hard to block from my mind. Though there had been threats online, and even some letters before then, that was the first time someone actually got close to me. That's when I started to get really afraid. "It's them," I say in a shaky voice. "Is it written in a red pen?"

Will hesitates but then nods.

"It's the same person," I say again, my voice rising into full-blown raging panic. I think I might faint, and I drop down into one of the kitchen chairs like a stone.

Will hovers behind me as I bury my head in my hands and try to control my breathing. He puts his hand on my shoulder, and immediately the constriction in my chest eases and I feel calmer. "I'll call Marty and let him know," he says.

"Why Marty?" I gasp, wanting to grab hold of his hand on

my shoulder and keep it there, because once he lifts his hand, the panic starts spreading again like a virus, multiplying in my bloodstream.

"Because . . ." He hesitates once more before finally admitting, "There have been other letters."

I start shaking again. "What?"

Will swallows hard. "I wasn't meant to tell you, but I don't like lying to you. There have been other letters recently. It's why they hired me, your mom and Marty. They were worried the threats were escalating."

His words sink in. My hands curl into fists. Why didn't they tell me any of this?

"They didn't want to scare you," he says, reading my thoughts.

I bounce up out of the chair as if I've been blasted, panic acting like rocket fuel. I just want to get out of here. The house isn't safe. They know where I live. I need to get Matias and Carla and go. "I have to leave," I say, turning in a circle, my mind desperately trying to process everything.

Will takes my shoulder again and turns me around to face him. "Luna," he says calmly, "just breathe. It's going to be okay. You're safe. I'm here. I'm not going to let anyone hurt you."

I look into his eyes. They're a smoky gray color that I've never fully appreciated until now, like sunlight caught in quartz. Just looking into them and seeing the calm radiating has a soothing effect, and my head stops spinning so wildly, or maybe it's his touch, grounding me.

"I need to get out of here," I wheeze. "Please. Can we go?"

"Where do you want to go?"

"I don't know," I tell him. "Anywhere that's not here."

WILL

Where are we going?" Luna asks, huddled into the passenger seat, her face pale and her eyes skittering as she glances out the window, scanning the traffic as if the person who is threatening her might be out there, following us. She doesn't need to worry. I had her duck down as we pulled out of the house, and I've been checking for cars following us, including Donny's, and we're clear.

"To my mom's," I say. She doesn't reply and, worried I've made the wrong call, I glance over at her. "Is that okay?"

She frowns. She probably wants to stay in a five-star hotel. "I guess," she says. "Are you sure she's okay with it?"

I nod. "I called her already. Her partner, Robert, has a few condos that he rents out, and one is empty at the moment. He said we can use it. I figured that way we could ensure complete privacy. No one will know where you are. And Matias will stay with Carla until your mom gets home."

She nods, but I'm not sure how much is going in. She looks terrified, sunk deep in her seat and gripping the door handle. I wish she would trust me when I say that I won't let anything happen to her.

Before we left, I went through the security tape. It turned out that one of Francisco's newest gardening employees had been handed the parcel at the gate and offered twenty bucks to leave it on the doorstep. Apparently, the guy who handed it to him was wearing a black hat, and that's about the only description he caught. He said the guy claimed to be a delivery driver for Uber Eats, and that he was in a hurry, which is why he couldn't deliver it to the door himself.

"I called Marty, too," I tell her. "He's going to speak to the police, and I'll put in better security protocols at the gate."

She nods again and doesn't say anything for a few minutes, but then she suddenly blurts: "Why does this person hate me so much?" Tears are rolling down her face. "What did I do?" she says, looking at me plaintively.

I feel a twist in my chest at hearing the pain in her voice. "Nothing," I reassure her. "They're just trying to upset you."

"So, you don't think they really mean to hurt me?"

I pause, not knowing what to say, and I can feel her eyes on me, see the glimmer of hope in them. But she wants the truth, and I'm torn between not exacerbating her fear and lying. "I don't know," I finally admit. "But better safe than sorry."

"Why would they want to hurt me, though?" she says, shaking her head and swiping at her eyes. "I don't understand."

All I can offer is "Try not to think about it."

She snorts. "Right. You try not thinking about it."

She closes her eyes, and I see her taking deep breaths in and out, using the breathing technique I taught her. When I look over again a few minutes later, she's asleep, her lips slightly parted, her eyeliner smudged where she's been crying, and her eyelids puffy and red. I feel a huge surge of protectiveness toward her and wish I could find the asshole who sent that dead bird and put my fist through his face.

It's late by the time we arrive in Oceanside, and I have to gently shake Luna awake. She startles in alarm, but when she sees it's me, she relaxes, then looks out the window, rubbing her eyes.

"We're here," I tell her.

Robert's left the key in a lockbox, and I let us in. Immediately I catch the smell of my mom's cooking and the scent of fresh linen. They must have come here earlier to make the place up for us. There's a note on the table from my mom telling me how to warm up the lasagna she's left in the fridge.

The next thing I do is open the doors to the balcony. The ocean breeze hits me, and I can hear the waves hitting the shore in the distance.

After a few minutes, I hear Luna step outside onto the balcony behind me. Her face is washed, and in the moonlight she looks almost translucent—more vulnerable—and as she nervously glances around, I sense she's still on edge.

"You okay?" I ask her.

She nods, wrapping her arms around herself, and I don't know if it's because of the cold or because she's afraid.

"We're safe here," I tell her.

She nods again, chewing her bottom lip, obviously not believing me.

"Are you hungry?" I ask. "My mom's made lasagna."

"A little," she says.

We go back inside, and after following my mom's step-by-step guide of placing a piece of lasagna into the microwave, I set the food in front of Luna. "Are you not eating?" she asks as I stand, leaning against the counter.

I shake my head. "I'll eat later."

A frown furrows her brow. I can't explain to her that I feel odd sitting and eating with her. Even being in this apartment alone with her feels strange and uncomfortable.

"You must be starving," she says quietly. She takes a bite and then smiles. "And this is really good. Have some, please."

I break at her small smile. Reluctantly, I take a plate from the cupboard and serve myself and sit down across from her. The food is good, as usual. Unfortunately, I didn't inherit my mom's cooking skills. We eat in silence until my phone rings. I pull it out. It's Kate, my little sister. I know what she wants—to grill me on Luna. I don't answer.

When Luna finishes eating, I take her plate to the sink, but before I can start the washing up, she edges me aside. "Let me do that," she says.

"No, it's cool. I've got it," I tell her.

She purses her lips and wrestles the scrubbing brush from my hand. "Please? You don't need to wait on me."

I nod and step aside. She washes up and I dry, and I wonder if she feels the weird tension of us being alone, acting like a couple, doing chores together. To my surprise, it's actually nice. She brushes my arm as she passes a plate, and when it slips through my fingers, we both grab for it, laughing. Catching my eye, she smiles before looking the other way, the haunted expression returning. I can't help but wonder what she's thinking. Is she glad we went away? Is she okay staying here, or does she wish she'd stayed home? Does she feel safe here, alone with me? I'm assuming she does, because she hasn't said she wants to leave.

The responsibility of keeping her safe hits me then. It's all very well acting normal and standing beside her drying dishes, but at the end of the day someone wants her dead, and who knows what they might be capable of beyond what they've already done? Their actions are ramping up, that's for sure. And a person who delivers a dead animal to someone's front door clearly isn't messing around.

I wish I had an idea of who they were and why they were doing this. I wish I could deal with it, remove the threat, so Luna could relax. Maybe then the haunted expression in her eyes would disappear. I'd really like to be the one to make that happen.

My phone buzzes again. Surprise, surprise. It's Kate. I decline the call again. Luna looks at me with a question in her eyes. "My sister," I explain. "I'll call her back later." Like next year later.

After we've washed up, I carry her bags into the larger bedroom and put them on the bed, and then I back toward the door. "Good night," I say, unable to look her in the eye. "See you in the morning."

Luna nods, and I catch her glancing at the windows, as though nervous someone might break in while she sleeps.

"I'll be right across the hall," I assure her. "Just shout if you need me. I'm a light sleeper."

"Okay, thanks," she says.

I leave, shutting the door behind me. I worry that she's not okay by herself, that her anxiety might overwhelm her, and I won't know what to do. She seems so on edge, so scared. Does she have her medication with her?

I think about that photo of her from the *National Enquirer*, drunk and passed out in a bathroom. What if she does something like that? What if I can't keep her safe from other people, or herself?

LUNA

I can't sleep, unable to shake the image of that dead bird from my mind. I lie awake with the light on, listening to Will as he takes a shower and then moves around in his room, getting ready for bed. I try not to imagine him lying on the other side of the wall, and I wonder, as the hours tick past, if he's sleeping.

I can't stop thinking, either, about the threats and wondering who is behind them, and why they hate me so much. What have I done to this person that they want to kill me? Are they serious about wanting me dead? Will says they're only trying to scare me, but I know he's trying to make me feel better. I can feel panic surging like a storm tide inside me, and it's as if my skin can't contain all the feelings and at some point they're going to burst out of me like worms erupting out of the soil after a downpour.

At around three, exhausted from thinking about it, I tiptoe into the kitchen for a glass of water. I open the freezer, looking for ice, and when I shut it, I scream. The shape of a man has materialized in the semidark.

The glass slips from my hand as my heart catapults into my

throat, and by the time I realize that it's just Will, hair mussed and wearing only a pair of boxers, it's too late and the glass is smashing against the tile floor.

"Shit," I hiss as glass splinters spray across the kitchen and both our bare feet.

"Sorry," Will says. "I didn't mean to scare you. I heard a noise."

"I'm sorry." I bend down so he can't see the panic on my face.

Will joins me to gather up the bigger pieces of broken glass in his palm. "Why don't you go back to bed and I'll clean this up?" he says gently.

"No, let me help," I argue.

"Why don't you find a broom, then?" he suggests, and I gingerly pick my way over to a cupboard and start looking for a dustpan and brush.

"Couldn't sleep?" he asks when I find one and hand it to him. I shake my head.

"It's hard with the lights on," he remarks.

"It's harder with the lights off." I reach for some jagged shards that have lodged under the sink and manage to slice open the top of my index finger. "Ow," I say, inhaling sharply.

Will stands up and takes hold of my hand to examine the cut. "Hold it up," he says as blood starts to pour down my hand. I feel light-headed at the sight of it.

"I'm fine," I tell him. Of all the things I can handle tonight, a cut is definitely one of them.

But before I know it, Will already has a dish towel wrapped around my hand as he leads me into the bathroom.

He sits me on the edge of the bathtub and roots around inside the cabinet, pulling out a green first-aid box. "Really, it's not a big deal," I say, embarrassed that he's having to save me not only from dead birds but broken glass too. He ignores me, easing the soaked dish towel away from my hand. "It's deep," he says. "But I think you'll live."

As he soaks some cotton with antiseptic, I close my eyes, surprised at how much it stings. "I ever tell you about the time I walked on a drill piece?" he asks.

I shake my head. "No," I whisper through clenched teeth, knowing he's trying to distract me from the upcoming pain. "I was eight and chasing my sister, and my dad had left it out in the middle of the living room floor. Sticking straight up. Went right through my foot."

"Oh my God," I say as he swabs my finger with the cotton. It feels as if it's been dunked in acid. "What happened?"

"My mom rushed me to the ER. I needed surgery. Had to wear a cast and use crutches for months."

"Ow," I whisper, both in sympathy and at the throbbing pain climbing down my finger.

"My dad was just pissed about the drill bit. The ER threw it away."

My eyes flash open in disbelief. My God. Will's smiling, though, albeit the smile doesn't reach his eyes. In fact, his eyes seem to darken at the memory, and I want to touch his cheek and find a way to bring the lightness back. Of course, I don't. Instead, I drop my gaze, but then it lands on his naked chest as he kneels in front of me, and holy shit . . . I mean, wow. He is ripped. I saw him with his shirt off when he was boxing, but I wasn't this close—barely inches away. I don't know if it's the sting of the cut floating through me, but all I want to do is trace the line of muscle across his shoulders with my fingertips. And for a second, I contemplate what it would be like to kiss him at the base of his neck, where it dips into shadow. And he smells so good. . . .

"There," he says, fixing the Band-Aid, and I startle. Did he notice me staring?

"Thanks," I say, jumping to my feet, ignoring the wooziness that hits me. I'm not sure if it's caused by the throbbing pain in my finger or by Will's nearness.

"Are you sure you're okay?" he asks, studying me.

I nod. It was just my finger. He's looking at me intently, as though he doesn't trust my answer. "Did you take anything?"

Why's he asking me that? Why would I have taken something? It dawns on me. Does he think I'm drunk? Or that I've taken some prescription drugs? I know he must have googled me and read all the gossip, and my face flames red-hot at the knowledge.

"Want me to get you a glass of water?" he asks.

"Did you see the *National Enquirer* article?" I ask, unable to keep the annoyance out of my voice.

There's a flash of guilt in his eyes. "Yes," he admits.

I knew it. "Normally, I don't drink," I tell him. "That was a one-time thing. I mixed my medication with alcohol and I passed out. And that asshole bodyguard took my picture and sold it and made it look like I overdosed." I say this all realizing I don't owe him, or anyone else, an explanation.

Will bites the inside of his cheek. "I'm sorry."

"I get it. Everyone believes what they read."

"I didn't believe it," he says.

I look up, my heart lurching. "Really?"

He nods. "I figured there would be another explanation." He pauses. "He shouldn't have done that to you. It makes me mad. If I ever met him, I'd—" He breaks off.

"You'd what?" I press, my embarrassment fading and the heat from my face flooding to other parts of my body.

"Give him a piece of my mind." He shifts the weight on his feet. "Want me to get you some water?" he asks again, changing the subject.

I nod and he heads off to the kitchen. He brings the water to me in my bedroom and hesitates in the doorway, not wanting to intrude on my personal space, I assume. He hands me the glass, and I carry it over to the bedside table.

"Good night," he says before moving to close the door.

"Will?" I call.

He opens the door again and looks at me, half-expectantly, half-warily.

"Can you turn the light off?" I ask.

He cocks his head at me. "You sure?"

I nod. "But maybe leave the one on in the hall?"

He gives a small smile and nods, turning off the light and then shutting the door, leaving it only slightly ajar so the light from the hallway shines through like a beacon.

"I'll keep my door open too," he says.

I slip back into bed, laying my head on the pillow facing toward the door. The light spills in through the gap, and I imagine Will getting into his bed. Is he staring at the same light, thinking about me? The thought makes my stomach flutter and a warmth spread down my limbs. I throw off the sheet as I'm so hot and roll onto my back to stare at the ceiling, only I don't see the ceiling. All I see is Will, with his shirt off, crouched in front of me. There's an answering dip in my stomach, as though I'm on a roller coaster.

I drift off to sleep, no longer thinking of the person who's sending me threats but thinking about Will.

When I wake, sunlight is streaming through the crack in the blinds. I stretch out like a cat, feeling weirdly refreshed, and when I check the time, I see that for the first time in ages, I've had eight hours of sleep. It's almost midday. I see that Jamie has texted me a half dozen times, wanting to know where I am and begging me to call. He must have heard from Marty about what happened. I contemplate replying, and for a moment the memory of the dead pigeon fills my mind with worry, but then I hear sounds coming from the kitchen, where I find Will with his head in the fridge as something burns on the stove.

I dart forward and yank the pan off the heat.

"Crap," Will says, coming to stand beside me.

"Mmmm, that looks delicious," I say, laughing at the blackened remains of what I can only assume were once scrambled eggs.

"It's this special cuisine: cordon noir," Will deadpans. "I'm an expert at it."

I laugh, then nudge him aside, aware of my bare leg brushing his and feeling a jolt that I try to ignore. I'm wearing pajama shorts and a baggy Blondie T-shirt. He's dressed in shorts and a T-shirt, the most informal I've seen him. I kind of miss the bare chest, to be honest, though.

"Let me," I tell him. I open the fridge and see there are half a dozen eggs left in the container, as well as milk and butter, and in the cupboard there are basics like flour and salt. "Pancakes?" I ask.

Will looks at me with a skeptical expression, like he isn't sure if I'm joking.

"I can cook. Carla taught me," I say indignantly. "You want American style or French?"

"I get a choice?" he asks, hopping on a stool and grinning. "I'll go with French. I've always wanted to go to France."

I get busy whisking up the batter, determined to make a good impression and to prove his image of me wrong. I know he thinks I'm just a spoiled rich girl who has people cooking for her and cleaning up after her, but I can look after myself. I had to when Matias and I were kids and my mom was working all the time. "We really need lemons," I say, frowning as the first pancake hits the pan and starts to sizzle.

"I think I saw a tree out in the front," Will says. "Let me go grab some." And he's off, making sure to lock the door behind him when he goes. I smile to myself and start to hum the tune that's been playing in my head for the last day or so, running over lyric ideas as I do. A sense of peace settles over me, which is weird considering the circumstances. I feel safe here, cocooned. No one knows where I am and it's freeing. Being away from LA and the pressure-cooker atmosphere might have something to do with it too. But, also, being with Will.

Back in less than two minutes, Will unloads the lemons he's collected in his shirt and watches me as I pour the batter and expertly flip the pancakes, secretly praying I don't mess up and end up with it stuck to the ceiling. He gives me an appraising smile that makes my stomach flutter violently. I cut up a lemon, letting out a scream when the juice of one finds its way into the cut on my finger.

Will is at my side right away. "Did you cut yourself again?" he asks.

I grip my finger. "No. Juice in the cut."

"Ow." He winces in sympathy, then takes the knife from me and slices the lemons for us.

We eat outside on the balcony, and I watch, nervous, for his reaction. He can tell because he deliberately takes his time chewing as I wait, knife and fork poised, before eating my own.

"These are really good," he finally says, grinning.

I smile to myself, enjoying watching him eat it up. He seems to have lost his resistance about eating with me and I'm glad.

"How's the finger?" he asks.

"Throbbing," I tell him. "But my surgeon did a good job."

He grins. "Medic training," he tells me.

"This place is really nice," I say, gazing out over the ocean and taking a deep breath of fresh air. There's no pollution haze like there is in LA. "It's nice of your mom and her partner to let us stay. Will you thank them for me?"

Will nods, then bites his lip and frowns. He glances at me nervously. "Actually, they've invited us for dinner." He squirms. "I'm sorry. My mom made me promise I would ask."

My heart does a little pirouette. He's ridiculously cute right now. "That sounds great," I say, hiding my smile.

"You don't have to . . . ," Will mumbles, looking at me like he thinks I'm just saying it to be polite.

It annoys me. "I know. I want to," I say.

"Great," he answers. But I can't tell if he means it.

WILL

Luna spends the afternoon on the balcony, her feet up on the ledge, scribbling in a notebook, and I don't disturb her until the sun's setting low in the sky and she finally puts the notebook and pen down.

When I step outside onto the balcony, she looks at me and smiles wide, and my heart skips. I try to avoid her eye, because it makes me uncomfortable, but in the late-afternoon sun her skin is glowing golden, and it's hard to tear my eyes off her.

"What are you writing?" I ask, nodding at the notebook as I lean against the balcony railing.

"Song lyrics. I'm working on some new material." She says it almost shyly.

"Is that what you were singing in the shower earlier?" I ask her.

She cringes. "Oh . . . yeah."

"It sounded really good."

She wrinkles her nose and shakes her head. "It's not. I don't know why I'm bothering, actually. Marty will hate it."

"Why do you care so much what he thinks?"

She stands up. "He knows the business. He's managed my career this far. . . ." She trails off.

"But you don't like what you sing." I know I'm right, even though she won't admit it.

Her lips part and her back straightens. "I . . ." She stops, then shakes her head again. "You're right. I don't." She looks startled at having finally admitted it out loud.

"So why do you let him dictate what you sing?" I ask.

"It's not as easy as that." She takes a deep breath and her shoulders sink. "I've tried bringing it up before, but every time I do, Marty tells me my songs won't sell, and then he goes and arranges these incredible partnerships with producers who most people would give their right arm to work with. So, I can't say no."

I study her. She seems frustrated and has started wringing her hands.

"People like Craig?" I ask.

She nods, her mouth downturned. "He's a hit-maker." She sighs and glances over at the notebook. She picks it up. "This is stupid, really. I don't know why I'm bothering."

I watch her walk back inside and over to the trash. She opens it and drops the notebook into it. Damn. I should have kept my mouth shut. An hour later we show up at my mom's place. Luna seems shy and self-conscious, and hovers behind me.

"By the way," I tell her before I ring the doorbell, "Kate's been warned to be on her best behavior and I've sworn her to secrecy, but you might find she's a little overexcited to meet you."

Luna lets out a long breath. "Never have heroes. They always disappoint when you meet them. It's happened to me so many times I've lost count."

The door opens. My mom stands there with her arms held

wide, and I hug her, then shake hands with Robert.

I don't know Robert that well, but from what I can tell, he seems like a decent man. He treats my mom well, and she seems happier than I've ever seen her. But I'm still wary on her behalf. I don't trust people lightly, especially not where my family is concerned.

"Hi," my mom says to Luna, and before Luna has a chance to reply, my mom sweeps her into a hug too. Luna stands like a stiff scarecrow for a moment, but then I see her relax, and her arms come up and she hugs my mom back.

"Hi," Luna says. "Thank you for having us."

Robert shakes her hand next with a grin that splits his face.

"Thank you so much for letting us stay in the condo," Luna tells him. "I really appreciate it."

He waves her off. "Anytime, anytime."

I hand my mom the lilies that Luna picked out for her, and her face lights up. "You shouldn't have," she says to me in an admonishing tone. She knows I'm strapped for cash.

"I didn't. They're from Luna," I tell her.

"They're from both of us," Luna interrupts.

"Let me find a vase," my mom says, carrying them off to the kitchen.

"Come in, come in," Robert says, ushering us inside.

"Oh my God! Oh my God! Oh my God!" Kate races out of her bedroom and tornadoes toward us like a flaming missile. When she reaches us, she freezes and stares at Luna as though she's face-to-face with an alien.

Luna forces a smile. "Hi," she says to Kate.

"This is Kate," I say, introducing them. "In case you hadn't guessed. And that's my brother, Cole," I say, pointing to Cole, who is hovering behind my mom. He's acting shy, which isn't like him, and I smile, realizing he's getting to that teen age where he's noticing girls. He stares at Luna like she's made of gold, and I almost laugh but then realize that's probably how I was staring at her earlier on the balcony.

"I thought he must be lying." Kate gasps. "I thought that he was telling me you were coming today as a joke. I can't believe it's true. But you're actually here. And you're actually real. And you're really short." She covers her hand with her mouth. "Oh God, sorry. But you really are, like, ridiculously tiny."

Luna smiles as I cringe beside her.

"How tall are you?" Kate asks.

"Five foot one," she says, laughing. "Five foot four in heels."

Kate grins at me, all teeth and excitement. "Do you know how popular I'm going to be at school when I tell them I've met Luna Rivera? I don't think they'll believe me. Can I take a picture to prove it?"

"No," I say, stopping her as she pulls out her phone. I've already talked to her about this, finally calling her back this afternoon to read her the riot act.

She pouts. "Okay, fine. You're so pretty," she says to Luna, putting her phone away. "Your skin is amazing. You look like Ariana Grande. Has anyone ever told you that? Only prettier. Are your lashes real?"

Luna laughs. "Yes."

Kate lowers her voice and leans in. "What's Jamie like?" she asks in a conspiratorial whisper. "I promise I won't say a word." She makes an elaborate cross on her chest. "Is he a dick? He seems like he might be. But everyone at school has a crush on him. Except me. I'm gay—did you know?"

"Kate," I growl.

She looks up. "What?" she asks, acting all innocent. "Do you want to see my room?" she says, turning back to Luna.

Luna nods. "Sure," she says.

You don't have to, I mouth.

She smiles reassuringly and heads off with Kate.

"Kate," I say in a warning tone.

"I know, I know." Kate grins at me. "Best behavior!"

I wander into the kitchen, where I find my mom and Robert serving up a pot roast.

"Can I help?" I ask.

"Can you mash the potatoes?" my mom asks.

I grab the masher from the side and get started, not sure what else is involved besides pulverizing them. My mom calls Cole to set the table.

"It's a shame that Tristan and Zoey had to go back to Florida." My mom sighs. "But I'm so glad you're home."

"How's the job?" Robert asks, lowering his voice.

"She seems sweet," my mom adds.

"Um," I say, not sure I want to be candid about the ups and downs. "It's fine. You know, it's just a job."

"Your mom said it's just for six weeks, is that right?"

"Yeah," I say, and for the first time I feel a prick of disappointment. In the beginning, I couldn't wait for this job to be done and was only in it for the money, but something has shifted in the last day or two. I don't know if that's because of the threat and feeling like I can't leave her, or something else.

"Did you figure out what you'll do after?" my mom asks.

I shake my head.

"You know you can stay with us," my mom says. And Richard nods and smiles at me.

"I know," I say. "And thanks. But I need to get my own place. Figure out what to do with my life."

I haven't told her about my idea, that I want to work with young people who are at risk of falling through the cracks. I don't know why. I guess, until I told Luna, I hadn't spoken of it to anyone. And I also didn't want my mom to ask why I wasn't pursuing it, because that would mean I'd have to explain about the debt, and I'm never telling her about that. But now that's not an issue. I'm going to be able to clear my debts before too long.

"Actually," I say, "I want to find a job working with kids. Maybe outdoor education or something like that."

My mom pauses what she's doing and looks at me. "That's a wonderful idea," she says, beaming at me so I feel like I'm in first grade and just came home with my first gold star.

"I think you're drawn to helping people," she says, squeezing my arm. "I'm so proud of you, Will."

I side-eye her, embarrassed. I don't know what she's got to be proud of. "Yeah, okay, Mom, thanks," I mumble, trying to move the conversation on.

But she won't let it go. She turns me toward her, still gripping my arms, and locks her gaze on mine. "I know how hard it was for you as a boy," she says. "You were so brave and so good. You were always looking out for your brother and sisters. And for me. I feel terrible about that. You shouldn't have had to protect us. It was my job." Her eyes well up with tears.

"Mom," I say, feeling a lump in my throat. I don't want to think about that time, or about my dad. And I definitely don't want to talk about any of it while Luna is around.

"I failed you," she says, her lip trembling.

"Mom, no . . . ," I say, shaking my head and blinking back tears, terrified that Luna might walk in and see. Why are we doing this now?

"Yes I did. I should have protected you. And I'm sorry."

My mom smiles through her tears, and then she pulls me into her arms for a hug. She has to reach up to put her arms around my neck, and I bend down. "I'm so proud of the man you've become," she whispers into my ear. "You're a good person. You're kind and thoughtful and you care about people."

Her words bounce off me, unable to penetrate. I don't know if I'm a good person. I'm half my father, after all.

She puts her hand on my cheek and strokes it. "I love you."

"I love you too, Mom," I say, the lump in my throat now more the size of a boulder.

Kate and Luna come back out of Kate's bedroom just then giggling, and I turn away and busy myself, trying to get a grip on my fluctuating feelings. I don't want Luna to see that I'm upset, but when I turn around, I can see she's looking at me curiously. She's picked up on something. It surprises me how in tune we are with each other's moods and emotions.

I pull out a chair for Luna at the table, and she sits down. "You okay?" she whispers.

I nod, forcing a smile, wishing my poker face worked better on her.

"How long will you be staying?" my mom asks as we all take our seats.

I look across at Luna. She returns the look, as if I might have the answer. But it's her call. "I don't know," I answer.

"I have rehearsals," Luna says, reaching for the mashed potatoes and dropping a lumpy mound on her plate.

"This tastes amazing," Robert says, smiling at my mom. "You're such a great cook. I've put on ten pounds since we started dating," he announces to Luna and me.

"What is this?" Kate asks, spooning the potatoes up and staring at them as if she's never seen mashed potato before.

"Mashed potato," my mom answers, frowning. She looks at me. "Did you add the butter and the salt?"

I shake my head. "Was I meant to?"

Kate turns to Luna. "Will didn't inherit the cooking gene from my mom. He takes after my dad in that department."

I look down at my plate, my hand gripping my knife and fork so tight my knuckles turn white. I hear my mom clear her throat awkwardly. Why did Kate have to bring up Dad? Or remind everyone I'm like him in any way?

"Oh, I discovered Will's cooking skills earlier." Luna laughs, glancing at me. I keep my face averted.

"So you're a singer, I hear," says Robert.

"Oh my God, Robert!" Kate exclaims. "She's not just a singer. She's the biggest singer on the planet."

"No, I'm not." Luna shakes her head.

"And she dates Jamie Whitstone."

I glance up at that, and now it's Luna who is looking down at her plate.

"Who's he?" Robert asks, glancing between Luna and Kate.

Kate rolls her eyes at him.

"Actually, we're not dating anymore," Luna says, cutting in.

Kate drops her fork with a clang onto her plate. "For real? That's true? Will said he didn't know for sure. And he made me promise not to ask."

Oh God. I'm going to kill Kate. I sense Luna's eyes on me, but I avoid her gaze.

"Do you think you'll get back together?" Kate asks, the flood-gates now open.

"Kate," I hiss, widening my eyes at her in a warning. *Please shut up.*

Luna sips from her glass, then lowers it, glancing briefly at me. "No," she answers. "I don't think so."

My heart gives a quick rebound into my ribs. Why did she look at me when she said it?

After dinner, Luna helps Robert and Kate clear the dishes and stack the dishwasher, and I help my mom make coffee.

"She likes you," my mom whispers.

I whip my head to her, then glance quickly over my shoulder to make sure Luna hasn't heard.

"What?" I say under my breath.

"She likes you. I can tell."

"Mom," I mutter. "No, she doesn't. I work for her. She's a client."

My mom smiles slyly like she knows a secret I don't. "Only for six weeks," she comments.

"She doesn't like me," I insist. Does she?

LUNA

notice Will whispering with his mom, and I know it's about me. I wonder what they're saying. His family is lovely, and I can't help but think how lucky he is to have a mom who so clearly dotes on him and cares about how he's doing. My mom hasn't even called me since she's been away, and I know Marty must have been in touch with her to tell her about the threat. I can't believe how much they've both been keeping from me. I understand why they hadn't told me about the threats—I know they didn't want to worry me—and I get now why they were so insistent on hiring a bodyguard for me. But the fact that they knew about the threats and kept pushing me out onstage and into the public eye makes me angry.

"Are you going to Jessa and Kit's baby christening?" Kate asks, shoving between Will and his mom. "They invited me."

"Hadn't planned on it," Will says. "I have to work."

It jars me, hearing him say that. It reminds me that I'm only a job for him. A couple of days ago I wanted him to quit the job, and now I'm upset that he thinks of me as a client. These feelings I'm having don't make sense. I keep trying to ignore them, tell myself that I'm being an idiot, but I know I'm starting to fall for him.

Seeing him and how he interacts with his family has only made him more attractive. He makes me feel safe, and his honesty is like a searchlight—I feel like I can't hide anything from him, nor do I want to. When he looks at me, I get a flutter in my chest that feels like a million hummingbirds taking flight, and I find myself wanting to confess things to him I've never told anyone before. He makes the truth come tumbling out, and that's uncomfortable and confusing and scares me, because the truth can be used as a weapon. And most of all, I'm worried because I don't want to feel like this, especially about someone who I don't think feels the same way for me.

"Don't let me stop you," I say, my voice cooler than I mean for it to sound. "You should go. Take a day off."

"Why don't you come too?" Kate asks brightly.

"No," Will cuts in fast. "I'm sure Luna wouldn't want to come."

Is he saying it because he doesn't want me to come or because he genuinely thinks I wouldn't want to go?

"Why don't you ask her?" Will's mom says, her eyes drilling into him.

Will turns to me. "Do you want to come?" he asks.

"Please come!" Kate says. "Jessa and Kit won't mind."

I glance over at Will. He's looking at me, waiting on my answer.

"Sure," I answer. "I'd love to." I don't know why I say it. Maybe it's because I want to see how he responds. His eyes widen slightly, and the smallest smile pushes at the edge of his lips. He doesn't seem mad about it, and that makes the butterflies in my stomach flutter again.

Later, as we walk back to the condo, I'm aware of the

butterflies still fluttering, especially when Will veers close to me.

"They seem really sweet together," I say. "Your mom and Robert."

Will shrugs. "I guess."

"You don't like him?" I ask.

"I don't really know him," he admits.

"But your mom seems happy."

He nods. "Yeah."

"I'm confused," I say, slowing my pace and turning to look at him. "You don't date because you say you're skeptical about relationships because of your parents fighting when you were a kid, but your mom's found love with a really great guy . . . so what's the deal?"

Will takes a deep breath and exhales loudly. "I don't know," he admits.

I think he's lying to me and it bothers me, because he doesn't usually lie. He's usually painfully honest.

"Can I tell you what I think?" I say.

He's been looking down at his feet, but now he looks up at me with a wary expression.

"I think you're scared," I tell him, blurting it out before I can stop myself.

His mouth falls open. "I think you're scared that you're like your father," I press on.

He comes to a standstill. "What? Why would you think that?" he asks. His voice sounds strained. I've hit a nerve. I start to wish I hadn't said anything, but now I have to keep going and explain. . . .

"Because earlier in her room, Kate told me about your dad and what he's in prison for."

Will's jaw clenches. His nostrils flare. I can tell he's ashamed, that he didn't want me to know, but I want to finish telling him what I think. "And then, at dinner," I say, "Kate said you take after your dad with your cooking skills, and you looked really upset."

Will starts to speak but then stops, slamming his mouth shut. We're standing under a streetlight, and in the amber glow of it, I can see the hurt and also the truth written clear across his face. I'm right. That's his fear.

"You tried to hide it, but I could tell it got to you. You don't want to be anything like him."

Will swallows and turns his head away.

"I get it. I don't want to be anything like my mom or my dad either," I tell him.

Will still says nothing, but I can see him processing everything. I don't know much about his father, it's true, but from what Kate told me, I understand enough to know Will is nothing like him.

"Am I right?" I push. I want him to admit it because I hate the idea that he thinks of himself that way. I see the way he is with his family, so sweet and gentle. And I know how he is with me.

Will nods, blinking fast as if he's fighting tears. He looks away. I don't think he wants me to see him vulnerable.

"You shouldn't worry," I tell him.

His head flies back to me, and I smile at him.

"You're not your father."

He shakes his head unhappily. His face takes on an intensity, and anger flares in his eyes. "How would you know?" he demands under his breath.

His tone is harsh, and I tell myself it's deserved. I'm meddling

Mila Gray

in things I know nothing about. But I swallow and continue on. "I don't know your father, but I do know you," I say. "And you've never made me feel afraid. You make me feel the opposite. You make me feel safe. I could never be afraid of you."

I see the shock cross his face. He blinks at me. Frowns. I resist the urge to put my hand to his cheek. I want to smooth away the frown. He searches my face, as though he thinks I'm lying, and it bruises. I smile at him, wishing my words would penetrate his brain and help erase the story wedged in there. For a moment it looks like they might. I can see him processing, wrapping his mind around what I've said, but then he shakes his head firmly.

"I get angry," he admits. "Lose my temper."

"We all get angry and lose our tempers," I say with a small laugh. "That's normal."

He contemplates me with a wry expression. "But I've lost my temper and broken things before, punched things."

"People?" I ask.

He shrugs, looking down at his feet. "I mean, not since I was in the ring for a match." He looks back up at me with alarm. "And I've never hurt a woman. I wouldn't." He says it with such earnestness that my heart swells.

"I know," I reassure him, fighting the urge again to reach out and touch him.

He looks away once more, deep in thought.

"Everyone gets angry," I say again. "It's how you handle that anger that matters."

He seems to ponder that, but he says nothing, and after a moment he walks on. I walk beside him in silence, wanting to say something but not knowing what. I wish I could peer into his head and hear what he's thinking.

When we get back to the condo, he goes in ahead of me and checks it's safe. I watch him, a warmth spreading over me at how looked after he makes me feel, and how cared for. It's the simplest of gestures, and he has no idea what it means to me. I wonder what it would be like to be held by him. To kiss him. To have sex with him. Oh God.

"All clear," he says, and I jolt out of my daydream, my face hot.

"Okay," I say. "Good night." I rush into my bedroom and shut the door. I really should not be thinking things like that.

When I turn around, I find my notebook, the one I dumped in the trash, lying on my pillow. I walk toward it shakily. How did it get there? I pick it up. There's a sticky note on the front.

Keep writing, it says. And Will has signed his name underneath.

WILL

"How's this?" Luna asks.

My jaw drops as I see what she's wearing. It's the moss-green turtleneck dress. The one I picked out for her when we went shopping.

"I bought it," she tells me, looking a little guilty.

"I thought you hated it," I tell her. "You said it made you look like a nun with no taste."

She shakes her head. "I was joking. It wasn't something I would have chosen for myself, but maybe you should be my stylist after all." She grins. "Is it okay?"

I can't believe she bought the dress. She looks amazing. "Um, yeah," I manage to stammer, trying not to be too obvious.

Her face falls.

"It looks great," I add with a smile.

She bites her lip, nervous. "Are you sure about this?" she asks. "I don't need to come."

"I want you to," I reassure her. "My friends are great. And Jessa is an actress, so you'll have something in common."

She smiles at me and my heart skips a beat. I think about the other day, about how she tried to convince me I'm not like my father. I've been playing the conversation over and over in my head, wondering at how easily she pinpointed my biggest fear, without me ever telling her. It scared me how perceptive she was, and it scared me even more how easily I opened up to her and admitted it. I dropped my defenses, and ever since, I haven't been able to shore them back up. The image of her looking into my eyes and telling me I make her feel safe is scored on my mind. Is she right? I want to believe her, but at the same time, I remind myself that she doesn't know me, at least not well enough to know who I am. Yet she seemed so convinced of it. I want to believe her. And I want to believe my mom, but they don't live in my head—they don't know how hard I find it to handle my anger.

But maybe that's normal, like Luna said. Maybe I've been wrong all along and she's right; being angry doesn't make you a bad person. Everyone feels anger. It's how you act on it that matters.

"Jessa's married to Kit, who owns the restaurant?" Luna asks.

I tune back in and nod.

"Who else is going to be there?"

"Jessa's best friend, Didi. She's engaged to Walker. Didi's a psychologist."

"And Walker and Kit were both in the Marines, right?"

I nod. It's nice that Luna is trying to memorize all of this.

"Yeah. I met them through Tristan. He's friends with Kit."

"And Tristan's your best friend and in the Coast Guard. He's based in Florida, learning to fly helicopters. And he's dating your sister Zoey."

I nod. "Yeah."

Luna picks up her bag and turns to me. "Okay, I'm ready."

When we arrive at the christening, all heads turn our way. It's the Luna effect. She draws the eye wherever she goes. I sense her tensing beside me, and when I look, she's plastered on that megawatt smile I saw on the red carpet. Immediately I recognize it as a defense mechanism. She's hiding behind the mask. What she doesn't realize is that the other Luna is so much more appealing. I wish I could say something to her to convince her she doesn't need it, but it's not my place.

Didi and Walker come over to say hi, and I'm grateful for Didi, who is so down-to-earth and normal, and so un-starstruck. Didi makes no reference to who Luna is and doesn't treat her different from anyone else, and neither for that matter does Walker. I knew I could rely on my friends for that. No one is trying to sneak photos of Luna; they're too busy taking photos of the baby, Lyra. As we chat, Luna starts to relax, and I see her dropping her guard, the megawatt smile turning into something more genuine, and I'm pleased.

"Who's the little boy?" Luna asks, pointing at Riley, who is running around the garden outside the church as Kate chases after him. She's his babysitter occasionally, which is why she got invited today.

"That's Riley," Didi explains. "Jessa's brother's son. His dad died in Afghanistan before he was born."

Luna presses a hand to her mouth. "Oh God, that's terrible."

Didi squeezes Walker's hand. He looks off into the distance and Luna catches it. "He seems like he's a happy kid, though," Luna says as we watch Riley climb onto a wall and start scampering along it, laughing.

"Yeah. He takes after his dad," Didi quips. "Looks just like him too."

We watch a gaggle of grandparents hovering, making sure he doesn't fall off the wall.

Jessa and Kit, who are holding the new baby and grinning proudly, are over by the door to the church, welcoming people. I wave at them and they wave back.

Kit's taken to parenthood like a duck to water. He doesn't know it, but I've always looked up to him. He's the life of any party, making others feel comfortable. I envy that part of him that's always been so confident in going after what he wants and never being afraid to admit it either. He never hides how much he loves Jessa, and he never gets embarrassed, either, about how much he loves to bake cakes. Most guys in my unit would snicker at any guy who showed himself to be that domesticated or who had a hobby that involved wearing an apron, but Kit has never cared what people think of him. He knows what he wants and goes for it.

When he fell for Jessa, he knew that was it, that she was the one. They were kids, really. Jessa was eighteen, and now, despite all the odds, they've been together for years and are married with a kid.

I'm not like him, though. I'm an introvert and I'm used to hiding my feelings. I learned very early on in life to put up a wall because showing how I felt was a weakness that could be exploited.

"Your friends are so nice," Luna says to me as Didi and Walker wander away to say hi to other people.

"I told you," I say.

"You're so lucky," she answers with a sigh, sadness in her voice, and I wonder if she has any friends. I've never heard her mention anyone. And she hasn't called anyone either while we've been in Oceanside, that I'm aware of. There's also the fact she went to the movies alone that time.

"You must have friends," I say.

She shakes her head, rueful. "Not really. I mean, not like this."

"What about Natalie?" I ask, remembering I took her number the other day. I was meaning to call her, but I haven't thought about her since.

"She's not really a friend. She works for me," Luna explains. "Pretty much all my friends are people I pay."

"That sounds lonely," I mumble.

She nods, and when I look at her, I see a hint of vulnerability on her face, as though she's opening a door and showing me a little more of the real Luna. "Yeah, it is. I guess I find it hard to trust people."

"I understand why," I tell her.

We stare at each other, neither of us saying a word, and I know I'm not imagining it. That chemistry or whatever, that feeling that's been growing between us, it's there and it's real.

"Are you friends with Natalie?" she asks out of nowhere.

The question startles me. Where did that come from? I've barely spoken to Natalie. Does she somehow know I took her number? Did Natalie tell her? I furrow my eyebrows, frowning. "No. Why?" I ask.

She takes a quick breath and pushes her hair behind her ears. "Oh, I just . . . saw you guys chatting once."

At the party after the award ceremony. She noticed? Luna's staring at her shoes. Is she blushing?

"She gave me her number," I say.

She looks up sharply. "Oh."

"I never called her, though," I say, holding my breath, waiting to see her response.

I open my mouth, wanting to tell her that I haven't once thought about Natalie, that the only girl I have any interest in right now is her, but I swallow the words back down. I can't tell her that.

"I think she likes you," Luna says, her gaze fixed on mine, as though she's trying to peer into my head and read my thoughts. "Like, *likes* you," she says, emphasizing the second *like*.

My heart slows its pace as it always does when my instincts flare. Why is she telling me this?

"That's nice," I say, clearing my throat, "but I'm not into Natalie."

Luna nods slowly. "Yeah, of course, I forgot you don't date."

"No," I say quickly. "It's not that. I just . . . There's someone else. . . ."

Luna's eyes widen. Shit. I should look away. I shouldn't have been so brazen. What am I doing? It's so unprofessional. Her lips part, as though she's about to ask who. But before she can, we're interrupted by Kit.

"Hey!" he says.

I turn and find him holding the baby, Lyra, in one arm. He hugs me and then hugs Luna.

"Is Will looking after you okay?" he asks her.

She laughs. "Yeah, he's doing a great job."

"We never thought he'd ever bring a girl to any of these things," Kit says, grinning at me.

"It's not like that," I interrupt quickly. "I'm working for Luna. Strictly professional."

Luna's smile seems to dim, more confirmation that she feels something between us too.

Jessa sits next to her husband. "Hi," she says with a huge smile, holding out a hand to Luna. "I'm Jessa."

"I know," Luna says. "I'm Luna."

"I know," Jessa says.

They both laugh.

"I think she needs a change," Kit says, nodding at the baby. "It feels pretty explosive. Good thing I have bomb disposal training." He grins.

Before he can move, though, Didi bustles over. "Did I hear there's a diaper that needs changing?" she asks with delight, wrestling Lyra from his arms. "I think that's a job for her godmother."

"I wanted to do it." Kit scowls as Didi disappears with Lyra, bouncing her on her hip.

Jessa leans her head on Kit's shoulder. "There are going to be a lot more diapers to change," she reassures him. "Let Didi take this one."

He frowns and kisses the side of her head. "You're right. With six kids there will be a lot of diapers to change."

Jessa whacks him with her hand. "If you want five more, you're going to have to find a way to give birth yourself," she laughs.

"What about you and Didi?" Kit asks Walker, who's come over to join us.

"What about us?" he asks.

"When are you going to pop the question to Didi?" Kit asks, seeming not to care how personal the question is.

Jessa rolls her eyes at Kit. "Subtlety is really not his thing," she says to Luna.

Kit grins at her like a Cheshire cat. "If I'd been subtle about my feelings for you, we'd still be smiling politely to each other across your parents' living room. And you'd probably have ended up married to that really boring guy, whatshisface."

Jessa rolls her eyes again, but she's smiling. "My dad banned you from the house, so that's doubtful."

"Where did the name Lyra come from?" Luna asks. "It's beautiful."

"I used to call Jessa my north star," Kit says, putting his arm around Jessa's waist and kissing her on the cheek. "Lyra's a constellation. It's brightest in June, which is when Jessa and I first got together."

Jessa smiles at Kit, and the love in the way they look at each other knocks the air out of my lungs. I look away, feeling a sharp pain in my chest, like a knife slicing between my ribs. Luna was right. The fear of being like my dad has stopped me from ever having a relationship. And seeing Jessa and Kit and Didi and Walker, I'm realizing how much I've lost out on, all because of that fear.

But just because I recognize where the fear comes from doesn't mean it isn't valid. Luna tried to tell me I'm not like my father, but what would she know? We've known each other only a handful of days. And yet the strange thing is, I've also opened up to her in ways I've never done with anyone before. I've never told anyone about my father or my fears, but she guessed it.

I look at Luna and find her looking back at me. My heart smashes like a hammer into my gut. The problem is, now that I've opened up to the possibility I could have a relationship, the one person I'd want to actually date is the one person I can't. Not unless I want to lose my job.

The party after the christening is at Kit and Jessa's place, which isn't too far from the restaurant. It's got a view of the ocean and a big yard with a pool. It isn't Beverly Hills huge, but it's not small, either.

Kit has a fire going out back, and we pull up chairs in a circle around it. I stare across the fire at Luna, who is sitting opposite me, talking to Jessa. Luna's glowing in the firelight, her skin golden, her hair rippling like copper waves, and when she laughs, tipping back her head, I feel a surge of protectiveness.

Walker appears with a guitar and offers it to Didi, who shakes her head and laughs. "No way. You think I'm going to make a fool of myself when Luna Rivera is sitting right next to me? That would be like acting alongside Emma Watson or racing Usain Bolt. It's not a fair playing field."

Everyone laughs and Walker offers the guitar to Luna, who freezes like a deer caught in headlights, but then she takes it, surprising me. Dahlia and Didi both clap with excitement. A hush descends and all eyes fall on Luna as she starts to tune the guitar, her head bent and her hair falling over her face like a curtain.

I sense the anticipation in the air, a hush of suspense. When she looks up at us all, it's with a shy smile that makes my heart rate double. She pushes her hair behind her ear and takes a deep breath. For a long moment the only sound is the crackle of the logs in the fire and the gentle rush of the waves lapping the shore in the distance.

When Luna starts to sing, though, the waves stop their jostling onto the shore and the fire falls still. No one breathes. The whole world seems to pause, listening to her. Her voice is pure, with a rasp at its edge that holds a trace of melancholy. As she sings, I'm mesmerized, not just by her face but by the words. It's the song I've caught snippets of her singing in the car, the one I think she was working on while she was outside on the balcony, that she wrote in her notebook.

She's singing about drowning and struggling to keep her head above water, and then about giving in and dipping beneath the waves, but as the song progresses, it becomes about finding the strength to swim because in the distance she finally sees a light.

Her eyes are lowered as she concentrates on the music, closed as she sings the chorus. But then, for the final verse, she looks up at me.

"You're the lighthouse, bringing me to shore" are the final words of the song, and she is singing them right at me.

My heart stills in my chest before throwing itself into a gallop.

As the music dies away, there's a collective holding of breath. No one moves. No one speaks. Luna looks around and I see the fear flash across her face, doubt starting to assail her, and I start to clap, but before I can, Didi is on her feet, cheering loudly and whooping, and the others are joining in. Luna glances at me and the look on her face is uncertain, like she wants my approval, so I smile at her and I nod, trying to silently convey to her how much I loved it. The fear and uncertainty in her face dissolve, and she smiles back at me.

"So, have you thought about a career as a singer?" Kit jokes once the applause dies down.

"That was amazing," Jessa adds, hand on her heart.

"Did you write that?" Walker asks, shaking his head in amazement.

The self-conscious smile returns to Luna's face. She nods,

obviously relieved at the reaction, but also slightly disbelieving that it's genuine.

"It's so different from your usual stuff," Dahlia comments.

Luna nods and glances my way. "I was inspired."

"Can you play some more?" Didi asks.

Luna smiles and lifts the guitar onto her lap.

LUNA

You want to walk or get a taxi?" Will asks as we walk out of Jessa and Kit's house, among the last to leave and with everyone's farewells still buzzing in my ears. I feel happier and more relaxed than I have in years and can't stop smiling. Will liked my song. They all seemed to as well.

"Walk?" I answer with a question in my voice, in case Will would rather take a taxi. The condo is only about a mile away, and I find I want to spend as long as possible with Will before the night ends.

He nods. "Sure, whatever you want."

I keep telling myself I'm imagining the way I've caught him looking at me. Sure, he's warmer and less guarded, and he's opening up to me more, but it could just be that I'm learning to read him better. I shake my head, disappointedly. It's wishful thinking that he would ever think of me that way. I'm his client, or his boss, as he keeps pointing out to everybody, and he made it very clear that he doesn't date. He's keeping a strong distance between us on the walk. I shake my head again. Why would he ever like me anyway?

As the thoughts take hold in my brain, like tiny worms

multiplying as they invade, the voice in my head becomes a mantra of self-criticism. And before I know it or can stop it from happening, all the happiness I was feeling when we left the party starts to fade away. I replay the night in my head. Everyone clapped, but what if they were just being polite?

The voice in my head laughs at me. Yes, that's why they clapped. I try to ignore it, to concentrate instead on remembering the way Will looked at me after I played the song. He seemed to genuinely like it.

But still, the negative voice becomes so loud it obliterates all my positive thoughts. Neither of us talk on the walk back home, which only confirms the feelings I'm having.

By the time we're halfway back to the condo, all my memories of the evening have completely reshaped themselves in my head. My good mood has vanished entirely, despite my best effort to try to hold on to it.

"You need to play that song for Marty," Will says, interrupting my dark spiral.

I turn to him and shake my head. "No, I don't think so."

"Why not? It's amazing."

I shake my head again, my inner voice drowning out his. "It wasn't."

"What are you saying?" Will asks, bewildered. "You heard everyone. They loved it."

"They were just being nice." I can't believe how fast my inner critic has surfaced and taken over the narrative. Why can't I believe Will? Why can't I believe the good stuff, only ever the bad?

"Luna," Will says, turning to face me. "They weren't being nice. They were being honest."

"No one's honest with me," I say, my throat constricting.

"I am," Will says.

I can't argue with that.

"Have I ever lied to you?" he asks.

I want to say no, but my inner voice won't allow me to. How would I know if he's lied to me? I wouldn't. I battle that inner voice because in my heart of hearts, in my gut, I do know.

"I've never lied to you," he says, his voice full of earnestness. "You know you can trust me to tell you the truth. And I'm telling you the truth now. You sounded amazing. You are amazing."

The butterflies or hummingbirds or whatever they are start rioting in my stomach, and my inner critic finally falls silent as I look at him.

"You need to play that for Marty," he tells me.

I roll my eyes. "He wants me to record a song with Craig Matthers."

"Do you want to?"

"He's kind of a big deal." I sigh. "I have to."

"No, you don't," Will argues. "You don't have to do anything you don't want to. It's your choice."

I snort. "Not really." I move to walk away. This conversation is too painful and too real, and it's making me feel all sorts of anxious thoughts. What if I put the song out into the world and people laugh? What if I fail?

I take a sharp breath in and look down. Will's hand is circling my wrist, and he's pulled me to a stop.

"What do you want?" he asks me, looking me dead in the eye.

My breath comes so fast I feel faint. I want him to kiss me—that's my first thought and my only thought right now. All the other thoughts in my head vanish. "I don't know," I mumble.

"Yes, you do," Will says. "What are you afraid of?"

"Failing?" I say, unable to look at him. "Not being good enough." I whisper the words to him. I've never admitted them to anyone before.

His expression looks pained. "You are good enough, Luna. You have no idea." He shakes his head. "Why don't you believe it?"

My lip wobbles. I don't know is the honest truth. It's that voice in my head, who I'm starting to believe is actually an enemy. If only Will's voice lived in my head, then maybe it would win out.

He's staring at me still, his expression complicated and hard to read. He's frustrated and impatient. I want to apologize. I want to pull away so he can't look at my face and see the shame I'm battling, but I also don't want to move.

For a second his gaze drops to my lips, and I see something else in his eyes. It looks like want. Need. My breath catches. His does too. But then he seems to realize how he's holding me, and he lets go abruptly.

I grab for him, stopping him from pulling away. I don't know what I'm doing. But before I can stop myself, my hand is against his cheek.

"Luna," he says with a small frown.

I kiss him before he can say anything more, pressing my lips softly to his, on my tiptoes to reach him. He doesn't respond, and my heart thuds like a bomb. I've totally misread things, I think. I jerk away, humiliation rising up and my inner voice already screaming at me for being a fool.

"I'm sorry," I say, shaking.

"It's okay," he says, looking shocked. "Um . . ."

Mortification is hot lava swamping me. Immediately the voice in my head, the inner critic, starts laughing, cackling loudly at my stupidity, reveling in the humiliation.

What if he posts something online about it? What if he tells all his friends? What have I done? I march off, almost running toward the condo, fueled by panic and shame. I can hear Will behind me, calling my name, but I ignore him. As I reach the stairs up to the apartment, a man steps out of the shadows in front of me, and I let out a scream. Will is right there, though, before I can even let out a shriek. He shoves the man against the wall, his arm locked against his throat.

"Jesus, get off me!" the man growls.

I recognize Marty. Surprised, Will lets him go.

Marty glowers at him, dusting himself off. "What the hell, mate?" he says, annoyed.

"I thought . . . Never mind," Will says, shaking his head.

Oh God. How long has Marty been there, lurking in the shadows, waiting for us to get back? Did he see the kiss? We were standing under a streetlight but not too far away. Was he a witness?

"What are you doing here?" I stammer. "How did you know where to find us?"

"Where have you been?" he snaps at us. "This is the address Will gave on his application. I've been waiting here for hours. And why aren't you answering your phones?" He glares at me.

I shake my head. I haven't checked my phone. Haven't needed to or wanted to.

"Has something happened?" Will asks. "Did you find the guy who sent the bird?"

Marty's jaw stiffens. "No. The cops say they don't have enough to go on. I've had a word with the staff. They know not to accept any packages and to make sure everyone signs in at the gate." He looks at me. "Don't worry about it. It won't happen again."

I swallow, feeling sick. The grim reality of my life has intruded, as I knew it would.

"You're needed back for rehearsals," he barks at me now. "And we've got some interviews lined up. One with Ally Friedman on her late-night show. And your boyfriend's worried about you."

"He's not my . . ." I trail off.

"What are you wearing?" Marty asks me now, his nose wrinkling.

"What do you mean?" I ask, tugging at the sleeves of my dress.

"It's . . . different, that's all. Not sure it's a winner."

"I like it," I answer feebly. Another wave of humiliation washes over me.

"Look, go and grab your things, I'll drive you back to LA."

I can't even look at Will. My whole body is on fire, not from the kiss but from the shame and embarrassment. It's good that Marty is here, I tell myself. Perfect timing.

"I can take her," Will says.

Marty narrows his eyes at him. "I've got it," he says.

WILL

I follow Marty and Luna back to LA, frantic with worry. Marty must have seen us kiss. He didn't say as much, but the suspicious way he looked at me tells me he knows. What was I thinking? I totally screwed things up, and I didn't even get to explain to her why I pulled away. Damn it.

Marty beats me back to the house. I'm half expecting to find my things chucked out on the street and Marty waiting to fire me, but he leaves without speaking to me, and I wonder if maybe he didn't see after all.

I throw myself down on the sofa and groan loudly. This is a disaster. How did I screw things up so badly? She thinks I didn't want to kiss her when nothing could be further from the truth. I groan even more loudly, remembering the feel of her against me, recalling the kiss. It took me completely by surprise. And I would have responded, if she hadn't pulled away.

I fall asleep on the sofa in my clothes and wake with a start to a banging on the door. I hurry down the stairs, bleary-eyed, heart smashing. It's Luna, wearing dark glasses and dressed in leggings and a leotard.

"I'm late for rehearsal," she says.

"Okay," I say, unsure what she's thinking after last night and the kiss. "I'll grab my keys."

"We're going in my car," she announces, tossing her head and walking away. Okay, I can tell she's upset—as frosty as a morning in the Arctic.

I pull on some shoes and chase after her, wishing I'd had a chance to at least shower and brush my teeth.

Luna throws me her keys and gets in the passenger side, then busies herself with her phone. The message is clear. She doesn't want to talk. And she's angry. The Luna from our time away is AWOL. She's back to being the Luna I met the very first day: prickly, cold as ice. My adrenaline fizzes. I don't know what to do. I'm not good at talking about feelings.

"I'm sorry," I blurt.

"About what?" she answers without looking up from her phone, her voice thick with boredom.

Oh, I get it. She's going to pretend nothing happened. I could just go along with it. It would make life easier. But that's not my style.

"I'm sorry," I say again. "I didn't mean to upset you."

"You didn't," she snorts scornfully.

"You don't understand," I say, desperate to make her see but not sure how.

Should I admit to her that I have feelings for her? I don't want her to think I rejected her. I want her to know that I didn't kiss her back because I was scared I was crossing a line that I couldn't cross back over. And I want to tell her that I wasn't around to protect my mom and my brother and sisters from my dad. And that if anything ever happened to Luna now, I'd never be able to forgive myself.

She tosses her head, still tapping away at her phone.

"Let's not make a big deal of it, okay?" Luna says with a huff.

I bite my lip, wanting so badly to tell her the real reason I didn't kiss her back.

I pull into the parking lot of the rehearsal venue and into the space reserved for her. Luna gathers her things up and moves to get out of the car. I grab for her arm to keep her there. "Luna," I say, desperately searching again for words. I've never been in this situation before, and I don't know how to handle it.

She looks down at my hand on her arm and lowers her sunglasses. "Please don't touch me," she says in an icy voice.

I let go of her arm. "Okay," I say. I know I've only got one chance to make this right.

I glance up, movement catching my eye. A short, skinny guy with limp, dirty dishwater–colored hair, wearing a trucker's cap and sporting a wispy blond mustache, is strutting toward the car with a sneer on his face.

I jump out of the car, yelling at Luna to stay put and lock the doors, and I walk toward the guy, putting myself between him and Luna.

"Stay back!" I shout.

The guy glares at me, and then tries to push past me. I grab him, spin him around, and shove him face-first against the car, leaning all my weight against his body to pin him there.

"Jamie!"

I process the name and then, after a confusing beat, the face. Oh shit.

"Stop!"

Luna, who has jumped out of the car, grabs my arm and pulls

me off him. "What are you doing?" she asks, staring at me like I'm a Neanderthal.

"I didn't . . . I didn't recognize him," I say, looking at Jamie, who is now clutching his arm and scowling at me.

The dancers are all gathering around now. One or two have their phones out. Did they film it?

"You?" Jamie shouts, obviously recognizing me as the guy from the party who almost broke his arm. "What the hell are you doing here?"

"I'm sorry," I say, holding up my hands in apology.

Luna darts between us. "He's just my bodyguard," she explains.

Jamie puts his arm around her shoulder and I stare at it, appalled, Luna's words ringing in my head. I'm *just* her body-guard.

"What are you doing here?" Luna asks Jamie. She seems thrown by his appearance, but she isn't pushing him away. "I thought you weren't back until tomorrow."

Heat flows through my veins. Why is she letting him put his arm around her like that? She told my whole family at the din-ner table the other day that they'd broken up for good. Was she lying? But they're not acting like a couple who broke up.

"I came home early because I missed you," Jamie says. He takes Luna's face in his hands and kisses her hard on the lips. Whoa. Okay. They're still together. She did lie to me. What the hell was she doing kissing me, then? Was it a game? Was she playing me this whole time?

Behind them more dancers have started to assemble, coo-ing and nudging each other, as if they're watching a soap opera. Scorching anger almost blinds me. I want to look away, but I can't.

Jamie, still kissing her, opens his eyes and stares straight at me. There's a smug look on his face, and I have to fight every instinct in my body not to march over and drag him off her, then punch a hole right through him. When they finally pull apart, Jamie loops his arm around Luna's shoulder possessively and grins at me.

Luckily, Marcello appears then, the choreographer guy, and claps his hands at the assembled dancers. "Come on, everyone, we've got work to do!"

The dancers hurry off, and Jamie leads Luna inside, his arm still around her shoulder. Luna glances back briefly, catching my eye before looking quickly away, and I don't know what the expression on her face is, because it could mean a thousand different things.

Part of me wants to quit right then and there, but I take a few deep breaths and follow them, walking the circumference of the rehearsal room on autopilot as I check for any threats. When I've ensured it's safe, I stand at the far back of the room, watching Luna take her place onstage, feeling the red-hot anger turn white-hot and even more explosive. I force myself to keep breathing slow and steady in an effort to calm myself down.

"Hi."

I turn and see a familiar redhead is sitting in the back row. It's Natalie. I didn't know she was here. "Hey," I say because it would be rude not to answer her, even though I'm in no mood for a conversation. There's also the fact that I'm embarrassed I took her number and never called her. A shit move on my part.

She points at her makeup suitcase. "Marty told me to come. There are photographers outside. I need to do Luna's makeup before she leaves."

I nod.

Natalie glances toward the stage where Luna is rehearsing. "It worked, then, huh?" she remarks.

"What worked?" I ask Natalie, not sure I understand.

"He came running back."

She's nodding in Jamie's direction.

"She does it every time. They fight. They break up. She figures she can't live without him, so she does something to make him jealous. And then . . . he comes running right back." She snaps her fingers. "Like clockwork every time."

Jamie looks over his shoulder, scanning the room. His gaze falls on me. He gives me a smug, satisfied smile, before returning his gaze to Luna.

"How did she make him jealous?" I ask, hearing my heart start to thump in my chest.

Natalie turns to look at me with a pitying glance. "She used you."

My mouth goes dry and I can feel the anger rising in me like I'm standing too close to a burning building. My skin is burning with heat.

"That photo of the two of you out shopping? And at the movies? Luna set them up," she explains. "She did the same thing last time Jamie cheated on her too. It was an actor friend of hers. They went out and got photographed together. It looked like they were making out. Jamie saw it and came running back to her. If he hadn't been on tour, he would have come back sooner, right after he saw those pictures of you two together."

I keep my expression rigidly blank and stare at the dancers on the stage, trying to process what Natalie is telling me. Warring voices in my head tell me simultaneously that it can't be true and that it's obviously true. I feel like a total idiot, and shame makes me want to rush outside into the cooler air, but I also feel like bursting out laughing at my own stupidity. I look at Jamie, sitting right by the stage, puppy-dog eyes following Luna as she dances. Another voice in my head tells me that I've had a narrow escape and should be grateful.

When the song ends, Luna flips her hair out of her face and wipes the sweat off with the back of her arm. She smiles at Jamie, who is on his feet cheering and clapping. He jumps onto the stage, whisking her into his arms and spinning her around. Over his shoulder Luna glances my way, and instead of meeting her eye, I turn and look at Natalie.

LUNA

Jamie's all over me like a rash, his hands climbing up inside my clothes, his lips on my neck. I want to push him off, but I feel like I'm floating above myself, looking down. I watch myself as I stare vacantly out the car window. I know I'm trying to avoid looking at Will, who is driving us home. He hasn't looked at me once, not since Jamie showed up and started acting like we had never broken up. Is he angry? But he rejected me yesterday. So why should he care if I'm with Jamie or not?

I should have remembered Jamie was due back from Japan, but his arrival at the rehearsal venue took me completely by surprise, and I was too stunned to know how to act or what to say to him. And everyone was watching, so I knew I couldn't make a scene.

Jamie puts his arm around me and pulls me toward him across the back seat. I let him, too exhausted to fight him off. He kisses me on the lips, but my memory immediately conjures the memory of kissing Will last night, so I pull back. His lips feel wet and slippery in comparison.

"Didn't you miss me?" Jamie asks, looking confused.

My mind blanks. I can't think of what to say to him.

"What?" he asks, staring at me like I'm crazy. "What's wrong with you? It's not about that picture of me with that girl, is it?"

I don't want to be having this conversation, least of all with Will listening in, so I shake my head, but Jamie ignores me. "It was a total setup," he explains to me. "Her friend took the photo. They wanted their five minutes of fame. She's a wannabe model or something. You know what it's like. You can't trust anyone."

I stare at him, feeling a strange numbness come over my body. His words remind me of what Will said to me last night—that I could trust him.

"Babe," Jamie says. "Don't be paranoid. You know I love you. I've really missed you."

I let Jamie kiss me again, closing my eyes so I don't have to see his face. But when I open them, I find Jamie holding his phone in front of us, taking a selfie of the two of us making out. "What are you doing?" I ask, pushing him away.

"We need to post something of the two of us, otherwise people will talk."

"I don't care," I say. And anyway, there were photographers outside the rehearsal space snapping pictures when we left, so I'm fairly sure that the entire world already knows we're back together.

Jamie ignores me, though, and starts swiping through the dozens of photos he already took.

"That's a great one of me," he says. "By the way, why haven't you posted anything about my clothing line? You were meant to post a picture of you wearing my hoodie."

"I'll do it later," I whisper, dreading the idea.

"You promised," he pouts, poking a sharp finger between

my ribs. "And if you tag me, you'll get more followers."

"Ow," I say, pushing his hand away. "Stop it."

"God, lighten up," he huffs.

The car brakes sharply. I glance at Will, who's eyeing us in the rearview mirror.

"What are you looking at?" Jamie shouts at him. "Just drive." He turns to me. "He keeps staring at us," he says. "Why'd you hire this guy anyway?"

"I've been getting threats," I mumble. "I thought Marty told you."

"Yeah, I heard about the dead bird. That sounds gross," he laughs.

I feel like there's something wedged in my throat, and in my heart. "It was pretty horrible," I say quietly.

"I'll look after you now, babe," he adds, hugging me tight. "Don't worry. You don't need a bodyguard."

I can't help but look in Will's direction. I felt much happier knowing it was Will who was looking after me, and I start to worry that he might quit. The thought makes my anxiety levels leap sky-high and my heart pound. I don't want him to quit. But at the same time, how can I have him around me all the time? It's impossible, either way. Every time I look at Will, I feel like I might dissolve with shame and self-loathing.

"Hey, you," Jamie says to Will. "Can you put some music on?"

Will hesitates but obliges, shooting Jamie daggers in the rearview mirror.

"Let's get lunch." Jamie nudges my side. "You hungry?"

Will sits at a table a few feet away from mine and Jamie's. He's not looking in my direction but is glancing around the restaurant, scanning it. His expression is inscrutable. I think it's annoying Jamie because he keeps trying to rub Will the wrong way, kissing me at every opportunity, though Will always stares off into the distance as if he doesn't care. Jamie's behavior makes it clear that he saw the photos of Will and me online and assumed we were together. I still don't know if Will has seen them. He's never mentioned anything and I never brought it up, not wanting to go there.

Once again, shame and humiliation threaten to overwhelm me. An ant colony is on the march across the surface of my skin, and my head is a cacophony of screams and inner criticism. I wish I had my anxiety medication with me, but it's back at home. Instead, I try to do the breathing exercise that Will taught me, but it doesn't work. I can't concentrate because so many people in the restaurant are looking at us and I have to force a smile. I can't fall apart in public.

I pull out my phone and start to scroll through social media so I have something to focus on and an excuse to look down and shield my face from scrutiny. Jamie keeps posting pictures of us together, including the one he just took in the back of the car. I glance at the comments posted below the picture. A lot are comprised of rows of heart emojis and comments of the *Back together again!* variety, but quickly the trolls have surfaced.

Why's he back with that bitch? She doesn't deserve him.

It's a stomach blow, one that makes me curl over myself as I clutch my phone. My heart starts to race. It's getting hard to breathe. I order myself to put the phone down, but I can't. The addiction kicks in. I have a need in me, a perverse desire, to read them all. It's a form of punishment, each negative comment a whip biting into my skin. And I deserve each lash.

She's so lucky.
She's so ugly.
Has she put on weight?
What does he see in her?
I thought they broke up.
Didn't he cheat on her?
Are they back together?
Again! LOL.
He's so gorgeous.
I want his babies.
She'd be nothing without him. She can't even sing.

The words jumble in front of my eyes. I want to kick myself for reading them, but the panic has already risen up my throat and threatens to burst out of me in one long scream. *This is the truth*, the voice in my head tells me.

I am nothing. I am nothing without him.

I look at Will, who is turned away from me. His voice in my head was a lie. Why did I ever, for even a moment, think he might like me?

WILL

The waitress comes over, asking if they want dessert. Luna looks like she's about to order when Jamie cuts in. "We're good," he says, snatching the menu from Luna's hand.

I glare at him, but he ignores me. Luna stares down at her lap, looking miserable. How can Jamie not see she doesn't want to be here? She looks like she might be on the verge of a panic attack, breathing fast, almost panting, but he hasn't noticed.

I seriously cannot understand what the hell she sees in him. He's an insecure idiot who spends most of his time on his phone. Who sees her as a prop, something beautiful to pose beside. And it strikes me that he's chosen this table in the center of the restaurant not so everyone can stare at him, but so everyone can stare at him *with* Luna. Even in her misery she outshines him. People aren't looking at him; they're looking at her. She's the draw, the one that everyone can't help but notice. Jamie's basking in her glow. Is that why he can't ever stay away from her? Not because he loves her, but because he needs her? And does she think she needs him, too?

Now that I've had the thought, I know it's true. His brash arrogance and swagger—they are all for show. All talk, no game.

I have to take a deep breath and uncurl my fingers, which are clenched into tight balls. I'm angry. This situation is triggering all my rage about my dad. Jamie might not hit Luna, but he's controlling her in the same way my dad controlled my mom: treating her terribly, cheating on her, disrespecting her and belittling her.

What kind of mind trick is Jamie playing on her? But then I hear Natalie's words in my head—*she used you.* I'm so conflicted. I'm furious and hurt and frustrated and confused. I want to wash my hands of Luna. I wish I'd never laid eyes on her, in fact. But at the same time, I can't stop looking at her, can't bear the thought of walking away from her.

Every time Jamie touches her, I have to resist the urge to leap between them and push him off her. I'm gonna have to quit, I realize. I don't think I can keep a lid on my anger for much longer, and at this rate I might end up punching Jamie.

But I can't quit yet. I need to find someone to replace me first. And until then I need to keep calm.

"Let's go back to your place," Jamie says as we leave the restaurant. His hand slides around Luna's waist. "I want to show you how much I missed you."

My stomach boils. I will myself to stay cool and not give Jamie the satisfaction of seeing even a flicker of annoyance across my face, though the idea of them sleeping together is like a bullet to the gut. I almost pull the door off its hinges when I yank it open. This is what I was afraid of—acting just a little bit like my father and behaving like a jealous, violent monster.

* * *

When we get outside, Jamie stops to sign autographs while Luna retreats to the back of the car. I get in the driver's seat and stare through the window, determined not to look at her. I watch Jamie as he poses for more photographs. I can't believe she was using me. The tumult of feelings I'm trying to stuff down inside me almost bursts out like that scene in *Alien* where the monster erupts out of the guy's stomach. Why did she kiss me? There weren't any photographers around to snap a picture, so she couldn't have been doing it to make Jamie jealous then.

I shake my head and eventually find myself eyeing Luna in the rearview mirror. She's locked to her phone. Her lip is trembling and she looks on the verge of tears. Despite my swirling anger, I feel a lurch of compassion. I almost ask her what's wrong, but I press my lips together and look away.

Not for long, though. I can't help myself and take another peek at her in the mirror. This time I catch her wiping away tears as they spill down her cheeks.

"What's the matter?" I hear myself ask.

She looks up in alarm. "Nothing," she mumbles, hastily wiping her eyes.

Frustration, not anger, bursts out of me. I can't contain it. "Is it because he's treating you like absolute shit?" I ask.

"It's not him," she sniffs.

I arch an eyebrow, not buying it. "What is it, then?"

"I told you—*nothing*," she says, a hiss of anger in her voice.

"So why are you crying?" I ask, more belligerently than I should.

She closes her eyes and leans her head back against the seat and doesn't answer. I turn my gaze back to Jamie, still chatting with his groupies on the sidewalk, openly flirting with them. He's such a jerk.

My eyes flash open, and I realize I said the words out loud. I'm usually so much better at holding my tongue and keeping my opinions to myself. I had a whole lifetime practicing, but this situation has overwhelmed my ability to bite my tongue. "You can do so much better than him."

Luna shakes her head, her eyes still closed. "No, I can't," she snorts under her breath.

My eyebrows shoot up. What the hell is she saying? That doesn't even make sense. A tapeworm would be better than Jamie. "What?" I say, turning around to face her. "What are you talking about?"

She hangs her head, and I see she's clutching her phone. After a beat, she looks up, her face shining with tears and with so much hurt and pain that my anger and frustration are immediately defused. I almost climb over into the back seat to pull her into my arms. Except very quickly my irritation rises back up and holds me firmly in place.

"I'm not a good person. I'm a terrible person," Luna mumbles, looking down at her lap.

I stare at her. Who is this person talking? I don't recognize her. Why on earth would she think that? I knew her self-esteem was rocky, but this is next-level self-hatred.

She swallows, still not looking at me. "And no one else would ever want to be with me."

"So, you're with him because you don't want to be alone?" It's hard to keep the scorn out of my voice.

Her face crumples. "I don't know," she says. "Yes. He was my best friend, before . . . everything. The fame. He's different now, but he's the only person who's ever cared about me." She looks up at me then, her brown eyes brimming. "And you have no idea what it's like to be alone, to have no friends. You've got a family that cares about you and friends that love you." Her sadness is replaced by anger. "Of course you wouldn't understand." She spits out these last words.

I'm rendered speechless, even more confused and conflicted than I was two minutes ago. I had some idea that she felt these things, but I don't think I fully appreciated the depths of her sadness or loneliness. How can someone so famous, known by billions of people, feel so lonely? How can someone so adored by so many people feel like she's a bad person? She's right. I don't understand. But I want to. How can she think Jamie is the only person who cares about her?

"He doesn't care about you, though," I say, aware that Jamie will be back in the car any second, and I only have a minute, maybe less, to try to get through to her. "He only cares about himself."

She shakes her head. "He wasn't always like this. He can be sweet."

"Because he buys you roses?" I snort. "You think that's romantic? It's easy to buy roses if you have money. What else does he do that shows you he cares about you? The guy doesn't even let you have dessert! What kind of an asshole doesn't encourage the woman he loves to have dessert?"

Her eyes widen as she stares at me.

"And it's not true about him being the only person who's ever cared about you—I cared about you." I stop abruptly. I didn't mean to say that. I wish I could take it back.

She stops crying and looks at me through wet lashes. She's

surprised, I can tell, but not as much as I am. I don't know why I admitted it. I'm still so angry at her, but at the same time I want her to know. I need her to know that there are more people than Jamie who care about her. I let out a long sigh, rub my hand over my face. "I wasn't rejecting you," I say, "if that's what you think."

She blinks at me and her lips part.

"It was the opposite."

The car door opens. *Goddamn it, Jamie.*

"I'd always want you to have dessert," I say quietly, under my breath to Luna, as Jamie climbs into the back seat, forcing her to move over.

Luna stares at me, her mouth still open. I turn my head to face the front, heart thudding and throat dry at what I just admitted, wondering if I was stupid to do it and desperately wishing I knew what she was thinking.

"I can't wait to get you to bed," Jamie says to Luna.

My jaw clenches so hard I swear I hear a tooth crack. My hands on the wheel are white-knuckled.

Luna says nothing. I start driving, refusing to even glance in the mirror, unable to stand looking at them.

LUNA

What does he mean, *It was the opposite*? He wasn't rejecting me. The realization takes a while to penetrate through the fog. I'm aware of Jamie beside me, trying to pull me closer, but I stay rigid, leaning into the door. I stare at the back of Will's head. He just told me he cared about me, but he used the past tense. And it's no surprise. I've been so shitty to him.

I blew it. I'm still blowing it, sitting here in the back seat with Jamie. Why is it so impossible for me to break up with him? Why can't I believe Will when he says that I deserve better? Why can't I silence the voices in my head telling me that Will's lying and that all the people online saying horrible things are the ones telling the truth?

I look at Jamie. I know he cheated on me and that he's lying to me. I know he's always lying to me. And then I look back at Will. He has only ever been honest with me. Why is it so hard, then, to believe him over everyone else?

When we get back to the house, I climb out of the car in a daze. Will goes ahead of us, without so much as a backward glance in my direction. He's making sure it's safe, and as I watch him, I know that so long as he's beside me, that's how I'll feel. But with Jamie at my side, all I feel is doubt and unhappiness.

Will checks the front step, no doubt for more packages, but there aren't any, and so he opens the door and we walk inside.

"I'm going to call Marty," he says, not looking in my direction.

I open my mouth to respond, wondering why he's calling Marty. Is he handing in his notice? But Will's already halfway out the door, and Jamie is tugging me toward the stairs.

Matias and Carla enter from the kitchen. Carla beams and hugs me, and Matias ignores me and goes running after Will, catching him on the steps. "Can we play soccer?" he asks, bouncing up and down on his toes.

Will hesitates. "Not right now, buddy, but later, okay?"

Matias's face falls. He turns to Jamie. "Will you play with me?"

"I'm busy, sorry." Jamie smirks. He pulls me again toward the stairs.

I catch Will's gaze and see the flash of anger in his eyes. I want to unpeel my hand from Jamie's, but I can't. Will looks away from me and to Matias, who is starting to look agitated and like he might be about to blow.

"Give me ten minutes, okay?" Will says, seeing it too, and Matias immediately brightens. "Why don't you go find the ball and warm up?"

Matias scampers off and my heart swells to almost breaking at how kind Will is. I watch him walk off, and I want nothing more than to follow him. But Jamie has a tight grip on my hand.

Carla looks after Will's retreating back, then at Jamie, and then back to me. She frowns at me. She can obviously see that I've been crying. "Are you okay?" she asks.

I don't answer.

"Are you hungry? Want me to make you something?"

I shake my head, thinking of what Will said. *What kind of an asshole doesn't encourage the woman he loves to have dessert?* Those were his words. And then he said he would always want me to have dessert.

He didn't reject me.

He cared about me. But I've treated him so badly. I've used him.

Jamie tugs impatiently on my hand. "Come on," he says.

"Are you sure?" Carla presses, with a determination in her voice that goes beyond her usual encouragements for me to eat.

"She said she's not hungry," Jamie snaps.

"I'm not asking you," Carla responds in a steely tone. She raises her eyebrows at me. "How about huevos rancheros?" she asks, turning back to me. "Extra spicy."

Jamie sighs loudly, making for the stairs and dragging me behind him. "She doesn't want eggs."

"No," I say. "I don't want eggs."

"Told you," Jamie gloats at Carla.

"No," I tell him, digging in my heels and then pulling my hand from his. "I want dessert."

His face screws up in confusion.

"You need to leave," I tell him, hearing my voice but not recognizing it as my own. I don't know where I'm finding the courage to speak, but somehow I am.

"What?" Jamie says to me, bewildered.

"Please leave," I repeat.

Jamie smiles in confusion.

"I don't want to get back together with you. We're done."

"You always say that," Jamie laughs. "Why are you still in a mood with me? I told you there was nothing going on with that girl in the photo." He rolls his eyes like I'm being a drama queen.

"I don't care about that. It's not about that," I say.

"So, what is it about, then?" Jamie asks, annoyed. He gestures at the door that Will just walked through, and then looks back at me with a mocking look on his face. "Is this about him?" he asks. "Are you dumping me for him?"

I shake my head. "No," I say. "I'm dumping you for me. I don't care if I'm alone for the rest of my life—I'd rather be alone."

Jamie backs away from me, emotions racing across his face, making him look like a toddler on the verge of a tantrum. I recognize disbelief and then anger and then spite. "Fine," he finally says, his expression settling into an undisguised sneer. "But good luck with your career without me."

I shake my head again. "I don't care about my career," I say, a weight lifting off my chest as I admit it. "I just want to be happy."

Happiness seemed impossible thirty minutes ago, but now I've caught a brief glimpse of it, like a candlelight flickering through a storm, and I know I have to chase it before it blows out, or I lose sight of it forever.

Jamie keeps sneering as he walks out the door. "We are done," he says. "I'm better off without you anyway."

WILL

I've just gotten off the phone when I hear a knock on the door. I head downstairs, expecting to find Matias with the soccer ball. It's not him, though. It's Luna.

"I wanted to say sorry," she whispers, looking down at the ground.

"What about?" I ask.

"I used you." She looks up at me through lowered lashes. The shame on her face is awful to witness and makes me want to immediately reach for her, but I resist the urge and instead cross my arms over my chest.

"It was a shitty thing to do," she says, her voice breaking. "I invited you to the movies because I wanted to be seen with you and photographed. I wanted to get back at Jamie."

"I know," I tell her, wondering what's caused this sudden admission and also wondering why she's here and not in bed with Jamie. Where is Jamie, in fact?

"I'm sorry," she says again, pitifully. "I'm a bad person. If it makes you feel better, Jamie and I were broken up this whole time—I didn't lie about that—and we haven't gotten back together either."

"What?" I say in disbelief.

"I just told him we're over for good." She looks up now, staring right into my eyes, unable to hide the nervousness.

"For real?" I ask. I can't help but sound skeptical, knowing what I do about them.

She nods. "Yes. You were right. He's a jerk." She says it with a slightly rueful expression.

Okay. I don't know what to say to her, and I keep my face blank. I have no clue where this conversation is going, or where she wants it to go. And my defenses are still up. Anger and frustration buzz through my veins. Is she only here to apologize or is there something else she wants to say? But she stays quiet.

"Thanks for the apology," I say in the awkward pause.

She swallows hard.

"Was there something else you wanted?" I ask.

She swallows another time "I want dessert," she blurts.

"What?" I say, unclear what she means.

"I want dessert," she whispers again.

My eyes widen. Wait . . . She stares at me and I'm stunned by the vulnerability in her eyes.

"Dessert?" I ask, my arms falling slowly to my sides as I try to gauge her meaning so I don't misinterpret things.

She nods at me, her gaze dropping for a second to my lips, before returning to my eyes, and it becomes clear what she means.

And that's all it takes for me to drop my defenses. I'm not making the same mistake twice. I pull her into my arms and my lips find hers, and she's kissing me with an intensity that makes me stagger back. Flames lick my body, lighting every nerve, scorching me from the inside, incinerating all my anger and frustration. I pull her inside, kicking the door shut behind her with my foot, and we stagger back into the wall, locked in each other's arms.

My hands trace the length of her spine, the curve of her hips, the flat of her stomach, feeling her tremble at my touch. She presses so hard against me that I groan, and now she's pushing me back toward the stairs.

Maybe this is madness and I'm crossing a line I promised myself I wouldn't cross, but I can't stop myself. My brain is instantly clouded with desire. I can't get enough of her, of her lips or her skin, can't stop kissing her, feeling her desire fueling my own so it seems at some point we might combust with it. She's pushing me up the stairs and we stumble, tangled in each other's arms, until I reach down and pick her up and she strad-dles me, her legs around my waist, squeezing tight, still kissing me as I carry her upstairs.

I lay her down on the sofa. She knocks a lamp off the cof-fee table with her foot. It smashes, but we ignore it, both of us breathing so hard and fast I can't hear anything but the sound of my heart thundering in my ears.

Luna is on top of me, peeling off her T-shirt, dropping it on the floor and now pressing her body down on top of mine, kissing my neck and my jaw, her fingers tracing my stomach muscles. Oh shit. I need to come to my senses, but how can I when she's almost naked on top of me and her skin is like honey and she smells so good and all I want to do is get closer than close, closer than this. I want to feel and taste and explore every inch of her.

She gasps as my fingers stroke over her stomach and then toward the waistline of her jeans. I want to hear her gasp again, and again and louder still. I want to hear her say my name. With one arm around her waist, I flip her over so I'm on top of her and she's lying beneath me. I dip my face to hers, kiss her collarbone so she arches up to press against me. I do it again and she arches again, her fingers biting into my shoulders, pulling me down so we're skin to skin and nose to nose and eye to eye.

I can't remember ever wanting anyone this much. She wriggles out of her jeans, and as she pulls off her underwear, the roaring in my head becomes a thunderstorm. I can't hear myself think. I can only focus on how close we are, how naked she is, how perfect she is, how much I want her. And she wants me, raising her hips to press into mine, her perfect legs wrapping around my waist. Shit. It would be so easy.

I jump up, stepping away, feeling immediately faint and having to fight the desire I have to move back toward her because now I've got a full view of her and my God, that's a body to die for. She sits up, though, covering herself with her arms, her hair a wild crown around her head, her face flushed, her skin glistening with sweat.

"I don't know if we should do this," I tell her, having to pace in order to stop from throwing myself on her.

"I want to," Luna says. "Don't you?"

She looks hurt and insecure, as though she suspects I'm rejecting her again.

"It's just so fast," I say.

"I want you." She says this last part so quietly I barely hear her. "I . . . want to be with you."

I'm kissing her before she can finish.

I pull her into my arms again. She's so soft, and the heat of her body makes it feel like she's melting into me. We're both breathless again in seconds, hands sliding everywhere, making each other groan and cry out and inhale like we're gasping for air.

Is it too soon to have sex? I don't know. Probably. Should we slow it down? Probably. But then she's asking me if I've got protection, and she's straddling me as she lowers herself down, looking me straight in the eye. There's so much openness and vulnerability between us, as though we're both showing each other the real version of who we are.

In my arms she seems to shake off the insecurities and come alive, her lips curling into a smile as I kiss her collarbone.

I want to make her happy, make her feel good about herself. I want to show her how beautiful she is and show her how she should be treated. More than anything, I want her to know how much I care about her.

LUNA

He sees me. I can see it written in his eyes, in his expression, can feel it too in the way he keeps my gaze, so fiercely. How he kisses me, holds me, touches me, makes all my worries float away. For right now, there's just the two of us and the world disappears. Will keeps checking with me that I'm happy, that I'm okay, that I want him to keep going, and I respond by wrapping my legs tighter around him, pulling him in deeper and closer. I feel a sense of safety and belonging in his arms, feel seen for maybe the first time ever.

I don't even know for sure how I got here, only that whatever force has been driving me toward him ever since I first saw him is now irrepressible and impossible to ignore. I could no more easily remove myself from him, disentwine myself from his body, than I could leap from a roller coaster mid-ride. And I don't want to stop because it feels so good, and so right, like this moment was always going to happen and there was nothing we could do to stop it. His hands are cupping my face, pulling me nearer, and his lips are on mine, warm and gentle, and for the first time in my life I'm lost.

Thoughts burn to fragments in my mind, become ash and spiral into nothing in the air. Nothing registers anymore except the sensations flooding my body, a series of electric pulses gathering in intensity until rainbows of color explode on the back of my eyelids.

I hear Will say my name, and then I feel his weight collapsing on top of me, his sweat-slicked body crushing mine. It's a blissful heaviness. My limbs dissolve, but I also feel light as a feather, as though I'm drifting on warm currents of air. I can't ever remember feeling this peaceful or content. The noise of the world has retreated.

Slowly I become aware of the sound of Will's heart beating against mine and the scratchiness of his cheek buried in the crook of my neck. I become aware of our sweat mingling on my stomach and the weight of his limbs twisted with mine, the broadness of his chest and the softness of his skin. I want to burrow into him, and when he wraps his arms around me and gently rolls so we're on our sides, I don't feel the normal claustrophobia that I experience when Jamie does the same. I feel safe. I feel like I'm home.

I close my eyes and breathe in deeply, smiling to myself as I feel Will's lips in my hair and his hand stroking down my spine, gently caressing my skin in circles that send ripples of pleasure through me. "Are you okay?" he asks.

Am I *okay*? I murmur yes, when the truth is that I'm far more than okay. I'm on another planet, completely tranquil. I don't want to pull myself back to earth. I want to stay floating, pressed skin to skin with Will for the rest of my life because nothing will ever feel this good again. I'm certain of it.

We lie in silence for a long time, our breathing finally slowing and unconsciously falling in sync. When I start to shiver, Will moves, leaping off the sofa and fetching a blanket. I watch him go, his body so muscular and so beautiful that I find myself staring in awe and also with a lust I've never experienced before in my life. He moves so confidently but without any swagger. He fully embodies himself, without any self-consciousness or arrogance.

When he walks back, he catches me drooling and smiles, then drapes the blanket over me and sits down, pulling me into his lap, cradling my head against his chest. He strokes my hair. "You're so beautiful," he says, leaning down and kissing my lips.

I cringe and try to collapse into his chest, but he won't let me. He forces my chin up with his hand.

"You're the most beautiful person I've ever seen."

I look at him skeptically. He can't mean that? He's just flattering me.

I frown and shake my head. "It's all makeup. Photoshop. I'm not really."

He looks at me in astonishment. "Are you joking? You're so beautiful and you don't need makeup. I'm serious." He strokes my hair behind my ear and looks at me with such intensity and seriousness, I half believe him.

His hand caresses the length of my body, down my arm until it reaches my hip, then down my thigh. "And my God, are you sexy."

"No, I'm not." I feel myself shutting down, wanting to pull away and hide myself. What if he sees all my blemishes? Jamie was always pointing out things that were wrong with me, like my knobbly knees, the birthmark on my shoulder, and the fact that one boob is slightly smaller than the other. I pull the blanket back to cover myself, trying to hide, but Will notices. "What's the matter?" he asks, nuzzling my neck. "I like looking at you." He tries to peel the blanket back.

I clench my jaw and start to get up, but he takes my wrist and pulls me down. "Don't go," he says quietly.

I relent because I don't want to go.

"Let me look at you," he says again.

Reluctantly I let him peel back the blanket, and whatever chill I was feeling dissipates almost immediately under the heat of his gaze as his eyes travel up my body, taking in every inch of me, making me shiver.

"You're so beautiful," he murmurs again, and when he notices me squirm uncomfortably, he asks: "Why don't you believe me?"

I shrug. "You should read the comments online," I tell him, avoiding admitting to him that the ones my inner critic makes are worse.

He looks at me in shock, then frowns. "You should stop reading the comments online," he answers. "And listen to me instead."

I lean up and kiss him. I cannot get enough of his lips. He's an amazing kisser, better even than I imagined. His lips are soft but firm, gentle but also demanding. And very quickly after we start kissing, things are heating up again, at least they are on my part. I can't get enough of him, and there's an ache rising in my body that I need him to fill, but Will seems to only want to keep kissing.

I worry that maybe he isn't as into me as I am into him. What if I'm losing his interest already? Maybe he's a one-and-done kind of guy. Maybe what he said about never dating still stands.

"What do you like?" I whisper to him, smiling seductively,

hating myself for my anxiety and how I'm letting it control me.

He pulls back and looks at me strangely.

"What do you want me to do?" I ask, biting my bottom lip in a way I hope looks sexy.

He shakes his head and moves to kiss me again. I stroke my palms over the hard flat of his stomach and chest, my fingers sliding into the grooves of his muscles, and I gyrate my hips. I can feel he's getting turned on, but he's frowning at me.

I throw my head back and arch over him, groaning loudly even though he isn't doing anything except holding my hips.

"Luna," Will says. "You don't have to do that."

"Do what?" I ask, heat flooding my face.

"That. It's like you're putting on an act, trying to please me."

My heart beats hollowly. I want to escape into a hole and hide from him. "What do you mean?" I stammer.

"I don't want you to pretend."

"I'm not pretending," I argue.

"Look," Will says. "What we just did, what happened, that was amazing. Incredible. And it was perfect. At least for me, and I thought you liked it too?"

I nod, flushing, feeling an urge to cover my body and hide. "I did," I admit.

He runs a hand through my hair and smiles. "You don't need to do anything but be yourself. That makes me happy. You don't have to be someone you're not around me. I know you too well by now. I see through it."

"But . . . ," I say, my face and body both in flames. "I thought . . . that's what guys wanted."

Will shakes his head again. "Maybe some guys who've watched

too much porn, but that's not really my thing," he explains with a one-shouldered shrug.

"It's not mine, either," I admit, feeling my body start to relax and the humiliation slowly beginning to fade. "I've only ever been with Jamie," I blurt, lying down and resting my cheek against Will's chest.

I feel Will tense with surprise at the admission.

"He liked it when I . . ." I blush and bury my head against his shoulder. "Did stuff like that," I mumble.

Will strokes my hair. "Well, you don't have to do that for me. I don't want you to pretend to like something because you think that's what I want. I want *you*. You don't have to fake it with me. I don't want you to."

I nod. He cups his hand behind my neck and pulls my face up to his. We kiss and the heat from my face expands down into my chest and core, spreading all the way down my arms and legs to the tips of my fingers and toes.

"Nothing could turn me on more than knowing you're turned on. For real."

"So that wasn't a one-time thing?" I ask him, hating myself again for sounding pathetic and needy.

"Do you want it to be?" he asks, his smile fading.

I shake my head.

"I know you don't date," I say with a shrug.

"I do now," he answers with a roguish smile. "If you'll have me."

The smile bursts on my lips. "If you'll have me," I answer.

He grins and I shiver as his fingers slide between my legs, and I bite my lip to stop from moaning.

"Is that good?" he asks.

I moan yes into his ear. He kisses my throat, and my whole body starts to hum with need. I grip his lower back as he keeps touching me. Jamie never touched me like this. I think I might die.

Will stops just as I'm on the edge and starts to kiss and lick down my body. The hum is now a full-on raging fire inside my body, a pulsing need for him that I don't think I can contain. "Please," I hear myself say, pushing my body up to meet his lips.

He keeps going down until I feel his tongue on me, and I let out a cry of surprise that quickly becomes one of pleasure. I tip my head back and cover my face, biting the back of my arm as the pleasure becomes too much to handle, and finally I collapse, boneless and insubstantial as water.

WILL

When I jolt awake, the room is partially dark. I'm still lying on the sofa with Luna, who fell asleep in my arms. I take the time to enjoy the feel of her body against mine, to admire the smoothness of her skin, the softness too, and to study every detail of her face up close. Her lashes are so long they lay shadows across her cheeks, and her chin has the slightest dimple in it. She has three earring holes in each ear, but she is only wearing a pair of studs. She has a freckle above her lip, and her lips are parted enough that I can see the tiny gap between her two front teeth. I listen to the sound of her breathing. It's rhythmic and deep.

I crane my neck to see the time on the oven in the kitchen. It's just past five o'clock in the evening. We've been asleep for seven hours. I blink a few times, trying to shake off the lingering fog of sleep. Luna stirs after a while, smiling as she presses her lips to my chest. My heart expands bigger than I have ever felt it grow.

"What time is it?" she asks, yawning and stretching.

"Late. After five," I answer.

"I can't believe we slept so long." She sits up suddenly. "I have to go." She looks around for her clothes.

"Luna?" I say, pulling the blanket around my waist as she starts to dress. "I have to quit."

She pauses, one leg through her pants, the other out. "What?" she asks.

"I'm handing in my notice. Effective immediately."

Her face turns pale. "Why?"

"Because I can't be your boyfriend and your bodyguard."

"So?" she says, stumbling into her pants and then toward me.

"I crossed a line," I tell her. "Marty already warned me away from you. And your mom did too. She only hired me because she thought she could trust me. I've broken both their trust. I need to tell them."

"No!" Luna says, looking even more alarmed. "You can't tell them! And you can't quit."

I stand up and face her. "I can't do my job, Luna, not properly. Not now."

"Why not?" she asks, her voice sounding anguished.

I chew my lip. How could I keep working for her when every second of every day that I'm supposed to be concentrating on the job, I'd be dreaming of her naked and imagining what I wanted to do to her? Not to mention there is a possibility of *over*protecting. "I just can't," I explain weakly.

She stands up and takes my hands. "I don't want anyone else with me when I go to these events. If they hire someone new, they'll be spying on me and on us. Please. I want you."

"I can't protect you if we're dating," I tell her. "If there are feelings involved, it clouds everything. I'll be distracted."

Her face falls. "But I'll help find a replacement," I tell her. "And stay on until then."

She frowns unhappily. "I don't know," she mumbles.

I stroke her cheek. "Even if you have a new bodyguard, I'll still be there."

She looks at me hopefully. "Really?"

I nod. But I'm conflicted. I can't leave her when I know there's someone out there trying to hurt her. If she's being threatened, I'm going to be glued to her side until the threat's passed. Whether there's another bodyguard or not. "I'm not going anywhere," I tell her, kissing the top of her head.

She smiles up at me. "You'll stay? You won't go anywhere?"

I start to shake my head but stop myself. A sudden dark cloud settles over me, a nagging feeling anchoring in my stomach. How can I be at her side all the time, if I need to get another job and work? But I can't not work and live off Luna. I still have to pay off my debt, and there's my future to think about. "Not yet," I say, hedging. "Not until you're safe."

"Okay," she replies, thinking hard. "And until we hire someone else to take over, you'll be on the job during the day. We keep our relationship a secret, and we just act like I'm your client. At night," she says, looking at me with her face lit up, "I'm yours. We can stay in, watch Netflix, and . . ." She trails off.

"Chill?" I ask.

She nods, grinning at me. I'm still processing that she said the word "relationship."

She reaches up on tiptoe and kisses me on the lips, her fingers stroking my jaw. My arms loop around her waist and pull her nearer so her body molds to mine. We're a physically perfect fit, and the feel of her in my arms causes an instant reaction in another part of my body. Luna pulls away, grinning at me. I grin back. "Do you have to go?" I ask, kissing her.

She smiles. "I've got a meeting with Marty. He'll be here any minute. But tonight I'll come over when everyone's gone to bed."

LUNA

I ring Will's bell every night at around midnight after my mom and Matias have both gone to sleep and I'm sure no one will hear me sneaking out of the house.

Whenever I arrive, though, Will is always awake and waiting for me. We tumble up the stairs, him pulling me by the hand or me tugging him by the wrist, and there's no Netflix. Only chill. And always dessert.

Will is the kindest person I've ever met, traits that roll over into the bedroom in the best possible way. Unlike Jamie, Will only seems to care about how I feel when it comes to sex. It's a novelty and something I still haven't gotten totally used to.

Jamie didn't once ask whether I liked anything or if I was having a good time when we were in bed. The whole experience was designed always for his pleasure, never mine, and the really annoying thing is that I never questioned it. I thought that was how it went. I never considered my own pleasure or what it was worth. I only wanted to keep him, and keeping him meant keeping him happy.

"I missed you," I tell Will when he opens the door.

"It's only been three hours," he answers.

"It felt like thirty," I say as his lips find mine. "I brought you something." I pull a box out from behind me.

He steps back, smiling at the gift-wrapped present I'm offering him. "What's this? It's not my birthday."

"I know. I wanted to get you something, to say thank you, for everything."

"I'm just doing my job," he says with a half smile.

"I'm not talking about the job," I tell him. I'm talking about what he's done to lift me out of the darkness, to help me feel alive. My confidence is growing, thanks to him, and I'm feeling more in control. I'm playing around again with writing and considering my options for after I finish the tour. I'm wondering if I might be able to extricate myself from my mom and Marty and follow my heart for once. So far, doing so has been a positive experience, so how can it go wrong if I do the same with my career?

I watch Will take the present, almost reverentially, and set it on the table in the living room.

"Are you going to open it?" I ask.

He nods and a look passes across his face, something of a dark cloud.

"What is it?" I ask, feeling a buzz of worry at the thought he's upset with me about something.

He shakes his head, and then seeing the worry on my face, he reaches for my hand. "It's nothing. Thank you. I just feel bad. I haven't gotten you anything."

I smile at him. "I don't need anything from you. Just you being here. That's enough."

He smiles at me, and I kiss him to make him realize it's true.

He pulls me close and kisses me back, his hands winding in my hair.

I pull back. "Open it," I tell him, clapping my hands together with excitement.

He does, carefully, like he doesn't want to tear the paper. "Come on," I say, encouraging him as he rips the last part to reveal a brand-new Nintendo.

"Are you for real?" he asks me, looking amazed, like a kid at Christmas who just got the puppy they'd wished for. My heart lights up. I got it right.

I nod. "It's the latest one. I thought about getting you the vintage one from when you were a kid, but you can't play any of the games on it. But you have to promise me you aren't going to ditch me for it."

He sets the box down and takes my hand, pulling me toward him. "No chance," he says. "Thank you." He kisses me on the lips. "I can't believe you remembered," he says, incredulous.

"Of course I remembered," I say. I remember everything he tells me. "Also, we're getting takeout tonight."

"What?"

"Sushi. I'll get it soon."

Will grins at me. "I hear the good thing about sushi is you don't have to worry about it going cold."

"True," I say.

His hands are already on my hips, his palms sliding across them and toward my waist as he pulls me against his body with a groan. I lead him into the bedroom and we tumble onto the bed. He might not be too expressive in normal life, but in the bedroom he's straight-up honest with how he feels. He doesn't hide his feelings from me at all, forever telling me how beautiful I am, and how he can't get enough of me. I'm starting to believe it too.

Lightning streaks across my body wherever his fingers go. He kisses my collarbone, tracing circles with his tongue. "Everyone knows," I whisper.

"Knows what?" he asks, his mouth on my neck.

"That Jamie and I broke up."

He pulls away to look at me.

"He's been posting online," I say. "Pictures of him with a new girlfriend. She's a Brazilian model."

Will nods but studies me carefully. "Are you okay about that?"

I smile at him. "I'm okay," I tell him truthfully. It still amazes me that I put up with Jamie for so long. I didn't know any different and I believed everything he told me—that I needed him and that we were meant to be together and that no one else would put up with me. Sometimes I question if Will is right that I'm a good person and deserve better, and I worry that I don't deserve him, but I'm slowly starting to believe more in myself. I'm ashamed I needed him for that, but sometimes you do need someone to hold up a mirror and help you see yourself in a different light.

"How are the comments?" Will asks. He knows how nasty people can be, as I've shown him what people have said online about me.

"I took your advice," I tell him. "I don't read them anymore." I'm also working hard to silence that inner critic, meditating, and even starting to work with a therapist. She's making me see that Jamie put me down in order to make me depend on him more, because he needed me to make him feel more important. I'm starting to believe it.

I haven't posted anything online either, and it's wildly

liberating. Marty's been on me about it, saying I can't afford to lose my followers, and I know that he's probably found out about Jamie and me splitting up, so will be on me even more to post. He thinks I'm worth more as part of a couple than alone. My monetary value on Instagram, my level of influence, is much less as a single person. But I don't care. I'm not letting him and my mom rule my life anymore.

I roll on top of Will and kiss him, loving the scratchy feeling of his beard and the softness of his cheeks and lips. I work my way down to his chest. "How are the interviews going?" I ask, wondering about the search for a new bodyguard, which seems to have gone silent.

"I'm still looking for someone. Marty's left it to me. I've seen a couple of guys, but no one I think will work."

I smile inwardly, wondering if he's finding it hard to replace himself because he worries no one will look after me as well as he can. I am not complaining, though. I still don't want him to quit. I go back to kissing him.

After we make love, I lie in his arms and he strokes his fingertips up the inside of my arm.

"Sushi!" I say, sitting up abruptly.

I throw on Will's T-shirt and a pair of sandals and race to get the sushi from the house. Carla's left it in the fridge for me, and I sneak it back over to the apartment over the garage.

As Will tastes his first California roll and sashimi, I ask him about his father and he starts to talk, opening up about what it was like growing up. I only have to prompt him a little and it all floods out of him: the terror he felt as a small child wanting to protect his mom and siblings and not being able to. I feel his body tremble as he talks about how he'd hide in the closet with

Zoey and Kate and do magic tricks to keep them distracted, and my heart cracks open at the thought. I press myself against his body, kissing his shoulder, wishing I could take the pain away.

"I'm sorry," I tell him.

He doesn't speak for a while and I kiss his shoulder again. Slowly I feel the tension leave his body. He leans into me. "It's okay. If I hadn't gone through that, I wouldn't be here, eating raw fish eggs, which are delicious, by the way."

I grin at him, then stroke his face. I look into his eyes and try to communicate with him silently that I'm here for him. I wish I could take all the bad memories from his head, and the bad voice in mine, and banish them all to some other galaxy.

We fall asleep around three in the morning and are woken hours later, not by the alarm, but by the sound of the door buzzing.

I sit up with a jolt, groggy with tiredness, my limbs aching and entwined with Will's. He shoots up too, reaching for his pants. He hops out of bed, pulling his pants on, and slides over to the window. He peeks out through the crack in the curtain.

"It's Marty," he says.

"What?" I hiss, grabbing for the sheets in a panic. "Oh my God, look at the time!" It's nine in the morning. We must have forgotten to set the alarm, and I'm late for rehearsal.

The buzzer sounds angrily. Will heads for the door.

"Wait!" I whisper. "You can't let him in!"

"I can't ignore him or he'll know something's going on," Will whispers. "Don't worry. I'll keep him outside. Just stay hidden."

He disappears down the stairs, and I frantically rummage for my underwear and clothes. I can't believe I overslept. Once I've pulled on my clothes and shoes, I tiptoe to the top of the stairs that lead down to the door so I can hear what's going on.

"Where the hell is she?" Marty shouts.

"What?" Will stammers.

I cringe. Will doesn't know how to lie. Honesty is his default position, but he can't tell Marty that I stayed the night with him, and neither can he say he doesn't know where I am as it's his job to know where I am and keep an eye on me. I can see this rapidly heading south, so I do the only thing I can think of doing. I walk down the stairs, hoping I don't look too much of a ruined mess. I haven't brushed my hair or my teeth or looked in a mirror, but I trust that I know how to play a part.

"Hey, Marty, sorry, am I late?" I ask, brazenly strutting toward them.

Marty looks taken aback to see me. "What are you doing here?" he asks, his gaze snapping suspiciously between Will and me.

"I came to ask Will to teach me how to box," I say. "I bought Jamie all that equipment and it's going to waste. I figured I may as well get some use from it."

Marty glowers at Will, who shrugs and says nothing. For the first time I'm grateful for his inscrutable face.

Marty grunts but still eyes Will with suspicion. It seems like he's going to call me on the lie, but then he jerks his head at his car. "Come on, move it. You're gonna be late for rehearsal."

I stride past, without giving a second glance at Will.

"Hurry it up," Marty barks back at him before running to catch up to me.

I let out a long exhale. We've bluffed our way out, for the moment at least.

WILL

Luna's onstage rehearsing with a dozen backup dancers. I'm aware that Marty is prowling around and that he keeps glancing over at me every so often. He didn't buy my denial earlier, I don't think. Or else he's just a naturally suspicious guy. I'm therefore trying to avoid looking at Luna so as not to give anything away, but it's not easy. She's wearing a leotard and leggings and looking so hot that I'm having trouble concentrating. She's also an incredible dancer. I didn't get that impression a week ago when she was struggling to stay focused and didn't seem to know the moves, but now she and the choreographer, Marcello, are constantly locked in conversation, working through moves together, and Luna seems much more relaxed. She's laughing with the other dancers, and although she's trying not to give anything away by looking over in my direction, she's failing miserably. We keep meeting each other's eye and she continues smiling.

"She's in a good mood."

I turn to find Marty lurking in the shadows behind me. I don't respond.

"Is she taking something?"

What does he mean by that?

"Have you seen her popping any pills?" he presses.

I shake my head.

"Well, she needs to be taking them," Marty grumbles. "Otherwise she'll go off the rails again. I need her on form for this tour. There's a lot of money at stake. I want you to keep a close eye on her. Let me know if she starts acting funny."

I glance at him. "You know, I think the pressure she's under might have something to do with the level of anxiety she feels," I say.

Marty shoves a piece of gum in his mouth. "Look at her!" He points at Luna, laughing on the stage. "She's fine. She's just a little melodramatic at times. All artists are. Up one minute, down the next." He knocks me with his elbow. "By the way, I need you to encourage her to get back together with Jamie."

I side-eye him, trying not to show my reaction. He's got to be kidding.

"It's bad for business if they break up for too long."

I grit my teeth and take a deep breath. "But he's a loser who treats her like crap. She's happier without him."

Marty stops chewing. "I didn't think you cared so much about Luna's happiness," he says, raising his eyebrows.

Damn. I should have kept my mouth shut.

I keep my expression blank. "He's mean to her. He treats her like shit. Why would you want her to get back together with him?"

"He's not that bad. A little immature, maybe. And obviously, he has a massive ego. But the fact is, she's better off with him, from a career point of view. People love to tune in to all the drama those two create."

I grind my teeth together, trying to hide my anger. He's talking about Luna's life like it's a reality show. She's the unwilling star, and someone else gets to direct and there's never a final season.

"*She* doesn't love it."

Marty gives me a funny look.

"And hasn't Jamie got a new girlfriend anyway?" I say.

"He's only doing it to piss Luna off," Marty says. "It's how they operate."

I purse my lips, knowing it is, because she used me the last time to get to him. I've moved past that, though.

"Luna's hiding away like a hermit," Marty continues. "People get easily bored. They'll turn to another channel if we're not careful. We've given them the cliffhanger; now we need to give them a reason to tune back in."

He really is treating Luna's life like something he can script. It makes me furious.

"A big twist, perhaps. Something dramatic. A reunion," he adds, talking now to himself, seeing the ideas form in his mind.

"So this is about keeping her in the public eye?" I say.

"You're catching on quick." Marty holds up his hand and counts down on his fingers. "Scandal and gossip and sex. A triple threat when it comes to selling records. Luna's got all three."

"But what if she wants to live her life in private?" I ask, my anger in danger of manifesting itself.

Marty scoffs. "You can't. Not if you're famous. The public owns you. That's the deal you make with the devil. If you want fame, you give up your right to privacy."

"Did she ever make that deal?" I argue. "Or did you and her mother make it for her?"

Marty gives me a disgruntled look. "What do you know about it? You don't think she wanted to be a star? Look at her up on that stage!" He points and I follow his gesture. Luna's singing over the track and dancing, and I know it's true. She exudes magnetic appeal and an x-factor that's undeniable. The other dancers all fade into the background beside her.

"She's got something most people would chew their right arm off for," Marty goes on. "And despite what you think, she was as eager as anything to make it. She wanted it and she's worked hard for it. Are you telling me she should give it all up and walk away? For what? To go and work in Target or McDonald's? You can't waste a talent like hers."

"No, but you shouldn't have to give up so much of your life either. It's not fair."

Marty shrugs. "The good outweighs the bad."

Does it?

"She needs this," Marty says, gesticulating in Luna's direction. I watch her attempt a complicated move, flying off a scaffold on the stage to land in the outstretched arms of six dancers. They set her down and she beams with delight as everyone claps for her.

"She needs this," Marty repeats. "Who would she be without it?"

LUNA

"W here are you going?" my mom asks, appearing like a ghost behind me.

I haven't seen much of my mother since she returned from her "spa trip." Between rehearsals, hanging out with Will, and her Pilates and shopping schedule, we haven't run into each other. I've also been trying to avoid her because I don't want her asking me about Jamie and our breakup or asking questions about Will. But she's caught me coming out of my bedroom.

"Where are you going?" she asks again.

"Will's teaching me to box," I say, deciding to opt for the truth.

"Then why are you taking your guitar?"

"Oh," I say, "he plays." It's a lie, but it's the only thing I can think of. "I said he could borrow it." The truth is that I've been writing more songs and I want to play them for him. With Will's encouragement I've been putting together a whole album. I want to perfect them before I play the songs for Marty.

My mom frowns. "You look tired."

I shrug. I don't feel tired, but I have been getting a lot less sleep than usual. Though I'm not complaining—it's been worth every second.

"I feel like we should have a mother-daughter date," she says to me. "It's been too long since we hung out and had some girl time."

I make a noncommittal grunting sound. It's been years since we hung out and talked. I can't remember the last time it felt like we were a normal mother and daughter and not a business manager and a client. I think it was probably around the time I turned twelve and got my first break and she started to see me as the way out of poverty and living paycheck to paycheck.

"I feel like you're a little distant," she adds.

I raise my eyebrows. I'm the one who's distant? She's the one who's always running off to the spa, or going on dates with asshole men, or doing a Pilates class. My therapist suggested I build a bridge with her, but I haven't yet felt any incentive to do so. She's the mother. Shouldn't she be the one trying to build a bridge with me?

"And Marty tells me you're behaving a little strangely," my mom continues. "He said that you want to change your appearance."

"I only said I don't want to wear so much makeup and I want to change up my style."

"Your image is important, Luna," my mom says with a sigh. "How you look is everything."

I exhale loudly.

"You know I'm right," she says. "And I just want the best for you."

I snort. Right. She doesn't care at all about what's best for me. She cares about what's best for her.

She cocks her head to the side. "You know that, right? Marty and I only have your best interests at heart."

"Sure," I respond tersely, and try to walk past her, feeling my previously good mood evaporate, but my mom blocks my path.

"Have you spoken to Jamie?" she asks.

"No," I tell her. "We're done. I don't ever want to see him or speak to him again."

I walk away before she can ask me anything about the breakup.

Will's waiting for me by the punching bag, his hands already wrapped. "What's up?" he asks as soon as he sees me.

I love it that he can tell my mood instantly and cares enough to ask what's wrong. I shake my head. "My mom. She's on me about stuff."

"What stuff?"

"It doesn't matter." I don't want to talk about it.

I've surprised myself and Will with my love of boxing. It could be the cathartic nature of smashing my fist into something repeatedly, or how it helps me get rid of any pent-up anger and rage. I didn't even know how much anger was built up inside me until I started laying into the bag. Every mean comment made on social media, every criticism Jamie ever gave me, every time I've been groped or openly leered at by men in the industry when I've only been trying to do my job, every time I've been told to shut up and put up by Marty when I've complained about it, every time my mother has told me I'm lucky to be where I am and how many people are relying on me . . . It's all been stockpiled inside me in a way I wasn't even aware of until I first put on a pair of boxing gloves last week with Will and hit this bag.

I imagined the bag was Jamie, and Marty, and the internet, and every person who'd ever said a horrible thing to me, and then I pictured Craig's face as he squeezed my ass, and my father's face as he pleaded with me over FaceTime for more money, and then I pictured my inner critic, and I punched that bag so hard, Will had to pull me away before I did some damage to my hands. I feel stronger, not just physically, but also mentally from these daily workouts.

I've been able to have a better handle on my anxiety since I started seeing Will. If anything, being around him and knowing that he's nearby acts as a kind of human Valium. I feel calm, more confident, and slightly more in control of my life. I feel freer, which is saying something when you consider the fact that I have a stalker sending me dead animals in bakery boxes.

But the thing with freedom is, you can't just be given a piece. If you're in solitary confinement and then you're given time outside in the yard where you can see the blue sky and feel the sun on your skin, you're going to start dreaming of digging a tunnel. That's what Will has done for me. He's brought me out of solitary and into the yard, and without knowing it, he's handed me a spade.

I've started to dig, and the more I dig, the more desperate I feel to get the hell out. It's only when I think of what life will look like on the other side of that wall that I begin to feel the familiar claws of anxiety digging into my flesh and my breathing starts to hike. So far I've tried to ignore that feeling. Whenever I experience the worry of what I'll do on the other side, I try to comfort myself that Will is going to be there to help me navigate it.

I realize I've stopped punching and I'm standing there, arms hanging at my sides, staring at the punching bag. I shake myself back into the moment.

"You want to stop?" Will asks, checking the time.

I nod. My shoulders are aching and I'm dripping with sweat.

Will glances around to make sure no one is around, and then pulls me toward him. His arm goes around my waist and he kisses me. I melt, like I always do, at the feel of him. When he holds me, when he kisses me, I feel like I can do anything, that nothing anyone could say could ever hurt me. He makes me feel protected, sure, but also, for the first time in my life, like I'm invincible.

WILL

Luna's slick with sweat and her lips taste of salt. I push her against the punching bag and hear her groan. It's the sweetest sound, always unleashing something in me that makes common sense disappear out the window. Anyone could see us, but I just don't care. I can't get enough of the way she feels or the way she tastes, and I run my tongue across her lips and then down her throat and between her breasts, my hands on her hips, gripping them tight. She throws back her head and moans.

I find her lips again. She presses her hips against me, and I know she can feel how much I want her. Her eyes are half-open, heavy-lidded. I kiss her neck again, then her jaw, then her cheek. Her lips are by my ear and she's breathing fast, almost panting.

"I love you."

I freeze. What? I can't ignore what she just said. She tenses in my arms. My heart is pounding like a freight train, and I feel the electricity jumping back and forth between us. *I love you too,* I want to say, but I can't. My throat is dry as sand and my voice has disappeared. I can feel Luna starting to shrink away from me, her hands dropping from my waist. Shit. I pull her closer, then take her face between my hands.

I look at her, waiting until she raises her eyes, nervously, to look into mine.

I love you.

I can't say the words. I want to. They're trying to burst out of me. But I can't. So instead, I kiss her again, with an even greater urgency, trying to show her that I love her because my words have failed. She takes a few seconds to respond, but my hand slides between her legs and she gasps, and then she's kissing me back, opening herself up, and I'm lifting her against the wall, where we're out of sight of the house.

Her breath burns hot in my ear; her nails scratch my back. She's tugging at my shorts and I'm pulling at her clothes, and she's grabbing protection; then I'm inside her and I can hear her breath coming in gasps and my own heart hammering against hers, and then she comes and I do too and it's the most incredible release but also entirely different from any other time with anyone.

She loves me? I let the knowledge seep into me. It's heat from a fire warming my bones after an endless trek through snow. It's midday sun on my back after a dip in freezing water. It's breathing in the smell of pine needles and woodsmoke infused in crisp fall air. That's the only way I can describe it.

But it's also terrifying. I've never experienced it before, and already I can feel myself starting to worry what it would feel like to have it taken away. For the fire to be extinguished, or the sun to sink below the horizon, or the crisp fall air to give way to the deadly chill of winter.

She's panting, her head on my shoulder, our bodies glued

together with sweat. She unhooks a leg from around my waist and leans back against the wall, out of breath. I push a strand of damp hair off her face and tuck it behind an ear. She smiles but doesn't look me in the eye.

Did I make a mistake? Should I have said it back? Is it too late to say it now?

"I'm going to go take a shower," she mumbles, giving me a quick smile before rushing off.

I watch her go. I do love her and I don't want to give her up ever, but that nagging feeling in my stomach hasn't gone away since my conversation with Marty. I only took this job so I could earn enough to pay off my debt and have some cash to get away from here. I planned to head north, to Oregon or Washington State, to find a little town in the middle of nowhere, somewhere with a lot of trees, near a lake, and I wanted to find a job working with at-risk kids. I had a dream and I still desperately want to pursue it.

If I say *I love you*, then it feels like I'm agreeing to stay here in her world, where I don't feel comfortable and where I don't belong. I don't want to be in the limelight.

But then I consider being apart from Luna, and I know that I'd rather be with her because of that feeling flowing through me right now. She feels like home. The roots I want to put down are with her.

And Luna can't come with me into my world, to follow my dreams. She wouldn't want to. And even if she did, it would be like pulling a fish from the water and expecting her to be able to survive on dry land.

Marty told me that she was made for the limelight, that she needed it, and I thought he was being over-the-top. But he was right. Performing is what gives her joy. I can't take that away from her.

I want us to be together, and if that means being in her world, then I'll be in her world. I don't have to love it. I just have to love her. And, of course, find a way to tell her.

LUNA

Marty is distracted, buffing the bumper of his Tesla.

"Marty, I'm talking to you," I say, annoyed at him only half listening to me.

"Yeah, I'm all ears," he mutters, taking out a cloth to rub at an invisible smear on the license plate.

"What is it?" Marty says.

"Did you listen to the song I sent you?"

"Oh, that. No," Marty says, not meeting my eye. "I haven't actually had a chance to. I'll listen to it later."

My heart sinks.

"You know I've still not seen you post on Instagram for a while. You need to be showing your face more before people forget what you look like."

"I don't care," I say, waving off his concerns. I love being free of the prison of social media. I love not worrying about how many likes I'm getting, and I love not wading through hateful comments. I've broken the addiction. Admittedly, it's not easy, but I'm getting there.

"Look, you make a lot of money from influencing," Marty

says. "And if you lose your followers, you lose your influence."

"I know how it works," I tell him. "You don't have to mansplain Instagram to me."

He looks up at that, taken aback. I've never talked back to him before. It gives me a thrill. "And I don't care if I lose followers," I add.

Frowning, he beeps open his car. "Let's talk about this on the way," he says, getting in.

Huffing, I get into the passenger side of the car. "What about Will?" I ask him, wondering where he is, as he usually comes with us. I'm anxious, haven't been able to shake the worry crawling through my gut and the buzz of hornets behind my rib cage, ever since yesterday when I blurted I loved him and he didn't say it back.

I should have kept my mouth shut. It just came out and I wish I could take it back. I've scared him away.

"I've given him the day off," Marty says.

That's weird. Will never said anything about having time off. But I can't make a big deal of it or Marty will get suspicious and wonder why I care. It nags at me, though. The voice of my inner critic starts to pipe up, reminding me that I was stupid to fall for him, telling me that he's just using me, because how could he ever love someone like me. I force myself to ignore the voice because deep down I know it isn't true. I focus instead on how to tell Marty that after the tour I want to take a break away from the spotlight and work on my new album.

No, I remind myself. You're not *wanting* to take a break. You *are* taking a break. You're not asking permission. I take a deep breath. No time like the present. "After the tour," I say, "I want to quit."

Marty's foot slams on the brake, throwing me forward so the seat belt cuts into my throat. "Ha ha, very funny," he mutters darkly. "I almost crashed, Luna. Don't make jokes like that."

"I wasn't joking," I say. "I want to take a break."

"Sure, sure, a little holiday, somewhere nice and sunny," Marty says, focusing on the road. "The Caribbean, maybe. Or Cabo? How about it? I'll book you into a nice resort somewhere on the beach. Somewhere with a spa. You can have a relaxing time. Chill out a bit. Then we can start work on your next album. Craig wants to talk to you about that actually today. We've got the whole concept worked out. We were thinking of something a bit Madonna in her heyday, a bit Ariana Grande, a bit Billie Eilish."

I close my eyes, wincing. This isn't going to plan. Besides the fact I have zero idea how he can mash those three artists and come up with a coherent sound, it's not what I want to do. I don't want to be a mash-up of three other people. I want to be my own person.

"I don't want to be those people. I want to be myself," I tell him.

Marty looks at me like he's talking to a toddler. "Why would you *not* want to be any of those people? They're richer than God. And Madonna's still going in her sixties."

"And she's always made the music that she wants to make," I argue. "That's part of her longevity. She's always trying new things."

"That's what we're doing with Craig. You're lucky he wants to work with you. He's got people queuing up around the block, begging for him to work on their albums. Guy's got his pick. And he's picked you."

I suppress a stomach heave.

"I don't think Craig and I are a good fit," I say for want of a better explanation. Telling Marty I don't want to work with someone who creeps me out won't be enough. "I want to do something more me, something cooler," I say, "almost unplugged. Just me on the guitar or the piano and vocals. More of a soul groove."

"That's not gonna sell," Marty snorts. "You're not Janis Joplin, Luna. You've got a following who expect certain things. And what do you mean, 'cooler'? You can't get cooler than Craig Matthers."

Marty's abrasiveness starts to overwhelm me. He's so loud and, trapped in the car with him, I don't feel like I can get a word in. "If you just listen to the song I sent you, maybe you'll see what I mean. I've been writing a lot. I've almost got enough for a whole album. Give me a month or two and I'll have it ready for you to listen to."

"Luna," he cuts me off with a patronizing tone. "I've got the best songwriters in the world sending me stuff, specifically written with you in mind."

"But—" I start to say.

"Stick with what you know best," he says.

Fully deflated, I sink into my seat and shut my mouth. That snide voice in my head tells me to try again, to speak louder, but what's the point? He's not going to listen. He's just a typical old man who thinks he knows everything, and I'm a young, naive girl who knows nothing. But then I hear Will's voice in my head, telling me to stand up for myself. I have the power in this relationship. Marty works for me, after all.

"I'm not doing it," I say, my voice ringing out as loud as a bell in the car.

"Gotta make a quick call," Marty says, ignoring me entirely and hitting dial on his phone.

For the rest of the car ride he stays tied up on work calls. I stare out the window, feeling my frustration building and then turning inward as doubt starts to creep in. It's my fault. Maybe Marty is right. What do I really know? He might work for me, but at the end of the day he knows the business side of things better than I do. And the work I've done on a new album probably isn't any good, anyway. My hand curls into a fist and I almost punch myself in the thigh, out of anger. Why do I always let the negative voice speak louder than the positive one? Why have I let my inner critic so easily take over again when she's been silent so long?

"Right, we're here," Marty says, hanging up his final call and pulling into a parking spot in front of a faceless building.

My phone vibrates, and I look down to see Will is calling, but I can't take the call, not with Marty right beside me, so I don't answer.

In Craig's office there are gold and platinum-plated discs on all the walls, Grammy Awards on a shelf, and a bookshelf containing no books, only photos of Craig grinning as he stands arm in arm with the biggest names in the industry.

Craig walks in, and though he's about forty, I think, he tries to dress like he's still a teenager. "Hey," he says to Marty, giving him a fist bump that Marty returns awkwardly.

"Luna!" he says to me, his eyes running up and down my body in a way that makes me feel very self-conscious. I feel like a gazelle in front of a lion, and my body freezes rigid as he pulls me into a hug, kissing me on both cheeks.

"You look bangin'," he tells me, his hands still glued to my waist as though I'm a butterfly he's pinning in place. Before I can stop myself, I find I'm smiling at him and saying hello because I don't want to be rude or cause a scene.

"Let's get into the studio," Craig says, gesturing to the door. "It's all set up. I want you to listen to what I've put together so far. It's cool. You're gonna love it."

And there I am, smiling again, following him, letting his hand trail down my back like a clinging vine, as he ushers me out the door. I can hear myself saying how excited I am to hear it, and my self-hatred threatens to strangle me. Why am I retreating behind the mask, putting on a show, and not just being myself?

In the studio Craig pulls out a chair for me and then perches on the desk beside me. He makes a point of leaning over me to play with the equipment, adjusting knobs and levels. It feels deliberate, like he's placed me here in this chair so he can have an excuse to brush against me.

He hits play on the track. It's synth-pop, heavy on the electronica and with a bass note that sounds like it's designed to bring on arrhythmia. It's so not me. In fact, when he layers a vocal over the top, I don't even recognize at first that it's me singing. It's my vocals that he's lifted from another track and heavily edited. It could be anyone.

"What do you think?" he asks.

"Bloody brilliant," Marty says, nodding along enthusiastically.

"Yeah," I hear myself say even as inside I wonder who it is that's talking. It's as if I've been invaded by a body snatcher who has control of my voice box.

Marty's phone rings and he steps out of the room. I stand up too because I don't like sitting where Craig keeps leaning over me and brushing against me, but as soon as I do, he steps closer, squashing me against the desk.

"What do you think?" he asks. "We're a good team, right, you and me?"

His hands are on my waist. I'm not even sure how they got there, and I freeze.

"Maybe we should think about partnering up in other ways."

Stop! Get off me. I say the words, but they're silent, trapped inside my throat.

His hands slide over my hips. "If you want, we can work together on the whole album. Guarantee you a hit."

He presses against me. I'm paralyzed. I start to detach from what is happening, to shrink inside myself, so I don't have to deal with the situation.

His hands now slide up my back. He must think that because I'm not moving or saying anything, I'm consenting.

Craig leans down as if about to kiss me.

And then the voice in my head pipes up. It shouts at me, *Jab. Cross. Hook. Uppercut.*

I twist my waist as Will taught me and throw all my force behind the punch, aiming for Craig's jaw. When my fist makes contact with Craig's face, pain explodes up my arm, radiating out from my wrist in concentric circles of throbbing. It feels as though I've smashed my hand into a metal wall. I still manage to follow through, though, with a left jab to his face. The satisfying crunch it makes and the sight of the blood spraying out of his nose makes any pain I feel inconsequential.

Craig staggers backward, falling against a desk, knocking over a monitor, which crashes to the ground and smashes at our feet. Craig doubles over, clutching his nose, grunting with surprise and anguish.

Marty bursts back into the room. "What the hell happened?" he asks, looking between us and the smashed monitor, bewildered.

"He touched me," I say, my voice shaking.

"She's fucking crazy," Craig slurs, cupping his hand over his bloody nose to catch the drips. "My Goddamn nose! That bitch broke my nose!"

I lunge at him, fists flying, fury unleashed like a hound. The self-hatred has morphed into straight-up hatred, rushing out of me and latching on to him like a gremlin. Marty jumps between us. "Whoa, whoa, calm down," he says, holding me back.

But I'm not going to calm down. "He assaulted me," I shout. All the buried silent rage I've been carrying around, stuffing down inside, is erupting out of me. All those places in me that felt hollow weren't hollow after all. It turns out they were filled with this anger, just waiting for the spark to ignite it.

"Don't you ever touch me again!" I scream at Craig.

"She's crazy. Get her away from me," Craig laughs.

Marty suddenly lets go of me and whirls around. He gets right in Craig's face, shoving him backward against the table. "Say that again, mate," he says in a threatening voice.

Craig puts his hands up in defense, looking alarmed. "What?" he asks.

I shove my way through the door and outside, and I don't hear what Marty says next, can only hear the sound of them arguing because my anger is a drum and it's beating so loud inside my skull that it drowns all the other noises out.

WILL

'm waiting in the driveway, pacing back and forth. Luna texted me from the car to let me know what happened with Craig, and I'm so livid that the only reason I haven't gotten in my Bronco and driven over there to break Craig's hand and then possibly every other bone in his body is because I want to see Luna first and make sure she's okay.

As soon as they pull up in front of the house, Luna jumps out of the car and runs toward me. I'm taken aback because we're on full display and Marty's right there, but she throws herself into my arms anyway, shaking all over.

"Are you okay?" I ask her, holding her by the tops of her arms and looking her in the eye, trying to get a read on whether she's more angry or upset.

"I'm fine," she says. Then she holds up her hand, which is swollen and red. "Actually, no, I hurt my hand. I punched him."

I take her fingers and slowly, gently, bend them to see if anything is broken. She winces but doesn't cry out.

"You hit him?" I ask with more than a hint of pride in my voice.

She nods, a smile brushing her lips. "Twice. I punched him. A right hook. And a left jab."

"She broke his nose," Marty snaps.

I smile at Luna. "Good. I'd like to go over there right now and break more than his nose."

She grins back at me.

"Just bruised," I say once I've finished flexing her fingers. "We need to ice it, though." She nods. "And follow up with a knee to the balls next time."

"There won't be a next time," she says grimly.

"You should file a report," I say. "What he did is assault."

Marty waves his hands, as though trying to damp down flames. "Let's all calm down, why don't we? I already gave him a talking-to. It won't happen again. He got the message loud and clear."

"He put his hands on her without her permission," I inter-ject. "She should file a police report."

Marty purses his lips angrily. "Stay out of it!" he says. "Besides, you're fired!"

"What?!" Luna shouts. "You can't fire him."

"I bloody can. And I bloody have." He turns to me. "Get your stuff and get out of here. What did I tell you about fingers and pies? You knew the rules."

"No!" Luna protests. "You can't fire him. I employ him. Not you. And I pay his salary, just like I pay yours."

Marty opens his mouth and then shuts it. He remains glow-ering at me, though, as if he'd like to rip my head off my shoul-ders. "How long has this been going on for?" he growls, gesturing between us.

"It's none of your business," Luna protests.

"That why you and Jamie broke up for real?" he asks.

I glance at Luna, but she shakes her head. "I broke up with Jamie before I got together with Will."

"I know you're the one putting her up to all this," Marty says, turning to me.

"Up to all what?" Luna interrupts angrily.

"Up to all this nonsense about wanting to sing your own stuff." He turns back to me. "And you're the one who taught her how to punch. Great move!"

"And thank God I did teach her!" I shout back. "What if she hadn't been able to fight him off? What might he have done?" The thought makes my blood boil. "You should be thanking me. Where were you anyway? How could you let him do that? If you had let me come today, this wouldn't have happened."

Marty has the decency to look abashed at this last part.

"He touched me," Luna hisses at Marty, and I'm gratified to see this new angry and alert version of Luna, one that's willing to stand up for herself, who's confident and knows she deserves to be treated with respect. "Was I supposed to put up and shut up? Is that what you wanted me to do? Smile and say *please*? Be grateful?"

"No," Marty protests. "I told you I gave him a mouthful. Told him he couldn't behave like that. He won't do it again."

I can't believe Marty still wants her to work with the guy. And I'm guessing he doesn't want her going to the police as he doesn't want the bad press that might go with it.

"No!" Luna shouts over me, shaking her head at Marty. "I'm not working with him. I'm done with all this! With the music, with being told what to do all the time by you. So you can choose: do what I want, support me fully, or walk. I know I don't have

Mila Gray

the power to fire you, but I also don't have to do what you say. You can't control me."

Marty looks like he's been slapped. "You know I only want the best for you."

"No, you want the best for *you*. Just like my mom," Luna retorts.

Marty takes a deep breath and weighs his words. "All right, from here on in, we'll work together. You call the shots and I'll support you, whatever you want to do."

Luna eyes him suspiciously.

"And the album I want to record?" Luna says.

"I'll take a listen," he says grudgingly. I wonder at his sudden change of tune. Is it because Luna is finally standing up to him, and he sees that if he doesn't back down, he'll lose her? Have her threats worked? Or is he just saying it for the moment, in order to get her to back down?

"I'm doing it, Marty," she tells him defiantly, "with or without you."

"Fine. I've said that I'll support you." He doesn't seem happy about it, though.

"And you aren't firing Will," she adds.

Marty glares at me. "Fine," he mutters under his breath. But I can tell from the way he looks at me, like he's weighing an opponent, that this isn't the end of it.

LUNA

My mom bursts into my bedroom, just as I'm getting changed. "What the hell happened?" she asks.

"Craig Matthers assaulted me, so I punched him."

"I heard," she says, looking concerned. "Did you have to hit him?"

I shake my head in amazement. The concern isn't for me but for Craig! "Are you joking?" I ask. "The guy touched me. You should be on my side. You're my mother."

My mom takes a deep breath and lets it out. She hangs her head and nods. "I admit what he did was wrong. But two wrongs—"

I cut her off. "Go away." I can't listen to this. But she doesn't go anywhere. She comes closer.

"Marty says that you threatened to fire him and that you want to record your own songs."

I nod, steeling myself for what's coming next.

"It's not a good idea, Luna," she says. "You need to let Marty and me manage your career," she says before I can get a sentence out. "We're the ones who understand the marketplace and how the industry works. And technically, as I employ him, only I can fire him."

I glare at her, biting my tongue. How have I let her take so much ownership of both my life and all my assets?

My mom sits down beside me on the bed, sighing loudly. "Luna, I've managed your career since you were a child. I know what I'm doing. You need to trust me."

"But Marty said he was okay with it," I argue.

"Marty shouldn't have said anything without discussing it with me first. Now we've talked, and we've decided this is for the best. You know the game. You know how it works. If you want to stay on top, you have to play along."

"I don't want to play the game anymore. I want to quit!" I shout.

My mom laughs and gestures at the room. "You don't want this? This house and those clothes and that car? You want to go back to living in a one-bedroom apartment in Glendale? Or a mobile home? You want Matias to survive?"

"That's not fair," I protest.

"Isn't it? He's only in remission because we can afford the treatment. It's out of pocket. It's hundreds of thousands of dollars a year. We couldn't afford it if you weren't famous. If we weren't rich."

I bite my lip.

"Family means sacrifice," she says to me, taking my hands. "It means giving up the things you love and doing things you don't necessarily want to do. That's what love is."

My insides clench. Is that true? It's how I felt about Jamie. That love was pain and sacrifice. But Will's shown me that love doesn't have to be that way.

"You don't think I sacrificed for you and your brother?" my mom asks, her voice raspy. "You don't think I gave up on my own dreams and worked terrible minimum-wage jobs to pay for you to succeed, so that we could all have a better life?"

I press my lips together tightly. I can't argue with her. She looks weary, and I remember how tired she used to be working all those jobs to put food on the table and to get me to auditions and Matias to his checkups. I remember how hard she fought and advocated for Matias to get the care he needed. Maybe I am being selfish to want to do my own thing. Marty and my mom have steered my career all this time, and there's no denying that I've been successful because of them and made a huge amount of money. And there's no denying that Matias is alive because of it. What if my own happiness and fulfillment is the price? It's surely a price worth paying.

"I'm not asking a lot, Luna," my mom says in a gentler voice. "Only for you to trust me. I'm your mom. I only want the best for you. Even if at times you don't believe it."

She brushes my hair behind my ear. I feel nothing. She didn't take my side with Craig, and that hurts more than I can put into words. And as I listen to her go on, trying to convince me of all the people who rely on me and all the things we're able to do because of my success, all my own dreams vanish. I watch them fade away like ash rising up a chimney and melting into darkness. Maybe it was stupid anyway. Just because Will's friends liked my music doesn't mean it was any good. I was being selfish to think I could do what I wanted, without considering how it might affect my family.

"And this thing with you and Will, it needs to end."

I tune back in. "What?" I stare at her openmouthed.

Did Marty tell her? He must have. Shit. I blink at her. "It's not a thing. I love him."

My mom strokes my hair. "Does he love you back?"

She may as well have slapped me. I swallow painfully. "Um . . ."

My mom makes a told-you-so face. "Luna," she says patiently, as though explaining rudimentary math to a two-year-old. "He's using you."

"No, he isn't!" I protest. "What would you even know?"

My mom sighs and hands over an envelope she's been holding. "I didn't want to show you this, but I think you should know. You're nothing to him but a means to an end."

I take the envelope. What is she talking about? I open it and pull out some glossy photographs and a printout of some emails. My eyes can barely take it all in. What is this? I scan the emails, trying to make sense of it.

"Do you see now?" my mom asks, putting her arm around my shoulder.

My stomach drops, and I think I'm going to be sick. The room spins like a fairground ride. How could Will do this to me? I don't understand why he would betray me like this. I trusted him completely.

I believed him when he said he would never hurt me, but he's turned out to be like all the others.

WILL

Luna storms into the bathroom as I'm getting out of the shower. "Why did you lie to me?" she yells.

"About what?" I say, grabbing for a towel.

"It was the money, wasn't it?" she asks, crossing her arms over her chest.

"Excuse me?" I say.

"You didn't quit when you should have because you needed the money. It wasn't because I begged you to stay on."

I take a deep breath.

"Is that why you still haven't found anyone to do the job? Because you wanted to last the full six weeks and get your bonus?"

"I should have quit, yes," I admit. "And you're wrong about wanting to stay on to get the bonus. I figured that I could still do a better job of protecting you than anyone else." I hang my head, staring at my feet.

"Why didn't you tell me you were in debt?"

Shit. She knows. I look up. She's staring at me stonily, hands on hips. "Because," I say. "It's not your problem or your business."

The hurt in her eyes is palpable.

"I didn't want you to know because I didn't want you to feel like I was asking for a handout. That's what your dad does. And I don't want your money."

She laughs, throwing back her head.

"And I'll quit now to prove it to you, if that's what it will take."

She studies me, her expression hard.

"Where's this coming from? Your mom?"

She doesn't answer. I sigh. "She and Marty are working together to manipulate you," I tell her. "They want us to break up because they need you pliable and doing their bidding—you're their cash cow. You stood up to them and they don't like it." I reach for her. "Come on, Luna. They're using you."

Luna takes a step away from me. "And how are you any different?" she spits, throwing something at me. I look down at photographs scattered at my feet, then bend down to pick them up. They're five-by-seven prints of Luna and me at the christening, including one outside the church of us facing each other, Luna's arms around my neck and mine around Luna's waist, and we're staring at each other like two people so in love they aren't aware of anything else going on around them.

I shake my head. "What are these?" I ask.

"You tell me!" Luna shouts. "How much did you get for them? Enough to pay off your debt?"

"I've never seen them before."

"Oh really?" she laughs angrily. "Your sister took them. And *you* tried to sell them to the *National Enquirer*."

"What?" I say, looking up in bewilderment.

"I saw the emails."

"What emails?" I ask. What the hell is she talking about?

Luna's bottom lip wobbles. "You lied to me. You said you saw the real me, but the whole time you were only with me because you wanted something from me. You told me you were always honest. What a joke! You're worse than the others. At least when they sold me out, they weren't sleeping with me too."

My mouth drops open. I have no idea what emails she's talking about. I look back at the photographs like they might have an explanation. Did Kate really take these? I specifically asked her not to take any photos, and I didn't see her taking any. But what emails is Luna talking about?

"Luna," I shout, taking a step toward her. "I don't know what is going on, but it wasn't me. I swear to God!" I can feel anger rising up in me like a red wave, almost blinding me. "Why the hell would you believe them over me?!"

She takes a step back, away from me, as though she's afraid of me, and I freeze in my tracks, realizing that I'm shouting. My fists are coiled, and the anger is coming off me like steam vaporizing off a hot engine.

She lets out another sob, turns on her heel, and runs out the door.

I stand there, dazed, for several seconds before I drop the photographs and run after her, but by the time I get outside, she's vanished. I hurry to the back door of the house, but as I open it, I hear the sound of the Porsche's engine purring. Damn. I race around to the front of the house and see the yellow car already flying down the drive.

Shit. I can't believe I blew up at her like that. I hold my head in my hands, feeling at a total loss for how to fix this.

LUNA

azed, I sit in front of the mirror as the makeup artist puts on my mask. I zone out, my mind on Will and the photographs. How could he do that to me? And then lie to my face about it. My mom showed me the emails he sent to various lower-level tabloids, trying to sell the photos as an exclusive along with lurid details of our relationship; *Luna gets over Jamie by getting under her bodyguard*. It was his name, his email address.

I trusted him. I believed him. I told him I loved him. I'm such a fool. There was a reason he never said it back to me! Because he didn't love me. He was pretending, just like my mom said. Of course he was.

My eyes look red, but I've stopped crying. Instead, a slowly creeping numbness is overtaking me. That could be the result of the two anxiety pills I took an hour ago. I couldn't handle the ants burrowing under my skin. I didn't want to feel the discomfort writhing inside my gut, and I wanted to drown out the voice in my head, laughing at me for trusting Will, for believing anyone could actually like me for real. All the thoughts and bad feelings are locked on the other side of a thick metal door now. I can hear the thuds and the scrapes, but they're muted, and if I try really hard, I can ignore them entirely.

"Are you almost ready?" a woman with an iPad and a walkie-talkie asks a girl opposite me, with dark hair flowing down her back and a bright smile on her face. It takes me longer than it should to realize it's me staring at my reflection and that the woman is talking to me.

"Yes," I say.

The makeup artist finishes applying concealer around my eyes and steps back to admire her handiwork. She makes me think of Natalie. Was Will lying to me about her, too? Was he dating her behind my back? I know she liked him and gave him her number. He said he never called her, but what if that was a lie too?

I frown. I'm being paranoid. But still, I can't quiet the nagging voice in my head telling me that Will was cheating on me. Jamie did, so why wouldn't Will?

"Okay, you're on in two minutes," the woman with the walkie-talkie says to me, "and these arrived for you too." She sets down a dozen bloodred roses in front of me. They're in a vase and tied with a black ribbon. I bet they're from Jamie. He's texted me regularly since I broke up with him and I've ignored him, until now.

I take the card that's propped among the petals and open it. In giant red letters someone has scrawled *I'M WATCHING YOU. GET READY TO SUFFER BEFORE YOU DIE.*

The words jumble in front of me. I drop the card to the ground like it's coated in radioactive powder.

"Ready?"

It's the woman with the walkie-talkie.

"Who sent these?" I ask, gesturing at the flowers, my voice shaking.

She shrugs. "Some guy delivered them to the stage door."

"What did he look like?" I can't breathe. My head is full of pins and needles, and it feels as if the room is shrinking in on me.

"He was wearing a black hat," she says.

It's him. It's the person who's stalking me. My hands begin to tremble.

"I didn't get a look at his face," she adds, before putting her hand on my elbow. "We need to go." She pulls me toward the stage, and I let her, too shaken to say anything, panic scratching inside my chest like a sack of rats about to be drowned. My brain screams at me to say something, to run, to escape, but my fight-or-flight response is dead. I'm frozen instead, paralyzed by fear.

"I need . . . I need someone . . . help," I stammer to the woman, but she is wearing an earpiece and not listening to me, and then she's busy talking into the walkie-talkie. I try to get her attention, but she's harried and I'm not making any sense. Where's Marty? He was here two minutes ago. He said he'd be right back.

I hear my name being called and the audience start clapping, and then the woman pushes me in front of the lights and I find myself stumbling across the stage toward the presenter. I squint into the house lights, a deer in headlights. I can't make anything out beyond a sea of black silhouettes. He's out there. He's watching me.

I can't even smile or wave.

I half collapse into the seat opposite the presenter, Ally Friedman, a woman with short cropped brown hair and a wicked grin. She's a comedian and a well-known late-night host. Marty said it was a huge coup to get on the show and was an opportunity not to be missed, but I really can't focus on anything other than the audience and the knowledge that among those five hundred pairs of eyes watching me, there's one person watching me who wants to kill me.

The interview passes in a blur. I think I mutter something about the tour and how much I'm looking forward to it, constantly taking my eyes off her to search the dark audience for movement, feeling my heart beating in my ears and my breathing starting to speed up.

"And what about Jamie?" Ally asks, leaning across the desk and whispering, even though we're live in front of a studio audience and millions of people are watching on TV and can hear her. "Is he your boyfriend or not? Just between us," she quips. "No one else needs to know."

I laugh nervously and glance toward the audience. The lights are blinding and hot. Sweat trickles down my back.

Ally leans back in her seat. "Because a little birdie told me you two were back together!"

I turn to her, not sure if I've heard correctly. Before I can reply, though, the audience suddenly roars with applause. I turn in my chair to see Jamie walking across the stage. He's grinning like a Cheshire cat. What's he doing here? I'm so stunned I almost fall off my seat. When he reaches me, he puts his arm around me and kisses me full on the lips. "Just go along with it," he murmurs, his lips sticky on mine.

I am completely paralyzed. I can't speak or move. I can only grin like a total idiot. My heart is beating faster than a hummingbird's wings. My body is drenched in sweat. The audience is a dark menacing presence beyond the blaze of lights.

I know I can't get up and walk off on live TV, and I'm not even sure my legs would obey me, so I stay sitting for the next few minutes as Jamie keeps talking, and I keep smiling and even let him take my hand and wave to the audience. I'm too numb and in too much shock and too terrified to do anything else.

"These guys love you!" Ally laughs. "The whole world just loves you."

WILL

As soon as I see Luna walk onstage, a sinking sensation washes over me. It's not that she doesn't look amazing—she does. It's that she looks and is behaving just like the Luna she was before. The mask is back on, and she's back to playing the role her mother and Marty created for her.

Maybe no one else notices, but I do. The smile is fake, and I know because I've seen her real smile. She seems muted somehow too, less alive, even with the glitter of all that makeup to disguise it. She's super distracted, her gaze wandering constantly to the audience, and she's barely able to string a sentence together. I wonder if she's taken some pills, and it makes me both sad and mad. Why did she have to listen to her mother and Marty? Why didn't she believe me or trust me?

I tune back in to the TV. Luna's smile has frozen onto her face. She is turning in her chair. The audience is clapping. And then someone is walking across the stage. It's Jamie. I watch, stunned, as he bends and kisses her on the lips, then takes her hand. She lets him. Why is she letting him? I can't hear what's being said as the audience is going wild, clapping and cheering.

My heart pulses in my throat. I think I'm going to be sick as I watch them on-screen together. It's as if none of the last few weeks happened, as if I dreamed it all. Luna and Jamie are back together; that seems to be the suggestion. But how? She was here not three hours ago, with me. Jamie was out of the picture. What's he doing with her now on national television? Why is he holding her hand? And why is Luna smiling like that and looking at him so adoringly? It must have been orchestrated by Marty and her mom.

I leap to my feet and press the off button on the TV. I can't stand to watch any longer. The room feels suddenly too small, like a cage. I have to get out of here, as far away as possible, in fact. I march into the bedroom and grab my bag and start stuffing all my things into it. My vision is a blur, my heart hammering so loudly in my ears that I almost don't hear the phone ringing. It's Kate, calling me back after I left several irate messages.

"Goddamn, Kate, what the hell?" I say, pressing it to my ear.

"What?!" she answers.

"The photographs."

"What photographs?" she says, her voice rising in response to my angry tone.

"The photos you took of Luna and me at the christening. You promised you wouldn't."

"I'm sorry," Kate stutters. "You looked so great together. I figured it would be okay and that maybe you'd like a photo of the two of you."

I throw back my head and run a hand over my beard. I can't believe it's true. "Did you send them to anyone? Or show them to anyone?" I ask. "Did you try to sell them?"

"No!" she says. "I only sent them to you. Didn't you get the email?"

"No. I don't check my email that often. You know that."

"I sent them a while ago," she says, her voice plaintive.

"You only sent them to me? No one else?"

"Yes! I swear! Why? What's happened?"

"Luna thinks I tried to sell them to the tabloids."

"Why would she think that?" Kate asks.

"I don't know," I say. "I can't figure it out."

"Did someone hack into your email?" she asks.

I go still, my mind zeroing in on a memory of Luna's mother when I interviewed for the job. She knew everything about me. She even admitted she'd done a background check. Could she have somehow gotten access to my phone or my email as part of that? But then what? Would she set me up like that, lie to her own daughter to get me out of the way? The answer is obvious. Yes, she totally would. Anything to protect the brand. She and Marty want Luna to be with Jamie because it helps sell more records. And if not Jamie, then they certainly don't want her dating someone who won't help her steal headlines.

A minute later I've hung up on Kate and am walking into the house, past Carla in the kitchen, who is serving up a bowl of ice cream to Matias. They both say something to me, but I can't hear them. I march into the living room, where I find Luna's mom sitting on the sofa, reading a magazine. "You set me up," I say.

She looks up and a flash of guilt crosses her face before she brushes it aside and stands up to face me. She lifts her chin in a defiant gesture and shrugs. "So what if I did?"

"You got someone to hack my email," I say.

She doesn't deny it.

"You saw the photos Kate sent me," I say.

She still says nothing.

"What did you do?" I press. "Write those emails to the tabloids yourself and send them, pretending to be me?"

"You need to leave," she says, walking toward me. "You're fired."

"You can't stop me from telling Luna what you did," I say.

"Oh, yes I can," she answers. "I've already filed a restraining order against you."

"What?" I say.

"You're not allowed within five hundred feet of her or to have any contact with her whatsoever." She stands in front of me with her hands on her hips.

"You can't do that," I say, totally blindsided.

"I already have. It's in both of your best interests that you leave Luna alone."

I scoff loudly. "Oh, come on, you don't care about her best interests at all."

"You need to leave or I'm calling the police."

"I haven't done anything!" I say, my anger finally bursting out of me. "You're the one who hacked my emails."

"Prove it," she says with a sly smile.

"What kind of a mother are you?" I ask her, shaking my head in bewilderment.

"I'm protecting my daughter," she says boldly.

"No, you're not," I argue. "You're protecting yourself and your life and your investment. You hate it that she was starting to push back and think for herself. You're terrified that she might stop living for you and start living for herself. If you were really interested in protecting her, you wouldn't be doing this, because

I'm your best bet. I'm the only person who does genuinely care about her and her happiness."

She purses her lips but doesn't disagree, except to say, "Oh, really? You aren't just after her money and fame like all the others?"

I literally take a step backward as if she's punched me. "Are you kidding me? You're talking about yourself. I don't care about any of that."

She looks momentarily abashed before she lifts her chin again defiantly. "Are you going to tell me that you love her?" she scoffs.

I open my mouth to say yes, but nothing comes out.

"No. Exactly," her mother says triumphantly.

"Have you even hired anyone to replace me?" I ask, frustrated. "Who's with her right now? There's someone out there making threats on your daughter's life, and you're more worried about her career."

"Jamie and Marty are with her," she snaps. "And I have a security company sending someone. Luna will be fine."

"She won't be fine." My fists are two tight balls. I want to kick my foot through the coffee table, but I keep hold of my temper. She must see that I'm on the verge of an explosion, all my pent-up rage at her just beneath the surface, because she pulls out her phone and starts to dial 911.

"It's all right," I say, making for the door. "I'm leaving."

"Good," she says, following me. "And don't ever try to contact my daughter again."

I nod and she smiles victoriously, seeing that she's won. I can't stand here another second, or I might do something I regret, so I pull open the door. As I step out of the house, I hear Matias call my name. "Will!"

I turn and see him running toward me. "Where are you going?"

"I have to leave," I tell him.

His face crumples. He doesn't understand. "Why? What about soccer?"

I shake my head. "I'm sorry," I tell him, and turn to go.

"No!" he shouts to my departing back.

"Bye, Matias," I say, hurrying down the steps as I hear him start to yell.

LUNA

W hat's going on?" I ask Jamie once we're backstage. "What are you doing here? What was that?"

Jamie puts his arm around me. "Surprise," he says. "I thought you'd be happy to see me."

"No," I stammer, the words thick on my tongue. "Get off me." I look around, feeling dizzy from all the lights. I can't think straight. It's too hot. I can't breathe. I'm stuck in a kaleidoscope that's spinning wildly.

"Luna?" Jamie asks. "What's wrong?"

I try to bat him away, but I can't. The room spins faster and faster. I stumble away from Jamie and toward an exit sign glowing green in the distance, but I trip over a cable and then slam into a woman carrying something. She drops it and swears and I hear my name being shouted, but I can't breathe. My vision is darkening and noise fills my ears, competing with the angry drum of my pulse. I need air. I need Will.

I'm suddenly outside. It's blazing hot and there's no shade. I stumble along, feeling as if I'm in a tunnel underwater, trying to fight my way to the surface, to oxygen.

I collapse to the ground, my head slamming into concrete with a jolt. The sky is pressing down and trying to swallow me. I want Will, but then I remember that he isn't coming to save me. I trusted him and he betrayed me, just like everybody else.

You're an idiot. You're stupid. You're a fool. The laughter in my head becomes a shriek that turns into a scream. *He was using you! He was laughing at you. Everything he ever told you was a lie.*

"Luna?" It's Marty. His face swims in front of me. His voice sounds like it's coming from inside a tin can. "Come on, let's get you up."

I try to push him away, make myself heavy as a boulder, but he lifts me easily. Jamie's there too. I can hear him saying my name, touching me. I try to kick him and gratifyingly hear him say "Ouch."

Somehow they get me into a car, and I'm aware of Jamie beside me.

"What's happening?"

"Wind down the windows," Marty says. "Get her some air."

When I wake up, I'm in my bed, and my mom, Marty, and Jamie are sitting around me like I'm a patient in the ICU. I feel groggy and weak, like I'm made of tissue paper and I might tear if I move too fast.

"Luna," my mom says when I blink open my eyes. She takes my hand. "You had a panic attack. You're home now. You're okay."

I frown. What? Then it all comes back to me. Will and the photographs. Jamie and the interview. The lights and the roses and the man in the cap, and the feeling that I was drowning. I struggle to sit up in bed, but I feel too weak.

"The doctor came and gave you something to help you relax,"

my mom tells me. "Some Valium to calm you down."

I take that in. How long have I been asleep? It's daylight outside. Is it tomorrow? How long have I been here?

Jamie takes my other hand. "I was really worried about you, babe."

I stare at him, then at Marty and my mother. All of them with looks of concern on their faces, but how many are genuine? Are they concerned for me or for the fact their precious money-maker might stop producing money for them?

"Leave me alone, all of you," I shout, yanking my hands from theirs and curling up on my side, with my back to them.

"Luna," my mother says, shocked.

I pull the covers over my head before drifting off, and when I wake again, it's early evening, judging by the pink light flooding the room. I feel less groggy, but a weight of sadness presses down on me so I can't move my limbs, and the thought of crawling out of bed is overwhelming. I don't want to think about anything, least of all Will and how he betrayed me, because when I do, it's like a fishhook being torn through my heart, then ripping through my flesh. All those moments we shared, all the times we slept together . . .

I told him I loved him. . . .

I'm such a fool.

There's a knock on my door.

I pull the covers back an inch to find Matias standing there. He comes racing over and jumps on the bed. "Hey, Matias."

"Are you okay?" he asks.

I nod. "Sure," I lie.

"Why did Will leave?" he asks.

A heaviness pushes against my chest. His name lands like a blow. "He . . . had to," I say, barely able to get the words out.

"Because Mom made him," Matias sniffs.

I turn my head toward Matias. "Mom made him?" I repeat. Sometimes Matias gets confused or doesn't explain himself clearly.

"But I don't know why," he says with a shrug. "She was shouting at him. And Will was angry and then he left and he didn't play soccer with me."

I struggle to sitting. "What?" I ask. "Say that again. Mom and Will had a fight?"

He nods. "Mom made him go. She said she'd arrest him and send him to jail if he didn't." He bites his lip, making a guilty face. "I was listening in the hallway."

I give him a reassuring smile, so he knows I'm not mad at him for spying. What he's saying doesn't surprise me. Mom must have been furious at Will for selling me out with the photographs.

"I wish Will didn't go," Matias says with a sigh. "I liked him."

I clench my teeth. I liked him too. But now . . .

My head throbs. I just want to sleep. I search around for the TV remote so that I can give it to Matias, hoping cartoons will distract him from talking any more about Will.

I find it and switch the TV on for him, before lying down and reaching for a pillow to throw over my head. I could sleep for a year.

"What's hacking?" I hear Matias ask.

I open one eye.

"What do you mean?" I mumble.

"When I heard them talking, Will said that Mom had hacked him. What does it mean?"

I sit back up and turn the TV off.

"What?" I ask.

WILL

How are you doing?" Kit asks.

I shrug. "Surviving," I answer. This is just about true. I'm crushed. It's as if I'm pinned beneath rubble after an earthquake has destroyed my world. But my most pressing issue is that I need a job. I still have a large amount of debt hanging over me.

"Listen," Kit says, "have you figured out yet what you want to do?"

I shake my head. Robert's letting me stay in the condo because I think they figured I needed some space, but I can't stay forever, not without paying rent.

"When I got out of the Marines, I knew what I wanted. To open this place," Kit says, gesturing around at the restaurant. "Do you know what you want?"

My first instinct is to say Luna. But she's chosen to believe her mother and has now gone back to Jamie, so I've tuned out everything about her. I've deleted my email account and changed my phone number, too, in case her mother is still hacking me. Even if I could contact her, I'd run the risk of being arrested for breaching the bullshit restraining order, and that could get me a criminal record, something that would make it even harder to get a job.

Although I'm tempted to search for news about her on the internet, knowing that all I'll see are pictures of her and Jamie makes it a whole lot easier to stay off the web. I can't seem to ignore the nagging worry I have, though, despite trying to. What if something goes down and I'm not there to protect her? What if her new bodyguard isn't any good? But if I dwell on all these thoughts, I spiral down into such a pit of anger and despair that I've had to learn not to. The only way through is to forget about her and to banish every single thought about her.

"Here."

I look down. Kit's holding out an envelope. I take it and look inside. "What's this?" I ask, staring at the thick wedge of notes inside.

"It's a loan. But it's interest-free."

I shake my head again and push the envelope back at him. "I can't take that."

"Yes, you can," he says, insisting. "Jessa and I want you to have it. And you can't say no to me." He pushes the money toward me again.

I frown. "I don't need it. I'm working here."

Kit smirks. "And you don't want to be here." He puts his hand on my shoulder. "Look, bro, take the money, get a new car, go on a road trip. Buy yourself a new razor."

I try to ignore the comment about the razor, even though he's right. I really ought to shave sometime. My beard is so thick I'm starting to look like a hipster, the kind that wear lumberjack shirts and own cool coffee shops where people come and play board games.

"Go find some wayward kids to keep on the straight and narrow," Kit says with a knowing smile.

I glance up sharply. How does he know that's what I want to do?

"Luna told me," Kit says, seeing my expression. "When she was here for Lyra's christening. She said it was what you wanted to do with your life. She told me that hearing you talk about it made her want to do something that mattered as well."

I exhale, knocked a little sideways by this revelation.

"We've all got to have dreams, right?" Kit says, pushing the envelope into my hand. "And sometimes we also need to have friends to remind us about them."

LUNA

The vodka is in a water bottle, so no one can tell, not even my unspeaking Israeli prison guard who I know is informing on me to my mom. I untwist the lid, my vision blurred, and swig back a mouthful, swallowing two pills with it. I get the vodka from one of the dancers, who sneaks it to me in an Evian bottle at rehearsals. I've stopped using the breathing technique that Will taught me, because it reminds me of him, and thinking of him only makes me more depressed.

After I found out from Matias about how my mom hacked Will's email and lied to me that he'd tried to sell the photos, I tried to call him and emailed to explain and apologize, and he never replied. Not that I blame him. He was so angry when I accused him. And no doubt he saw me on TV with Jamie and made an assumption, like the rest of the world has—that we're back together.

But we're not. I haven't seen Jamie since I told him to get lost after the Ally Friedman show. Not that he's listening. He's like my mom in that regard. Nothing I want seems to matter.

He keeps texting me and sends me flowers every day, though I have no idea why he's so persistent when there are a million other girls out there with posters of him on their walls who'd happily throw themselves into his arms.

I frown at the bottle in my hand. It is half-empty already and my eyelids are drooping, my brain starting to crash like a computer going into shutdown mode. I should really be more careful with keeping track of how many pills I've taken, I suppose, and not mix them, but my anxiety is through the roof and my prescription meds aren't working as well as they used to, so I've taken to washing them down with vodka. Not only does that combination hold the terror at bay just long enough to get through two hours of performing, but they also help me stop thinking about Will all the time and about the fact that the man in the black cap is still out there.

I stare sullenly at my guitar. It sits in its stand, a glaring monument to my failure. I haven't picked it up since Will left. And I haven't been able to finish my album, not that there's any point now. I don't even think Marty ever listened to the songs I sent him, not that there's any point to that, either, because he quit after the TV interview, completely out of the blue and without any explanation, and I haven't seen him since.

My inner voice tells me that it's because he's found some younger, prettier, more talented musician to manage and can't be wasting his time on me anymore.

There's a knock on my bedroom door. I ignore it. Carla enters anyway, and I hastily shove the vodka bottle out of sight behind my pillow. She sits down on the edge of my bed and strokes my hair. "Are you hungry? Can I make you something?"

she asks. She takes care never to mention spicy eggs anymore. I shake my head, which feels leaden, and the vodka sloshes in my stomach and almost halfway up my throat.

"How about ice cream?"

I shake my head again, fighting back nausea. "I'm not hungry."

"You never eat these days," she says. "You're too thin."

"There's no such thing," I quip, quoting my mother.

"You never go out anymore either," she adds. "You're just stuck in the house all day every day. It's not good for you."

I never go out because I'm too afraid to. My mom employed this fifty-year-old Israeli bodyguard who has the personality of a sledgehammer and the body of one too, but I still don't feel safe out in public. And I also don't trust him not to either report back on me to my mom or sell me out to the press. I shrug at Carla.

"You're so unhappy," Carla says. "It breaks my heart."

I slump against her shoulder, so glad I have her in my life and ashamed at how much I took her for granted until recently, how I treated her. Yet she's become my only ally.

"You shouldn't let your mother control you so much," she says.

I pull away. "It's not that easy," I explain, hoping she can't hear I'm slurring my words. "I'm not you. I can't just quit. Everyone's relying on me."

She stares at me hard. "I can't quit either," she says, annoyed. "You think I could leave you and Matias?"

I frown, not understanding, my head feeling too fuzzy to process her words.

"You're the only reason I stay," she says. "It's not for the paycheck."

My heart cracks and I almost burst out sobbing. I had no idea she thought of me that way.

"I don't know what to do," I admit to her, and now the sob does come bursting out, like an animal that's been caged too long. Carla puts her arm around me and pulls me in close against her soft chest. At once I feel relief, like she's a rock at sea that I can cling to, giving me time to catch my breath.

"You know what you need to do," Carla says, soothing my hair out of my face. "Follow your heart."

My heart wants Will, but it's too late for that.

"Listen," she says, turning me around to face her on the bed. "I know you miss Will, and maybe he is gone forever." She sighs sadly. "That's the way sometimes."

My stomach clenches at the thought of him being gone.

"People come into your life for a reason," she continues. "And maybe the reason Will came into yours was to show you the way."

Her words slip through the fogginess in my brain and resonate somewhere deep in my memory. I dredge up the words that Will once said to me. "To be the lighthouse," I murmur.

"Yes. A lighthouse." Carla nods, smiling. "He showed you what was possible. Showed you the direction you needed to head in."

I nod too. He did.

"And he gave you the courage to believe in yourself too, no?"

I nod again, slightly less happily, thinking of the songs I wrote while I was with him and the dreams I started to imagine for myself. All of them have drifted away like dreams do when you wake up.

"Maybe you need to swim to shore by yourself," Carla continues. "Maybe that's the lesson in this. He was never meant to save you. Because you have to learn to save yourself."

As soon as she says it, I feel a wave of light wash away the shadows in my mind, leaving startling clarity behind. She's right, even though it's painful to accept it. Will was never meant to pull me to the shore. He was never meant to save me. He was only ever meant to help light the way. I've spent my entire life letting other people control me and the direction I swim in. I've never had any sort of freedom, but I've constantly blamed everyone else, instead of myself.

I don't know, though, if I have the strength to succeed in fighting my way to shore. It feels like such a long way and against such strong currents, but maybe I could try.

"But what if it goes wrong?" I ask, turning to Carla. "What about Matias?"

"He's not your responsibility," Carla says gently. "You're not his mother. And he will be fine. You have enough money to never have to work again and to take care of Matias."

"I do?" I ask in surprise. How does she know that?

She raises a wry eyebrow at me. "You should be managing your own finances—then you would know all this. But I hear things. I see things. You'd be surprised what people say when they think no one is listening."

I frown. It all feels overwhelming again. Carla sees the shadows of doubt creeping in. She pats my arm. "I'll be there cheering you on every step of the way."

I nod at her, feeling the shadows slink back, and then I turn my face to the window, to the sunlight pouring in. I need to start swimming.

"And no more of this," Carla says disapprovingly, pulling the water bottle out from behind my pillow. "You need to start eating properly and taking care of yourself."

I feel like a scolded child. But I don't mind, not one bit. I lean into her cushiony side. "Can I have some eggs?" I ask her.

TWO MONTHS LATER

WILL

When I walk out of my cabin, all I can see is the glitter of the lake and the rich green of the forest pressing all the way down to the shore. The sun's fierce and I turn my face to it, closing my eyes, hoping for once it will chase away the shadows lingering over me, but they're still there. It's been months of not seeing her, not hearing her voice, not even looking her up online, forbidding myself to, and still I can't shake her off me. She's a virus I can't clear out of my blood. And I hate it.

That's not to say I haven't found peace of some description. As I step off the deck of my wooden house and listen to the wind whistling through the trees and the chirping of the birds, I can't help but smile. For the first time in my life, I feel like I'm in a place I want to be. Surrounded by nature, fully immersed in it, living off the grid and an hour from the nearest town, I know I'm home. And I'm doing a job I was made for.

In the distance I can hear the kids, starting to wake up, their calls and yells and laughter filling me with a sense of satisfaction and purpose I've never had until now. Not only did Kit set me up with the loan, which I'm working on paying off, but Walker had a buddy who runs a camp in the High Sierras, north of Lake Tahoe. In summer they mainly take kids from all over, but for the rest of the year they run programs in partnership with social services and the juvenile justice system. They're wilderness adventure therapy programs, and it's working with those kids that I'm finding I can really make a difference. I'm actually helping transform lives.

We currently have our last group staying with us before the official camp program begins. Thirty kids, all teenagers in juvenile detention across the state, most who grew up in the foster care system, arrived a week ago with a vast amount of attitude and anger issues. But within the space of six days, where we've pushed them to their limits physically, we've seen a huge shift in their behavior. A job I used to dream about is actually my dream job. I get these kids. I get their pain and I get their anger. I get that for most of them, not having a father figure to look up to has left them struggling to know who they are or how to figure life out. I also get that having people believing in them and showing them they can master things, like Joe did for me, is a powerful tool in raising their self-esteem and their ideas of what they can achieve in life.

It might not be the kind of work that requires a PhD or some wild talent like Luna's, but it feels like it's something I can do well. I'm already signed up to start a learning degree in social work in the fall. Eventually I hope to specialize in supporting children in the foster and juvenile system. But honestly, I can't see myself ever wanting to leave this place. The fact it's miles from anywhere and has no cell phone service or internet connectivity makes it even better.

Every weekend I drive into the nearest town and spend an hour or two in a coffee shop catching up on calls to friends and family, and I've found that living away from all the noise makes me happy. I don't know how I put up with LA for so long, other than the fact that Luna was there. But I try not to think of that, or of her and what she's doing. It hurts too much. I know she's back with Jamie because Kate blurted it out to me. The knowledge weighs on me. I wonder all the time if when she was with me, she always intended to get back with him.

Ultimately, I've come to accept that we're two very different people, on very different paths. Our lives crossed briefly, and I'll never regret falling in love with her. I'll only ever regret not telling her.

I stop on the shore of the lake. The water's like ice. Every morning I take a swim to wake myself up and to wash away whatever lingering dreams of Luna are hanging around. I dive in and the water slaps the air out of me. I break the surface, gasping, letting out a holler that echoes off the ribbon of trees surrounding the lake. When I swim back to shore, I find someone waiting for me.

"What are you doing here?" I ask as I pull myself up onto the dock.

Marty scowls, looking around at the forest and the lake with distaste. "Could say the same. Took me a bloody age to hunt you down."

I grab a towel from the rail and wrap it around my waist.

"That looks bloody freezing," Marty says, nodding at the water.

"You should try it sometime," I say, my heart hammering wildly, not from the shock of the cold but from the sight of Marty after so long. What's he doing here, looking so out of place in his tight trousers, gold jewelry, and Rolex watch?

"Not bloody likely," he grunts.

"What are you doing here?" I ask.

"Luna," he says, and my heart stops.

"What's happened?"

LUNA

Turns out swimming to shore is a lot harder when you're in shark-infested waters. My mom is Jaws. She's fighting like a great white scenting blood in the water to stop me from emancipating myself. Even though I'm nineteen and technically an adult, my entire life is wrapped up in a trust that she controls; all my finances, the corporation that controls the rights to all my music, is in my mom's name and control, and furthermore, since I have a diagnosis of anxiety, she's using that to try to enforce a conservatorship, telling the court I'm not mentally capable of making decisions about my life.

I have, however, found a lawyer to fight her so I can win my freedom and control of my assets and finances. I know my mom is hurt and angry. She honestly thinks she is doing the right thing to protect me, that left to my own devices, I might go off the rails. Her version of that, though, is that I quit the career she's carefully honed for me and take a riskier, less financially solid path.

I've been on tour for a month around the US, so I haven't had a chance to push forward with anything and am too tired most days to think about the next steps, but for now I'm happy that I'm finally swimming at least, not drowning, and the shore is getting closer. Once I'm done, in a few weeks' time, I'm planning on moving out of LA and finishing work on my next album. I want to take some time for myself, get my head straight, focus on self-care and doing more therapy. I've even started thinking about new managers, but I'm not in a hurry to sign with anyone, not given my experience with Marty.

My anxiety hasn't magically gone away. I'm just learning to manage it in healthier ways that don't involve unhealthy habits. The threats from the man in the black cap haven't materialized, which helps, as does stepping back from social media. I leave that to a new social media manager to handle.

Beyond that, I'm also meditating. I wish I could tell Will. I'm finding it so useful for helping reduce the anxiety attacks I was experiencing. I haven't had an attack since the one after the Ally Friedman show.

I'm playing LA tonight. It's my last show. Matias and Carla are coming, and I can't wait to see them. Carla doesn't know it, but I've also invited Francisco, the gardener. If I leave it to the two of them, I'm guessing neither will make a move, so I'm nudging them in the right direction. I've reserved them a box, and they'll get the full VIP experience.

All in all, though, I feel good. Better than I have since the breakup with Will, but still not as happy as I was when I was with him. I doubt I'll ever feel that happy again. That was once-in-a-lifetime happiness. But as soon as I think of him, I push the thought away. I can't go there. Not when I have to perform tonight. It takes a lot to get through these shows, both mentally and physically, and I need to stay focused. I can't allow that negative voice to gain a foothold.

I get up from where I'm sitting cross-legged on the floor of my dressing room, having been meditating, and look in the mirror. I'm dressed for the show, covered in glittering makeup, my hair slick and shiny in a ponytail down my back. I smile and for the first time in forever I recognize the girl in the mirror. It feels as if the smile is real, and that it isn't for anyone else but me. It's a smile that says: You're doing it. You're surviving. You are worthy of love and of happiness.

There's a knock on my dressing room door and I turn around. It's Marcello. My bodyguard is posted outside the door, and I nod at him that it's okay to let him in.

"These came for you," Marcello says. He pulls a large bouquet of dark crimson-colored roses from behind his back. They're from Jamie. He still hasn't let up with sending me flowers, even though I never respond or even let him know I've received them. I'm hoping he'll get the message, and I'm confused as to why he hasn't. I read the note with disinterest. *Good luck tonight, babe. Can't wait to see you perform, Love, Jamie xx*

I read it again. What? He's coming tonight? I didn't know that. When will he get the message we're over? I scrunch up the note. I'll have someone deliver the flowers to the nearest hospital to cheer up the nurses. It's what I always do with the flowers he sends.

"What's this? Did someone send you cookies?" Marcello asks as he sets the bouquet down on my dressing table.

I look over and see that a box has appeared there: a cake box, wrapped in a pink satin ribbon. Trembling, I reach for the ribbon, tugging on the end. It slips undone easily, and then I lift the lid off the box.

Marcello lets out a gasp. "Oh my God!" he says, his hand flying to his mouth. The stench billows up and smacks me in the nostrils. Vomit lurches up my throat.

A dead rat lies in the box. I reach for the note attached to the ribbon. In large red letters that look like they've been scrawled in blood, it says THIS IS YOUR LAST DAY ON EARTH. SAY GOODBYE, BITCH.

WILL

I stand opposite Marty on the jetty, dripping wet. "What do you mean she needs me?"

"She needs you. Let's go." He starts to march away.

"What's happened? Has there been another threat?" I ask.

Marty shouts over his shoulder, "We need to go. I'll explain on the way."

I stare at his retreating back. Why isn't he telling me? She must be in danger. Why else would he come get me like this? My feet are itching to run after him, but my stubbornness roots me to the ground. That and the knowledge she's with Jamie.

Besides, I'm working. And she has security. They can handle whatever threat might have come up. I've also got a restraining order and can't go near her, or did Marty forget that fact?

Marty glances over his shoulder and sees me standing there, not moving. "Are you coming or not? Plane's waiting."

He came in a private jet? What the hell? A sense of foreboding grabs hold of me. She must be in danger for him to come here like this. I battle warring instincts. I swore I'd never let anyone hurt her. Even after everything that's gone on, I can't let that promise go. I've already failed once with my family. I can't break a second promise to someone I love. But at the same time, what would I be running into?

"What's happened?" I ask again.

Marty throws up his hands. "She's not with Jamie, if that's what you're worried about."

His admission shocks me because it wasn't even what I was asking.

"She never got back with him," Marty goes on. "That whole stunt on the Ally Friedman show, that was just a PR move. I'm sorry. I should never have tried to break you two up. You were good for her."

I blink in astonishment. "They aren't together?"

He shakes his head. "No. So, will you come now?"

Marty's private plane is waiting at an airfield in Tahoe to fly us back to LA. I tell my boss that it's an emergency, and he kindly lets me take a leave of absence for twenty-four hours. I'm still fighting some warring instincts. This could go horribly wrong if her mother sees me and calls the cops, but that concern falls away.

"Are you ever going to tell me what's going on?" I ask Marty for the twentieth time as I strap into my seat and glance around nervously at the white leather interior of what is a very small plane.

Marty looks out the window as we take off and exhales loudly. "It turns out maybe I was wrong," he says once we're off the ground and juddering into the air. "I had what might be called a come-to-Jesus moment."

I know I must look confused as hell because he continues. "I saw the damage that was being done to Luna." He squirms in his seat, uncomfortable at the admission. "I think, until then, I hadn't wanted to face facts, because . . . you know . . ."

"All the money you were making off her?" I suggest.

He nods, grimacing a little in shame. "Yeah. But after the Ally Friedman show, when she collapsed—"

"She collapsed?" I interrupt.

"Yeah," he admits a little sheepishly. "She had a huge anxiety attack, couldn't breathe. I honestly thought she was having a heart attack."

I feel my hands crunching into fists and have to restrain myself from getting up and pummeling him backward into his seat.

"What happened?" I ask through gritted teeth.

Marty winces. "I took her home, called a doctor. She was fine. Don't worry."

"Fine?" I run a hand through my hair. "You don't have any idea, do you, of what you put her through? You and her mom both. You're a piece of shit, Marty."

"Yeah," he acknowledges with a nod. "Worse than that. And that's why I quit. I tried talking to her mother afterward, telling her that enough was enough and we needed to rethink the strategy for managing Luna, but she wasn't having it. She told me I could either get with the program or take a hike, so I quit."

"You had a crisis of conscience," I sneer, shaking my head in disbelief, "so you quit and abandoned her to her mother. That's a great move. Well done."

Marty hangs his head in shame. "I know," he says. "Which is why I have spent so much time trying to find you. Your family wouldn't speak to me or tell me where you were. I had to hire a private investigator to track you down."

Once again, I'm surprised. I gave my family orders not to talk to anyone who came around asking questions about me and Luna.

"Why were you trying to find me?" I ask. "What do you think I can do? Her mom put a restraining order on me. She set me up, hacked my emails. Made Luna think I'd sold her out. If I go near her, I'll be arrested."

His eyes widen with shock. "I didn't know about the restraining order. I knew she hacked your emails—"

"Who told you about that?" I ask, stunned he knows about it.

"Carla."

"How does she know?" I ask, bewildered.

"Matias overheard you arguing with her mom before you left. He told Luna about it."

I sink back in my seat and try to process that. Luna knows that her mother set me up? That changes things, though I'm not entirely sure how. If she knew the truth, then why didn't she reach out to me? Before the question fully forms in my mind, realization hits me like a bucket of ice water. Shit. I changed my email and my phone number. Maybe she has been trying and she thinks I've been ignoring her. I can only imagine how that's made her feel.

I open my eyes wider and look at Marty. "I still don't know why I'm here," I say angrily. "Has she had more threats? Have they found the guy? Is she in danger?"

"No," admits Marty, wincing again. "I mean, I wouldn't actually know because, like I said, I quit."

Shit. He made up the urgency. He deliberately made it sound like something had happened or was about to, and I was needed, and he did it because he knew it would be the only safe way to make sure I got on this damn plane. And I fell for it like a total idiot. I was so desperate to run back to her, to act like some stupid hero, and I've been made a fool of. Luna isn't in danger. She doesn't need me. She hasn't asked for me.

"Once again," I ask even more angrily, "what the hell am I doing here, then?"

Marty stands up, his head almost brushing the top of the plane. "If Luna's still in the same boat as she was a month ago, then she needs help. The last time she was in a dark place, she spiraled out of control; started abusing her prescription pills, mixing them with booze. I'm scared for her, honestly. What with being on tour—that's what happened last time. The pressure got to her. And I'm guessing because you're here on this plane with me, that you still care about her. . . ." He looks at me hopefully.

He isn't wrong. Of course I still care about her. I've tried to move on, but this whole time away from her, she's been a near constant in my thoughts. I look at Marty, harder. I can see now what this is.

"Are you telling me this is some kind of rescue mission?" I ask.

His eyes light up. "Exactly, mate. Knew you'd get it, being an ex-soldier and all."

"Marine," I reply under my breath.

He makes a "whatever" face, then leans toward me. "It's a rescue mission. We're going into enemy territory and we're going to rescue the target—the hostage—and get her safely back home. That's with you."

I raise an eyebrow at Marty, whose gung-ho expression

makes me want to both laugh and roll my eyes. He's watched way too many movies.

He sees me hesitate. "Don't worry about the restraining order. If you're caught, we'll tell the judge all the lies Luna's mother told. I'll be your witness." He pauses. I'm not sure that would count for much, but it doesn't matter. I've already made up my mind.

"So, are you with me?" he asks, grinning.

I nod. "Yeah, I'm with you."

LUNA

The noise of the crowd is a deafening roar, so loud it's like being inside the barrel of a wave, but it still can't silence the screams in my head.

Twenty minutes ago I was feeling calm and confident, and now I'm falling apart. It shows me just how shaky my new sense of self was. I was a badly constructed Jenga tower, and someone has pulled a block from the very bottom and I'm collapsing in slow motion.

Adrenaline pounds furiously through my veins, making it hard to breathe or think straight. I take a swig from my water bottle, hoping it might drown the million ants that have started to burrow and scratch beneath my skin. I thought I had it under control, was managing to swim with my head above water, but just like that, I've been dragged under.

The idea of walking onstage in front of seventy thousand people is suddenly an impossibility. How can I—knowing someone out there wants to kill me?

How did they slip unnoticed into my dressing room? How did they get past my bodyguard? Everyone with backstage access is meant to have been security-checked. No strangers should be able to get back here, so whoever it is must work for me. But who do I know that could secretly hate me that much?

The roar in the distance grows louder, making me think of a hungry crowd baying for a gladiator's blood. I have to go out there. I don't have a choice. The clock is ticking.

I think of Will to help calm me and wonder where he is right now. If he's happy. Closing my eyes, I allow myself to picture him—focus on recalling every detail, pulling them out of my memory like treasures from a box. I see the soft curve of his lips and the rough scratch of his beard, how it felt when he kissed me. I remember the exact sensation of his hands gliding down my body, coming to rest on my hips, the way he'd tug me toward him. I can visualize the warmth in his smoky gray eyes as he looked at me, seeing all the way through the outer layer to the real me inside.

For a while we were free, on the run together, never glancing over our shoulders or looking back, but only focusing on the present and each other. The rest of the world could have gone to hell. It was just us. I smile as I recall those days of dizzy escape, but then the smile fades. I always knew deep down that they'd have to end. You can't be a fugitive from your life forever. One day you'll get caught and sent back to do your time. I just wish it hadn't happened so soon.

I wish we'd had longer.

Every breath is a ragged gasp. The air isn't making it into my lungs, and black spots swirl in front of my eyes. I stumble over to my bag and root through it in growing desperation, looking for my anxiety medication. After what feels like ages, I find it, popping the pills from their silver packet and dry-swallowing them.

They get stuck in my throat, so I search for a water bottle. I cross to the mini-fridge beneath the dresser that the stadium staff make sure is filled with cold drinks for me and any guests I might have.

Inside, I find a dozen miniature bottles of vodka, gin, and whiskey as well as beer and sodas and flavored water. I grab for the water but then hesitate, and instead reach for the liquor.

WILL

Marty tells me to duck down low as he drives into the stadium's VIP parking garage. He's waved through easily enough, and I glance at him in surprise. He clocks my look and shrugs. "Most of them still think I'm Luna's manager," he says. And he points to the security pass he has that gives him backstage entry. "And I know the stadium manager." So much for Luna's new security—the thought doesn't sit well with me at all.

He parks in the VIP area, which I take as a bold move, but hardly expect less from Marty. We get out of the car and stride toward a back entrance between trailers and two dozen or so backstage workers. All I can hear is the roaring of a crowd that's so loud it could be mistaken for thunder rumbling overhead. The ground shakes with it. It takes a few seconds before I realize everyone is chanting Luna's name. I stare up at the vast stadium ahead of us in awe.

I knew Luna was big-time huge, but the thought that she can fill a stadium this size is mind-blowing. It makes me see her in a whole new light, appreciate even more the pressure she is under. I can't imagine performing in front of a crowd as big as the one I can hear screaming her name. No wonder she has anxiety.

It also makes me realize just how hard it would have been for her to walk away. How do you walk away from this? Where do you go?

Now that we're actually here, I'm wondering what Marty and I are doing. Seeing Luna's face illuminated on the front of the stadium and hearing all these people chanting her name like she's a deity is a hard reality check.

"What are we doing here?" I find myself asking.

"We're going to find Luna," Marty says, striding toward the entrance.

I slow my pace until I come to a standstill. "I don't know about this," I admit, having second thoughts.

Marty turns and marches back over to me. "We didn't come this far for you to back out now."

"What if you're wrong and she doesn't need rescuing?" I ask.

Marty opens his mouth and then shuts it. "Well, you're here, so . . ."

Something catches my attention over his shoulder. "Black cap," I say, blinking in astonishment.

Marty turns to look.

I'd been scanning the faces of everyone around, something I always do, without even realizing it. "That guy," I say, nodding my head at a man in the distance. "Five ten, wearing the red plaid shirt and the black cap."

"He's a roadie," Marty says, clocking him. "They all wear caps."

"The guy Natalie said she saw hanging around the dressing table was wearing a black cap."

"And the man who delivered the note at the Ally Friedman studio was too," Marty adds, his voice rising.

The man is striding among a dozen trailers, and I sprint to catch up to him, grabbing him by the shoulder and hauling him around to face me.

He's about thirty, everyday-looking, nothing that would make him stand out in a crowd. He's startled, his eyes flaring with panic. "What?" he asks.

"Where's your security pass?" Marty demands.

The man pulls a laminated pass out of his pocket. Marty grabs it, then looks at me. "It's legit," he says to me, and I let the man go, disappointed.

He scowls at us both, mutters under his breath, and walks off. But something about the way he moves like a scuttling insect, his head lowered, and the nervous way he glances back at us, sets my inner alarm system off. I've seen men like that before, when I've been on guard duty at the base. We're taught to scan body language for cues, and his is screaming that he's up to no good. We know whoever's been threatening Luna is someone who has access to the backstage areas. And this guy has a security pass.

I start running after him again. He glances back, sees me coming, and runs between two huge trailers. I sprint after him, spotting him as he rounds a corner and races for the stadium's backstage entrance. A dozen roadies are milling around, and he disappears into their midst.

I burst through the crowd seconds after him, looking around desperately to spot him. I catch sight of his back, disappearing through the door, but before I can run after him, a stadium security guard catches my arm.

"Stop!" he yells. "You can't go in there, not without a pass."

LUNA

'm unscrewing the cap on the vodka bottle and am about to tip it down my throat when there's a knock on the door. I drop the bottle in fright and leap back as the door flies open. "Luna?"

It's Matias. The relief almost knocks me to my knees. Carla is behind him, and behind her is my bodyguard. Carla sees at once that I'm not okay and rushes over to me. "What's happened?" she asks.

"There was another one," I stammer.

She knows immediately what I mean, and worry floods her face. "Where was your bodyguard?" she asks, both annoyance and worry in her voice.

"We think someone slipped in while I was onstage doing the sound check. They must have a security pass, though, to be able to get back here," I say, starting to pace. I feel as if I'm trapped inside a giant anthill, being eaten alive by insects.

"Cartoons!" Matias yells, leaping for the TV remote, trying to turn it to the Cartoon Network.

"I can't go on," I murmur to Carla as she takes my hands and tries to ground me.

Carla looks me in the eyes. "Breathe," she says. Hysteria grips me. I can't breathe. I'm almost dizzy for lack of oxygen.

How can I walk out there?

Carla glances down and sees the vodka bottle on the floor. My face flushes. She looks up at me, but instead of consternation, I see only concern on her face. "You don't have to go out there," she tells me.

I shake my head emphatically. "I have to," I say.

"That's your mother's and Marty's voices. You don't have to do anything you don't want to."

I frown. Is that right? I can't not go out there, though. People have paid money to see me perform. I can't let them down. "What if he's out there?" I say in a voice that's barely a whisper. How will I manage to sing if I can't even talk?

"What if Will was here?" Carla asks.

I shake my head again, not wanting to imagine it, but she persists. "What would he say to you right now?"

I swallow the lump in my throat and find my voice. "He'd tell me I didn't have to go on."

Carla nods. "Exactly."

"But I have to," I sob as the din above our heads seems to amplify. "Listen to everyone! I have to go on."

"Okay," says Carla, looking me calmly in the eyes. "And if you told him that, what would he say?"

"He'd tell me to take a deep breath and count to seven."

Carla nods again. "Can you do that?"

I do, breathing in through my nose, holding it for four, then letting it out for eight. I do it a few times until I start to feel calmer. Having Carla here, holding my hands, looking into my eyes, helps enormously. The black spots dancing at the edge of my vision slink away, and my heart is no longer crashing into my ribs quite as hard.

"One more night," I whisper to myself. "Just one more night and then I'm done." The shore is so close.

"You can do it," Carla says.

I take another deep breath in. Yes. I can. I'm not going to let this person terrify me any longer. I'm not giving them the satisfaction. For too long, I've allowed others to control my life, and I'm done with it. This is the last time I'm ever going to perform these songs. I'm retiring the old Luna, but tonight I owe it to her to pay homage, to send her out with a bang. "Okay," I say.

Carla smiles. "If you're going out there, will you play that song?" she asks, pointing at my guitar sitting in the corner of the room.

"Which one?"

"The one you wrote for Will. The one about the lighthouse?"

How does she know I wrote that song for Will? I frown at her and she shrugs at me. "You hum it all the time. You should play it tonight. It's my favorite."

"I don't think so," I say, not wanting to have to explain to her that tours don't work that way, that we have a list of choreographed songs that we work through.

"Please," she says.

"Wrong audience," I tell her. "They won't like it."

"Or maybe they will," she says.

It's so silly, but I honestly hadn't thought that my fans would like it. I'd assumed that, like Marty and my mom, they wouldn't. But what if Carla is right?

A knock on the door interrupts us. "Time," the stage manager says, poking her head inside the room.

WILL

Marty intercedes with the security guy and he finally lets me go. Luckily for him, as I was about to break his arm. The guy in the cap is getting away.

I chase him inside, darting around men carrying cables and dancers rushing to take their places.

The guy in the cap slips through a doorway up ahead, and I race and manage to catch the door with my foot just before it slams shut. I dart through, following him into the area beneath the stage.

Overhead, the cacophony of the crowd beats like a drum. There are cables and what look like sets, and so much equipment that the man slips from my sight, sneaking into the shadows. I creep forward slowly, trying to adjust my eyes to the gloom, my hearing useless as the music and chanting above my head is so loud.

I catch a glimpse of red and dart forward just in time to grab the collar of the man's shirt. I haul him backward, tripping him and throwing him down on the ground, pressing my knee to his chest and my forearm to his neck. He struggles.

"Why did you run?" I ask, patting him down with my free hand, in case he has a weapon on him.

"Because you were chasing me."

"Only guilty people run." I'm having to shout over the sound of the crowd above yelling Luna's name. "Did you send Luna those letters? And the dead animals?"

The man grunts. I push my weight down further onto his chest.

"Yes!" he shouts. "Please, get off!"

"Why?" I ask, digging my knee even harder into him. I can feel my anger getting the better of me. He threatened Luna. He wanted to kill her. Rage blackens my vision, muddles my thinking. But I'm not my dad. I breathe deep and wrestle back control before I lose it completely.

The guy's saying something that I can't hear over the screams of the audience above us. I lean closer. "What did you say?"

"It wasn't me!" he yells. "I was just the delivery guy."

LUNA

The thunder was deafening but has now started to take form, and I can hear it's not an endless roar, but rather there's a rhythm to it. They're yelling my name. Luna. It's a wave that keeps crashing to shore, drawing me closer even though the weight of it may crush me. For once I'm going to let the voices that are filled with love and support drown out the one voice of hate.

I step onstage, feeling light-headed and light-limbed but refusing to give in to my fear or let it control me any longer. The stage is dark and the audience, too. I can only make out blackness punctuated by the starlight of twenty thousand or so phone flashes, held aloft.

Every step toward my starting place among the dancers feels impossible, and at one point I freeze, before forcing myself onward, taking deep breaths as I go, needing to remind myself that I'm not letting this person win, that I owe it to myself and my fans to do this tonight.

The backup dancers are ready. When the stage lights go up in thirty seconds and the music starts to play, I'm meant to be in position, in the center of the stage, standing on a plinth that will rise with me on it.

I find my mark. I take my place.

The lights go up.

WILL

find Marty scouring backstage trying to find me, I'm guessing, and I run over and grab his arm. "Marty," I say, shouting to be heard over the furious screams of the audience. "I found out who's behind the threats."

"Did you get the guy? Where did he go?" he says, looking over my shoulder for the guy in the black cap.

"It wasn't him," I say. "He was just the delivery guy."

"Well, did he tell you who he was doing it for?" Marty asks.

"Yeah, and you won't believe it."

The audience is screaming so loud that I have to lean in close and shout it in his ear.

Marty reels back, looking at me, blinking. "Are you serious?" he asks me, seeming like he doesn't believe me for one second. Then he turns and marches off.

I run after him. "Where are you going?" I shout over the roar of the audience's cheers.

"I'm going to go and find that little pillock," Marty says.

"He's here?" I ask.

Marty nods. "Yeah, I just found out. When you took off after that guy, one of the roadies let me know he'd just seen Jamie."

"Where is he?"

"Probably gone straight to Luna's dressing room." He starts jogging, and I join him.

"I thought they'd broken up," I say.

"I thought so too," Marty growls.

"What are we going to do when we find him?" I ask, wondering if he means to bring in the police.

Marty doesn't answer. He charges down a corridor like an angry bull, sending roadies and other backstage staff scurrying to get out of his way. We weave our way through a maze of backstage corridors, and Marty stops outside a door to a dressing room. A huge security guard stands in the way, guarding it. My heart starts racing at the thought I'm about to see Luna, but then I hear her voice, booming through the speakers overhead. She's onstage, above me. The crowd is going wild, the decibel level doubling. It feels as if the ceiling is going to collapse with the thunder of feet and the roar of voices.

"Stand aside," Marty barks at the security guard, who, not recognizing him, shakes his head.

"I'm her manager," Marty huffs, conveniently leaving out the *ex* part.

"And I'm her manicurist," says the man with a snicker.

"No, seriously," Marty says.

The guard looks pissed, then impatient. "IDs please."

"Is Jamie in there?" I ask.

The guard looks me over. "ID please and security pass."

Before we have to reply, the door to the dressing room opens. It's Jamie, sticking his head out with a frown, wondering what the commotion is. Marty lunges and grabs him by the collar.

"You little shit!" he says, dragging Jamie out into the corridor.

The bodyguard goes for Marty, but I drag him back. He shoves me against the wall, and I protest. "It's not what you think!"

The security guard reaches for his radio to call for backup.

"He's the one sending Luna the packages—the threats . . . ," I say.

The security guard looks at Jamie and then at Marty. "He's right." Marty's still holding on to Jamie, who looks like he might be about to collapse in tears. "This is the guy who's been terrorizing Luna."

The security guard gives me another look, then lets me go, warning me with a look and a gesture to stay where I am and not move an inch. I nod. It's for the best I stay here because there's a very real danger that I might try to rip Jamie a new one.

Marty pulls out from his pocket a handful of the letters Jamie has sent to Luna and shoves them in Jamie's face.

Jamie feigns incomprehension. "What's this?" he asks.

"Don't you give me that bollocks," Marty shouts back. "I know it was you that sent them. And the dead animals. Let's see what the cops have to say about it, shall we, as well as the SPCA?"

Jamie turns pale. "What are you talking about?" he croaks.

Marty pulls one of the letters from an envelope and reads it out loud: *"I'M GOING TO WATCH YOU DIE, YOU UGLY BITCH. I'M GOING TO MAKE IT SLOW."*

Jamie cringes, a red bloom coloring his cheeks.

"Another one just came," the bodyguard says, showing Marty and me a white envelope in a plastic baggie.

Jamie takes a step back, away from Marty's flying spittle and the bodyguard, who is now getting in his face.

"Telling us you don't recognize any of these?" Marty asks.

Jamie shakes his head mutely and takes another step backward, looking between the three of us.

"Shame you don't write songs with half as much sentiment," Marty laughs. "You might still have a career."

Jamie flushes, his mouth pursed with indignation.

"Because that's what this is about, isn't it?" says Marty. "I should have known. You can't stand the fact that Luna's getting more successful than you."

"No!" Jamie protests. It looks like he might be about to burst into tears. "It's not that."

I don't believe it for a second.

"I love her," Jamie argues.

"Funny way of showing it," I snap.

"The flowers didn't work. Nothing I did worked," he says in a whiny voice.

"What are you talking about?" I ask.

"Every time I sent one, she'd come back to me."

Marty and I stare at him, then exchange a bewildered look. "Are you saying you sent her death threats so she'd get back together with you?" Marty asks.

"Out of fear?" I add, still trying to wrap my head around it all. I suspected him at the very beginning, when I interviewed with Luna's mother, and she dismissed my theory, but I was right! Why did no one spot the pattern—I suppose the breakups were so frequent that no one saw the correlation. But the dead pigeon did arrive when they were broken up.

Jamie shuffles his feet. I keep a grip on the raging anger that's doing its best to Incredible Hulk its way out of me.

"You deliberately tried to scare her, so she'd look to you for support?" I ask.

His shoulders slump. It's not a nod, but he doesn't deny it either.

"That's messed up," Marty says, shaking his head in disgust.

"She's on anxiety medication. She's lived her life in fear because of this," I say, stepping toward Jamie, feeling the rage building like a tsunami inside me.

He shrinks away from me. "I didn't mean to upset her. I love her."

I grab him by the collar and twist it. He lets out an alarmed yelp.

"That's not love. You don't even know what it means," I shout.

"She needs me," he whimpers.

"Or is it that you need her?" I spit through a clenched jaw. "You're afraid that you're nothing without her. She doesn't need you to be successful. But you need her. The only way you could feel big was by making her feel small."

I'm right. I can see it in his face. The way the muscle in his jaw spasms and the truth flares in his eyes. I let him go, chucking him backward and away from me with revulsion.

Marty pokes Jamie in the chest with his index finger. "Hate to break it to you, mate, but once the world hears about this, your career is canceled. The only thing you're going to be starring in is *Celebs Behind Bars*."

Throughout the confrontation, Jamie has been shrinking smaller and smaller into himself, and his face has been scrunching up tighter and tighter. I wonder if he may explode or try to rush past us, but no, he collapses crying to the ground.

Marty stares down at him in open disgust, as though he's looking at a slug.

"I didn't mean it. I just . . . It's not fair," Jamie says, sobbing.

He looks up at me, glaring. "You took her away from me."

It's tempting to kick him.

"You couldn't bear someone else being with her, not even if it made her happy," I tell him. "You are a selfish asshole."

He swallows and can't meet my eye.

"I guess, though, I should actually thank you," I say.

He frowns up at me. I smile at him. "I was only employed to protect Luna because of the letters you were sending," I explain. "If you hadn't sent them, I would never have met her."

What I don't add is that I would never have fallen in love with her either. I would never have gotten to know what it was like to love someone as extraordinary as that girl whose voice I can hear above us right now. The girl who is so close to me and who I suddenly have an overwhelming urge to see.

"Are you going to tell Luna?" Jamie asks, his voice trembling.

"Tell Luna? I'm going to tell the bloody police!" Marty bellows.

Jamie throws himself forward. "Please, don't!" he cries.

"You're pathetic, you know that?" Marty says, trying to kick him off.

I walk out the door, done with listening to Jamie's sniveling excuses. Marty can handle it from here.

LUNA

finish the first song and we roll right into the second. I drop a few lines, distracted by worry, but it doesn't matter because the audience is screaming the lines anyway, filling in the gaps for me. I can do this. I can hold it together. The audience is lifting me up, making me feel stronger. And I have to trust that my bodyguard and the security team are doing their jobs and keeping me safe from whatever threat is out there.

There's a break between this song and the next. I'm meant to make a quick costume change in the wings. When the song ends, though, I don't run offstage as I'm meant to. No. I walk to the center of the stage instead. "Change of plan," I say.

I look up at the box where the sound and lighting guys are sitting, mouths falling open. I've gone off script. They don't know what to do. But they're pro enough at their jobs that they switch on a spotlight and center me in it.

The crowd is screaming and applauding, and I smile and thank them and then I say, "How would everyone like to hear something else? Something new? Something I've been working on?" My voice sounds strong, stronger than I feel.

Focus, I tell myself. "Good!" I say, my voice trembling. "Because I have something special I want to play for you."

I turn around and look into the wings, where among the shocked backup dancers, all of whom are standing around bewildered, wondering what the hell is happening, I can't make out anyone because of the glaring lights, but I wave toward where I told Matias to wait in the wings.

A second later he rushes out onto the stage with my guitar. I put my arm around him. "Everyone, this is my brother, Matias!" I say to the audience. "Say hi!"

The crowd roars hello and Matias grins from ear to ear, delighted.

"Thank you," I whisper to him.

He runs offstage.

"Thank you all for being here tonight," I say to the audience once he's gone.

I look down at my feet, feeling a little dizzy all of a sudden. What am I doing? But then I push on. I look up again, into the diamond glittering lights, and my smile fades. I let it. I let it all fall away. I force away the fear, and I force the Luna that's been stepping out onstage every night on tour, the Luna everyone here knows, or thinks they know, out of the way too. I tell her thanks, but it's time to go. I don't need you anymore. I take off the mask and drop the facade, and as I face the audience, blind, I feel more vulnerable than if I were standing here naked.

"I want to sing you something that I wrote for someone, someone who changed my life. Someone I loved very much—" And here my voice cracks and I have to take a deep breath. "Someone I'm still in love with, if I'm honest."

Someone in the audience yells "Jamie!" and I could ignore it. I could choose to keep the truth hidden, but I don't. I look out into the audience and I say, "No. This song is for Will."

WILL

My whole body goes into a state of paralysis. Did Luna just say my name? I must have misheard. But suddenly I see Matias waving at me from backstage. He runs over to me. "You're here!" He slaps me on the shoulder. "She said your name! Will! Will!" he shouts.

We both turn toward the stage. There, through the wings, I can see a single spotlight illuminating her. Luna. My breath catches in my chest. She looks so beautiful, glowing gold beneath the lights. She strums a chord and I recognize the tune. It's the song about the lighthouse.

She's singing it for me. Does she know I'm here? She stands on the stage in a single spot of light in an ocean of dark. With no backup dancers or other musicians, the focus is purely on her, and it's as if all seventy thousand or so people in here are holding their breath, watching her, listening as her fingers strum the chords. And her voice . . . it sounds like nothing on earth. She's so tiny and yet her voice fills the entire arena, starting off low and husky before swelling to the high notes with a burst of electrifying energy. It's heartbreaking and poignant and imbued with a sense of sadness that brings tears to my eyes for a moment. You can feel the waves of emotion rippling around the stadium as people listen, drawn into the story she's weaving.

Tens of thousands of people hold lighters and their camera flashlights up.

The feeling of pride I have when the final note dies away leaves me breathless. It's as if the world stands still and time stops. I want to rush onstage and pull her into my arms. The need propels me and I take a step out from the wings, but then the stadium erupts into applause and screams and I freeze. The ground shakes, the air splits with the thunder of clapping, and I watch Luna's face as she blinks and takes in the crowd's reaction, as if she doesn't quite believe it. But then her timid smile becomes wider, before splitting into a grin.

"Thank you," she says to the crowd, her hand cradling the microphone. "That one is called 'Lighthouse,' and it's going to be the first track on my new album."

More whoops and cheers.

She turns and walks in my direction. Halfway across the stage she stops, freezing like a deer in headlights. She's being tracked by the spotlight and so she's blinded by the lights, but she must have seen my silhouette, standing on the edge of the wings. I step forward, toward her, and I see her flinch in fear. Shit. She thinks I'm him.

I take another step forward, this time into the light, and watch the fear on her face transform immediately into disbelief. She takes a huge, gasping breath, as though she's seen a ghost.

I take another step forward and she does too. We're both in the spotlight now. There's maybe a foot of space between us, but I feel the invisible barrier that's suddenly appeared between us.

"What are you doing here?" she stammers.

"I love you," I blurt out.

She takes a step back, looking at me in total shock, her guitar hanging limp in her hand. Oh God. I realize I'm standing onstage in the spotlight and we're being watched by tens of thousands of people. The cheering and the clapping seem to be subsiding, but I can't really tell because all I can focus on is Luna and the fact that she's so close but still so far, like on the other side of a black hole. And I just admitted I loved her. And she's not saying anything. Is it too late?

But the next thing I know, she's taking a step forward and falling into my arms and we're kissing, and it feels like no time has passed at all since the last time, but also like a thousand years have, because I've missed her so much, more than I think I knew, and the feel of her in my arms again is tugging at the knots, and all the stifled longing and heartache I've been carrying around inside me is finally coming loose.

I can feel tears against my cheek and I don't know if they're hers. I pull her even closer. I'm never letting her go again.

Vaguely in the background, I can hear a roar gaining in magnitude, screams and clapping that are so deafening they almost drown out Luna murmuring "I love you" with her lips pressed to mine.

We're on a stage in front of seventy thousand people, but it's just the two of us, alone, locked in our own world, spinning in our own orbit.

EPILOGUE—
SIX MONTHS LATER

WILL

She's sitting on the deck in the morning sun, bare legs and bare feet balanced on the rail as she strums her guitar, a sweater she's knitting on the floor beside her. In the distance the lake glitters like frost, and I smile as I do every morning taking in the view—not just of Luna but of the green forest forming a barricade to this private galaxy we've created.

It feels like we're the only people in the world, even though on the other side of the lake the camp is in full swing. I'll take the canoe over there in half an hour and go to work while Luna stays here making music, reading, and relaxing. At lunch I'll come back and we'll swim together in the lake, sometimes more than just swim, lie naked afterward on the dock, and let the sun dry us. After I'm done with the kids in the evening, I canoe back over and Luna and I fish for our supper, and then we sit around the campfire wrapped in blankets, beneath a ceiling of a billion stars, and Luna sings me what she's written that day. Her album is almost ready. She's working with Marty to put the finishing touches on it.

I never knew life could be so simple and so perfectly blissful. We'll be staying here for a while. Luna plans to record her album here in the woods. She's set up a recording studio in the cabin. LA feels a world away. The whole drama surrounding Jamie and the letters never followed us here. When Luna found out Jamie was the one sending them, she told Marty that she didn't want to press charges because she didn't want to be dragged into anything messy and complicated—she wanted to stay out of the limelight and focus on being happy instead.

So that's what we've been doing: focusing on being happy. And it's working.

In the fall we're planning a trip to Florida to see Zoey and Tristan. And at Christmas we'll be back in LA for Carla and Francisco's wedding.

I don't wonder what would have happened if she hadn't seen me, though, because I know that one way or another, we would have found our way back to one another.

LUNA

Once Will has gone to work, rowing across the lake, I sit outside in the rocking chair on the veranda and tweak a few verses of what is going to be the final song on my album. I've promised Marty I'll send him the full track list next week. Despite everything, I'm still working with him. I couldn't be too mad with him given that he's the one who went and found Will and brought him back into my life on a rescue mission.

The big difference, however, is that now he's no longer driving the car. I am. He sometimes likes to back-seat drive, but I'm the one with my hands on the wheel and my foot on the gas, or more often than not, my foot on the brake.

It's good to coast idly for a while, windows down, no sense of having to be anywhere at any particular time and only a vague idea of the destination. I'm living free. And the best thing is that I'm not on the run.

Living out here in the forest with Will is the perfect antidote to the last nineteen years. Here, beneath a blanket of stars at night, lying in Will's arms, it feels as if the world has stopped existing and it's just the two of us, floating in space.

There's no more chorus in my head telling me I'm worthless or that I'm not good enough, and in that silence my own voice is getting stronger.

I've shed the old Luna completely and am someone new, someone stronger and happier and, above all, surer. If before I was balancing on a high wire, trying desperately not to lose my footing, now I'm standing on solid ground and I could never fall with Will beside me, as I know he'll always be there to catch me.

The only piece of my life that still feels like it hasn't healed is the relationship with my mom. She hasn't forgiven me for firing her as my manager and freeing myself from her control, but I haven't forgiven her for the lies and the pressure she put me under.

I promised to still support her, but I took control of my finances. I gave her a credit card with a limit on it and the house in Beverly Hills, which I never felt was home anyway, and I've promised her that I'll always take care of Matias. I'm also happy knowing that Carla is there to take care of him too. Maybe one day I'll be in a better place with my mom, but until then I'm going to live my life without apologies. I think I've earned that.

When Will arrives back for lunch, I'm waiting on the dock. I help him pull the boat in and tie it up to its mooring post. He brings mail: a FedEx package from Marty, which I open with shaking hands right there on the dock. I pull out the vinyl record inside. It's the first single of my new album, *Fall into Me,* and it's the first record I've ever been truly proud of. The album cover is a picture of a shooting star over water.

I stare at it for several seconds, before I hand it to Will and delve back into the envelope again, this time pulling out a piece of paper, which I also hand to him.

He takes it, frowning. "What is it?" he asks, scanning it.

"It's the deed to this place," I say, gesturing at the cabin. "It's in your name."

He looks up at me. "What?"

"I bought it for you."

He blinks at me, not understanding.

"I think you belong here," I tell him with a shrug, because it's true. He's so at home here that uprooting him would be like pulling up a cactus from the desert and planting it in the ocean. I step closer, brushing my cheek against his shoulder. "I can see you here as an old, old man, can't you?"

Will stares down at the piece of paper, his fingers gripping it so tight that I worry it will tear. He stares for so long without saying anything that I start to worry that I've done the wrong thing. He can be funny sometimes about money and the disparity in our incomes, not that it means anything to me, but I know that for him it's important that he can provide and stand on his own two feet. But finally, he looks up at me, and I can see his eyes are wet with tears.

"I can see me here, yes," he says, and with that, he smiles and pulls me toward him, his hands resting on my hips. "With our grandchildren playing on the dock and you sitting in that rocking chair, right here, playing guitar."

My face splits into a smile so wide my face hurts. I kiss him, tasting the sun and lake water on his lips.

"I love you," he murmurs.

The words are like helium injected into my bloodstream. Every time he says it, I think I could rocket into space but for Will's hands around my waist now, anchoring me to earth.

"You are amazing," he says, pulling away to stare at the piece of paper. "I can't believe you did this."

"I figured we could live between here and Oceanside," I say, looping my arms around his neck.

"Oceanside?" he says. "For real?"

I nod. "I've been talking to Robert. I'm going to rent his place. So we have a place at the beach, too, by your family and our friends." I smile, a little shy still to claim Will's friends as my own, but he seems happy.

His face lights up, but then he stops smiling. "Are you sure?" he asks. "I mean, it's not LA. It's so far from that world."

I grin and reach up on tiptoe.

"You're my world," I say to him.

He leans down. "You're my whole galaxy," he says, grinning, as his lips meet mine.

Heartfelt thanks to my editor, Nicole, and the team at Simon & Schuster, including Elizabeth Mims, Heather Palisi, Tom Daly, Jen Strada, Penina Lopez, and Amanda Ramirez.

Thanks to Amanda, my agent at LBA, and to all my readers, whose love for these characters inspires me to keep writing.

Turn the page for a sneak peek at
Watch Over Me

The End

ZOEY

see the decision get made—the resolution crosses his face, and in the same instant I move in front of Tristan to shield him.

There's a deafening bang, followed closely by a second bang, and I fly sideways and hit the ground. Tristan falls too.

Pain shoots through me like comets streaking across a black sky. My vision turns starry.

I look up and see the monstrous shape of my dad looming over us. He blinks, seemingly astonished. Maybe it's shock at what he's done. Maybe it isn't. Light bursts around him in a dazzling halo. I can't breathe—the pain is almost as bright as the light.

I've been shot, I realize. But what about Tristan? Is he okay?

Thoughts dart like eels through my mind so fast and so slippery I can't grasp on to them. The only thing I can hold on to, like a beacon in the darkness, is the thought of Tristan. Please let him be okay. I don't care if I die. Just let him be okay.

My dad drops to his knees in front of me like a dark avenging angel. For a moment, I think he's about to beg forgiveness for what he's done. I stare up at him, but his expression shows no remorse, not an ounce of sorrow. He's baring his teeth like an animal about to shred his prey.

My ears are ringing so loudly that all other sounds are dulled. Time has slowed to a near stop. My heart seems to be following suit.

Tristan is all I can think of as the light starts to fade. I led him here. This is all my fault. Where is he? I desperately want to see him. I can feel something behind me. Something heavy and unmoving. A body? His body? I want to roll over and reach for him, but I'm paralyzed.

I desperately need to know that he's okay.

But what if he isn't?

What if he's dead?

What if I'm dying too?

The Beginning

ZOEY

There's no dark in Las Vegas. It's the brightest city on earth, and I haven't seen the stars in three years because of it. So bright, in fact, the city can be seen from outer space.

There's no quiet in Las Vegas either. Even out where we live, miles from the strip and its herds of tourists, there's constant noise: the roar of traffic sliced with sirens, thumping music; arguments interspersed with cackles of laughter and the incessant drone of TV chatter drifting through open windows.

I miss quiet, but I don't miss the dark.

I finish the washing up and tidy Cole's homework away into his backpack. His notebooks are covered in colorful cartoon doodles, but as I shove one into his bag, I pause, realizing they aren't cartoon doodles at all. Underneath his name—COLE

WARD—written in big block letters of uneven sizes, he's drawn a man holding a gun. Bullets are flying from it, and half a dozen stick figures lie sprawled across the page, tongues lolling, limbs severed, and red marker used for blood.

My hand shakes a little as I study the picture. Why is a nine-year-old boy drawing pictures like this? Is it normal? Perhaps all nine-year-old boys who spend time playing video games draw pictures like this. But even as I try to excuse it, I know deep down that it isn't normal.

I sink down at the scarred kitchen table and debate what to do. I can't tell my mom, that's for sure. It'll be too much for her to deal with. She's finally managed to get on a good track, and I'm anxious not to do anything that might send her plummeting back into the dark place.

The best thing to do, I decide, is to speak to Cole. The violence could be Will's influence. It makes sense, given that our older brother is a marine and Cole hero-worships him. Or it could be he's just copying something he saw on TV or online. I try to police his screen time, but I'm not always home, and my mom isn't great with discipline. She doesn't like conflict. Maybe I should speak to his teacher, even though last time she made it very clear that it's my mom who should be taking responsibility for Cole—not his teenage sister.

I shove the book in Cole's bag and make a mental note to talk to him tomorrow before school—if I have time, that is. I have an early shift at work. Which reminds me that I need to get moving so I don't end up too late to bed. There's still laundry to do and lunches to prepare for tomorrow.

I stick my head around the bedroom door and see Kate isn't yet asleep. She's sitting cross-legged on the top bunk wearing the unicorn onesie I gave her for Christmas. She's texting on her phone, her fingers flying at five hundred emojis a minute. I swear that phone is glued to her hands, and not even a crowbar could remove it.

"Hey, it's late," I say to Kate, but she's wearing her headphones and can't hear me. "Kate!" I say louder, and she glances up, her hair blazing around her head like a fiery sunset. "Bedtime."

She rolls her eyes as though I'm just one big annoyance, put on earth to end her Snapchat streak, but miracle of miracles, she stops texting and yanks out her headphones.

"Good night," she says, and reaches for the little unicorn reading light by her bed, twisting its horn to dim the brightness. When we first moved here, I tried making the room nice for her. She was unhappy about the move and even more so about having to share a room with Cole. The books on the shelf are gathering dust, though, because the only thing she reads these days are texts and Instagram stories.

She shoves her phone under the covers, and I know as soon as I'm gone she'll be back to texting. I make Cole's bed on the bottom bunk. He sleeps there normally, but he and Kate had a screaming argument earlier, so he went to sleep in Mom's bed.

As I close the bedroom door, my phone rings. It's another call from an unidentified number, the third one today. The first one I answered, hoping it was about a job I'd applied for at a restaurant closer to home, but it wasn't—only silence greeted me on the other end. I hung up fast, before it rang again a few seconds later. And when I finally answered, all I could hear was someone on the other end, breathing loudly.

There was no answer when I said hello, just more breathing. Whoever it was proceeded to call a few hours after that.

And now, at ten o'clock at night, they're calling again.

My breathing hitches, and my heart beats abnormally fast. It's not him, I tell myself angrily. If it were him, I'd hear the pip-pip-pip of the federal inmate phone system and then an automated voice asking me if I wanted to accept a call from a prisoner at the Penitentiary of New Mexico. I know this because a few years ago he tried to call me. This was when I still had my old phone number. I rejected the call, then changed my number.

It can't be him, I repeat to myself. There's nothing to be afraid of. I switch off my phone and put it down on the table, trying to shake off the bad feelings slinking over me. Without warning, memories lunge out at me from the darkness, where I've tried to bury them: Cole's screams, Kate's sobs, my mother's face bursting under a flurry of punches, the fridge door hanging on one hinge. Then the blue and white and red flashing lights outside; my dad's angry roars. *You bitch! I'll fucking kill you.*

The phone rings again. I startle. How long have I been standing here staring into space, remembering things I'd rather forget? It's the landline this time. I walk toward it, debating whether I should answer. Something tells me not to, but another voice in my head, a belligerent one, demands that I do. I grab the phone. "Yes?" I say.

Silence greets me.

"Who is this?" I whisper, heart hammering furiously.

There's another second's silence, and then I hear the click as whoever is on the other end hangs up. As I stare at the phone, there's an enormous BOOM. The window shatters, and glass flies across the room. A wall of heat rushes toward me as a crackle and a deafening roar fill my ears.

Shielding my face, I squint through the broken window. Oh

my God. It's my car, parked just outside on the driveway in front of the house. It's on fire.

I stumble back from the window, chased by smoke and heat, and run to the bedroom, throwing open the door and screaming at Kate to get up.

"Fire! Move!" I yell before rushing out and into my mom's room to wake Cole. I come to a halt in the doorway. The room is empty.

"Cole?" I shout, ducking down and looking under the bed. He's not there. And he's not in the closet, either. I ransack the room looking for him.

Smoke is now billowing in through the broken window, and I start coughing. I push past Kate, who has staggered from bed and into the living room.

"Call 911!" I shout at her.

The front door is the only exit, and we can't get out, thanks to the fact the car is parked right in front of the door. Behind me, I can hear Kate on the phone to the dispatcher. "F-fire," she stammers. "Th-there's a fire."

"Cole!" I scream, turning every which way, trying to figure out where he might be. I check the bathroom, the kitchen, the closets—everywhere I can think of—but he's nowhere to be found. Coughing, I yell his name again, but he doesn't answer. The smoke is so thick and choking we can barely breathe. I grab Kate by the arm and drag her back into Mom's bedroom.

"Come on," I say to Kate, pulling her over to the window. "We need to get out of here."

The neglected courtyard outside is shared by the two dozen or so houses that back onto it. It's meant to be a communal meeting area with grills, concrete picnic tables, and a play area for little kids, but the play area is taped off because the rusting climbing frame and broken swings are a liability, and the only people who use the picnic tables are drug dealers.

Someone in the courtyard runs over and helps Kate out of the window, catching her as she stumbles. The person then helps me. I recognize him as a neighbor, a guy in his fifties, who I think works as a bus driver. His name is Winston.

"Have you seen my brother?" I ask him as he helps me down.

He shakes his head as panic ripples through me. I scour the crowd of a dozen or so neighbors—some in pajamas—rushing out of their houses to see what's happening. There's no sign of Cole. In the distance, I can hear the sirens of the fire truck.

I take Kate's hand and pull her around the side of the house, to the street. The car is still burning furiously, and the flames have started to stroke the roof of the house and melt the guttering. As I watch, sparks dance through the broken window and land on the curtains in the living room. They burn so fast and so brightly that they incinerate in seconds, and now the flames, hungry for more, leap toward the sofa.

Two fire trucks screech to a halt in front of the house, and we watch as firefighters go running past, carrying a hose. One team douses the car, and in less than a minute the blaze is under control, sputtering and finally vanishing with a hiss and a billow of black smoke.

The other firefighters have turned their hose on the house—sending the spray through the window and on the flames consuming the living room, while two others have taken an axe to the front door. They smash it down, then rush inside. I sink to my knees on the sidewalk, Kate collapsing beside me, sobbing. What if Cole's inside? What if he was hiding?

The fire in the living room is quickly put out, but it feels like we wait hours until the firefighters exit. One of them approaches Winston, who I see point me out to him. He walks over with a solemn expression on his face, and my heart starts to hammer. Kate grips my hand tight. The firefighter kneels down beside me. He's about fifty years old with a bushy moustache and blue eyes. "My name's Lieutenant Franklin," he says. "This your house?"

I nod. "D-did you find . . . ?" I stammer. "My brother. I don't know where he is."

He frowns and shakes his head. "There's no one in the house."

I let out a sob of relief. Kate does too.

"How old is he? Can you give us a description of him?"

I turn back to Lieutenant Franklin and try to focus. "His name is Cole. He's nine. He has brown hair, brown eyes, freckles. He was wearing Spider-Man pajamas."

Franklin repeats all of this into his radio, and the dispatcher confirms it.

"Is that all?" Franklin asks me. "Any other identifiers?"

I open my mouth, but nothing comes out. How else to describe my little brother? I haven't done him justice. He's smart as a whip, I want to say, even though he hates school. He loves to make up jokes, really bad ones. He's currently obsessed with Genghis Khan and LeBron James and Lionel Messi and he wants to be a race car driver when he grows up, unless of course he can be a famous soccer player. None of this information is going to help them find him, though. But how many nine-year-old boys in Spider-Man pajamas must there be walking around Vegas at this time of night?

"When did you last see him?" Franklin asks me.

"I put him to bed around seven thirty. I went to look for him after the explosion, but I couldn't find him. I don't know where he is."

I'm fighting back tears. I want to go and look for him—I *should* be looking for him—but Kate is gripping my arm, holding me firmly in place. She hasn't said a word this whole time. She seems to be in shock. Someone has placed blankets—those foil ones—over our shoulders. "Please," I whisper to Franklin, "you need to find him."

"Don't worry," he tells me. "All the patrol cars in the area are looking for him. We'll find him." He nods at me reassuringly.

"Where's your mother?" Franklin asks.

"She's at work," I tell him. "She should be home soon."

He frowns at that, and I sense he's making a judgment. He's probably thinking, What kind of a mother leaves her children at home to work a night shift? It irks me. I'm almost nineteen, and I'm not a kid. There are no laws being broken. Besides, he doesn't know anything about us. He doesn't know that my mom's job is the best thing that's happened to her in a long time, that it's given her back a sense of purpose and self-confidence. She might not be earning very much money, but she's earning something—enough to put a roof over our heads and get us off food stamps. This is what I want to say to him, but I don't.

"And your father? Is he around?" Franklin asks.

I shake my head. "No."

"You should call your mother," he says to me.

"My phone's inside," I say, nodding at the house.

"Okay, I can have someone contact her. Where does she work?"

"The Luxor," I tell him. "She has a job doing hair and makeup for the show there."

"That the aerial one? With the acrobats and the trapeze people?"

I nod. My mom got us tickets for Kate's birthday a few months ago. Special-rate ones. It was one of the best nights we'd ever had. Afterward, Cole spent two months swinging off every pole and rail he could find, until he fell leaping from a wall and took a chip out of his elbow.

"What's your mom's name?" Franklin asks me.

"Gina Ward," I tell him, mumbling it, my mind back on Cole. Where did he go? And more important, *why?*

"Does she have a car?" he asks.

"No. She takes the bus."

Franklin nods. "I'll have someone pick her up." He steps away, and I watch him talk into his radio, and then I just sit there on the curb, trying to comfort Kate and not to think about what might have happened to Cole.

Ten minutes later, as we watch the firefighters roll up their hoses and wait for my mom, Franklin returns. He crouches down beside us. "They found your brother," he tells me.

The relief bursts out of me. Beside me Kate clutches my hand. "Oh, thank God—where was he?"

"A few blocks away. A patrol car spotted him. He ran. They had to chase him down."

"What?" I ask, stunned. Why would he run?

"They're bringing him here," Franklin tells me. "Do you mind . . . ?" Franklin says, gesturing with a nod of the head for me to follow him a few feet away, out of earshot of Kate.

I prize my arm out of her grip and follow him. He gestures toward the car. "It looks like arson. It burned with the kind of intensity we normally see when an accelerant is used."

Arson. I say the word in my head as I stare at the smoking, mangled ruin that was once a Toyota Camry with 175,000 miles on the odometer.

"You're lucky," the fireman goes on to say. "If you'd had more fuel in the tank, it would have been an inferno. It could have taken out the entire block."

"Oh my God," I whisper, my heart clanging in my chest.

"Know anyone who might have a grudge against you?"

I open my mouth to say no, but then stop. Yes. I do know someone with a grudge against me. Someone who threatened once to kill me. But he's in prison. And he doesn't know where we live. It can't be him. But that's the second time I've thought that tonight, and I'm not a believer in coincidence.

Franklin shrugs. "Might just be bored kids. It happens." His eyes drill into mine as he says it. "Young boys in particular often go through a phase where they get interested in fire, playing with matches and things."

I don't understand what he's implying at first, and then it hits me with a jolt. "You think it was my brother who started the fire?" I ask, a note of anger in my voice.

He's quick to walk it back, shaking his head. "That's not what I'm saying."

But it's what he's thinking. I scowl at him, angry but also wrong-footed, because I'm wondering if Franklin might be right. Is that why Cole ran away? Because he didn't want to get into trouble? I can't believe that Cole would ever do something like this. I mean . . . I don't *think* he would do something like this.

"You got renters' insurance?" he asks. "The house has got a fair amount of fire and smoke damage."

"No," I say, my heart sinking.

He squeezes my shoulder. "The place isn't going to be inhabitable for a while," he says. "Do you have somewhere you can stay?"

I stare at the broken front door and the soot-covered walls of the living room. "No," I tell him. We don't have anywhere.